The Moonlit Warrior

Book 4 of The Shendri Series

E.P. Stavs

To all the readers who've shared this adventure with me.

Lehi

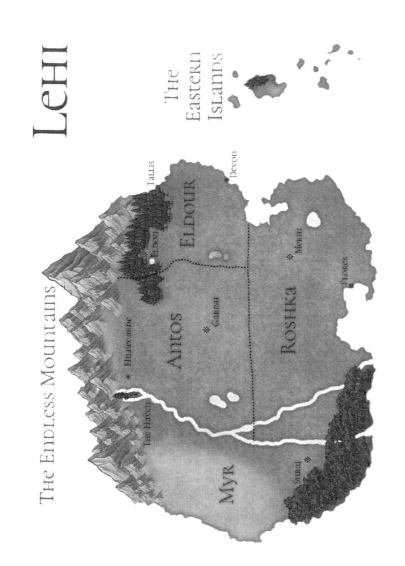

The Eastern Islands

The Endless Mountains

Tallis

Devon

Eldour

Eldon

Hildecarde

Antos

Garesh

Merith

Roshka

Flores

The Haven

Myr

Surai

Character Index

The Current Shendri Warriors

Josselyn deLure – current hellcat Shendri from Eldour, sword warrior

Lily Delaney – current phoenix Shendri from Roshka, healer

Maya – current wolf Shendri from Myr, archer

Fia Brendarrow – current dragon Shendri from the Eastern Island of Kreá, twin daggers

The Original Shendri Warriors

Fiona – Josselyn's ancestor and original hellcat Shendri

Cateline – Lily's ancestor and original phoenix Shendri

Sumeria – Maya's ancestor and original wolf Shendri

Aoi – Fia's ancestor and original dragon Shendri

Goddesses & Demigods

Luxeos – goddess of the sun & creator of the Shendri

Lunares – goddess of the moon, gifted Mihala with caeruleum

Bade – demigod of the moon, Lunares's son

Lumeria – demigoddess, ???

Prologue

Northern Antos, Two Hundred Years Ago

The dragon's fire spread in a ring around his battered form, fencing him in as Fiona and her hellcat stalked toward him. Sheathing her sword, Fiona issued her command in the steely voice of a hardened warrior.

"Finish him."

The hellcat snarled, displaying her vicious teeth, before leaping at his throat. Death was but moments away, and Bade welcomed the thought. Death would be a blessed relief after watching everything he'd worked for, the peace and equality he'd yearned for, spin out of control. The creature he'd unwittingly released upon the world was determined to destroy it, and he'd become nothing more than its puppet.

Yes, he would welcome death if it meant freedom.

Giving up so soon? the creature hissed, filling his mind. *Pathetic.* Taking control of his weakened body, the creature poured all of its remaining power into a single word.

"Reilentah."

The hellcat's paws hit his chest, knocking him backwards, but its jaw remained locked in place as its green eyes blazed with fury. It was frozen in place, along with every other man, woman, and beast within a thousand feet.

Bade pushed weakly at the massive beast, attempting to roll out from beneath it, and the creature snapped at him to hurry up – the spell would only hold for so long, and, broken as they were, there would not be enough power left for another. This was their only chance to escape.

When he failed to move the beast, the creature took control once more, exerting his body to the max as it heaved the beast off to the side and brought them staggering to their feet.

Do you even want to escape? it hissed, propelling them toward the fire that continued to burn in a ring around them. *After everything I've done for you,* it continued. *You can't even be bothered to survive.*

"Breathos," the creature commanded through Bade's lips, causing the flames to briefly flicker green. The spell didn't hold, however, and they soon returned to a vicious orange. Bade's well of power had officially run dry.

There's nothing else for it, the creature murmured. *Better a little singed than disemboweled by the beast.* It shoved Bade forward, pushing him through the flames. A scream tore from his gut as the fire burned his flesh, but he stumbled forward, falling to the ground on the other side and rolling in the dead grass until his burning clothes were fully snuffed out.

On your feet, the creature snarled. *We have to get to the mountains before our spell is released.*

"But the mountains are cursed," Bade argued, even as his legs pushed him forward, propelling him toward the misty peaks. "We'll lose ourselves and die in there as surely as we'd be killed out here."

A risk we'll have to take. Now hurry, the Shendri will not be held long.

Shaking with pain and fatigue, Bade ran across the field, heading for the path he knew would lead him into the mountain's enchantment. Despite being raised in the Eastern Islands, he had spent every school break and holiday at Hildegarde with his friend Darius's family while studying together at the University and knew these northern lands like the back of his hand.

What lay beyond the path's barrier, however, was a mystery even to him.

Shouts sounded behind him as he approached the shimmering wall, alerting him to the fact that there was a mobile army at his back. Without time for second guessing, he threw himself at the barrier just as the great white wolf's face appeared in his peripheral, the wolf Shendri perched atop its back, arrow nokked and aiming straight at him. The arrow clipped his shoulder as he passed through, and he cried out in pain as he fell onto his hands and knees in the dense air.

Keep moving, the creature demanded. *They may decide to follow us despite the risk.*

He crawled forward, his hands scraping against the rough stone and dirt of the path. How long he went on like that he couldn't say. Everything blurred together, and it was as if the heavens themselves were pressing down on his back the air was so heavy.

Collapsing onto the path, he rolled onto his back, wincing as his shoulder wound pressed against the ground. "No more," he whispered through cracked lips. "No more."

The creature remained silent for once, it too suffering from the overbearing exhaustion and retreating further into his mind. Bade closed his eyes, a sense of peace falling over him as he embraced his fate – he would die here, and with his death the creature would finally be destroyed. He inhaled, relaxing into his dusty grave – that is, until something tickled his cheek. He cracked one eye open, and spied a beautiful, blue butterfly with a flowing tail fluttering around his head. And was it... glowing?

He lifted his arm, unable to resist the pull of the strange creature. It landed on his fingers, and a melodic voice filled the air, compelling him to rise off the ground despite his complete and utter exhaustion and follow the butterfly toward the rocky walls of the mountain's cliff.

Hero brave, hero true, come to me now; I have need of you.
Though the mountains trap and bind, a worthy soul will surely find,
The weeping lady left for dead beneath the river's icy bed.

The glowing butterfly disappeared from view inside the stone, and as Bade staggered closer he discovered a crevice in the cliff's wall that had been previously obscured from view. Squeezing into the tight space, he shuffled sideways, maneuvering his way through the narrow chasm until he found himself stumbling out into an open meadow on the other side.

What in the world?

He paused, looking around the swath of grass and wildflowers that lay nestled between the rocky walls of the mountains like a secret sanctuary. The butterfly fluttered back in his direction, flying in circles around his head until it had his undivided attention then darting off across the meadow and diving behind a bush nestled against the far wall. He followed, fingertips brushing the tops of the grass as he cut a path through their wavy stalks. Upon reaching the bush, he discovered a tunnel leading below the mountain hidden behind it, with the butterfly's blue glow lighting the entrance, inviting him in.

A part of him balked, confused as to why he was following this strange, glowing butterfly in the first place, but the larger part was too entranced to question it deeply. The creature inside him remained unusually silent on the matter, which should have been a warning in itself. And yet...

Into the tunnel he went, half crawling, half sliding down the narrow opening until it finally grew large enough for him to stand. The butterfly led him down tunnel after tunnel lit only by the eerie, blue glow of crystals embedded into the walls. Mindlessly, he followed, until at last it ended and he found himself standing inside a cavern with a cathedral-like ceiling covered in blue lights and a bubbling creek passing through on the left.

"Well, now, aren't you a sight for sore eyes."

He turned to the right and found a stunning woman with ebony skin and long, golden hair staring at him with blatant appraisal. He opened his mouth to ask who she was but found his throat too dry to speak. She smiled, gliding toward him as she continued her inspection.

"An impressive physique, though perhaps not as muscled as I'd prefer. Still, you've got excellent height and those legs..." She licked her lips. "I quite like those legs." She circled him as she spoke, the yellow silk of her sleeveless gown brushing against him as she moved. She hummed in satisfaction as she came to a stop in front of him and lifted her hand to take hold of his chin. "Those eyes of yours are magnificent," she murmured. Her hand slid down to his throat, and she paused, brows lifting in surprise. "But what's this? There's power here, real power. Or should I say, magic." Her finger wrapped around his throat, and he fought the sudden urge to gag. "How does a Lowlander such as yourself have such pure magic inside him? Unless..." She hesitated. "Unless you're not an ordinary Lowlander at all?"

Unable to speak, he merely stared back at her, a prisoner to her delicate hand. There was nothing left, not a single ounce of strength for him to draw upon. He was entirely at her mercy, and he waited with anxious excitement for her to tighten her grip and end his miserable existence once and for all.

Only she did not.

Releasing her hold on his neck, she glided over to a large, wooden chest sitting off to the side and lifted the lid. After digging around inside, she finally straightened, and Bade caught sight of a gold-handled mirror in her hand.

"Normally, I play with my guests until I grow bored and they become too weak to hold my interest. The enchantment surrounding this rocky prison was designed to sustain me for as long as I live, but anyone else would require nourishment to survive for more than a few days. You, however, are far too interesting to waste with idle games. No, I do believe I'd like to keep you around for awhile. Something tells me it'll be well worth the investment."

She pressed her lips to the mirror's face before turning it in his direction, and he watched in frozen horror as a hazy, white mist leaked from its surface, slowly creeping toward him. When at last the mist touched his skin, it was if a thousand hands had reached out to grab him, pulling him toward the glass. He dug his heels into the ground, but the mist sucked him, imprisoning him in a void that he would not be soon released from.

Chapter One

The Endless Mountains, Present Day

It'd been years since he'd stepped foot inside this forsaken place, with its damp chill and eerie lights, and yet it still felt strange to be on the outside of things, instead of trapped in the witch's mirror. Two hundred years spent waiting upon her pleasure, providing the wit and conversation she craved while stuck in her own prison. He'd actually come to anticipate her summons, the glimpses he caught through the mirror's surface the only break in the otherwise constant darkness. When at last he'd convinced her to release him, with a promise of securing her freedom, the touch of sunlight on his face as he'd crawled back into the meadow had been the most blissful experience of his life. Two hundred years spent in the dark would make even the hardest of men appreciate the simple things.

"You came."

The witch rose from her pile of furs and smiled. There was a rustle of silk as she floated toward him, her sun-rimmed eyes drinking him in with an eagerness that set his teeth on edge. "I should never have doubted it for a moment." Her hands slid up the fabric of his charcoal gray coat and cupped the back of his neck as she raised herself up, pressing her cold mouth against his own. "I should have known you'd keep your promise, my love." Another kiss, harder and more demanding than the first. "My Bade."

This was a mistake.

He needed to turn back, to leave her to her underground prison. Harmless and alone.

Don't you dare.

The voice was harsh as it filled his mind and internally he winced at its intrusion, though his face gave nothing away. It never did. *We need her, and you know it. She has power the likes of which hasn't been seen in centuries. Once you undo the curse those damned Mihalans placed on her, she will be free to use that power for our cause.* There was a pause before the voice spoke again, accusation sharpening its words. *You do want to fulfill your mother's wishes, don't you? To cleanse these lands and start anew?*

Did he? He hardly knew what he wanted anymore. Not that it mattered anyway. He'd lost the ability to choose the moment he'd let that vile liquid pass his lips.

"A new world," he murmured, reaching his hands up to layer against the goddess's as he loosened her grip. Pulling her hands free of his neck, he gentled the action by pressing a kiss against her knuckles before releasing them altogether. "What do you think, Lumeria? Are you ready to rebuild these lands together?"

"So long as we're rebuilding from ashes, I'm in." Her eyes flashed. "Tell me there will be ashes, Bade. I've been longing to see this place burn. Starting with those pompous hypocrites sitting up there in their precious Mihala."

Did you order that attack, Bade?

Did you tell the Dredgers to burn down the Haven?

There were children, Bade. Innocent babies.

It was the memory of Fia's words, this time, that froze him to the spot. The look on her face when she'd asked about the attack... her eyes had begged him to tell her it wasn't true, and so he had.

How he wished it'd been the truth.

At least she wouldn't have to play witness to what was to come. He'd managed to spare her that. And if she did, she would be on the side of justice. If she regained her strength, she might even be the one to bring him down. He smiled.

Death would be so much sweeter if it were at her hands.

He reached into his coat pocket and pulled out a small, moleskin pouch. Lumeria's eyes widened when she saw it, and she licked her lips. "If they come to my side freely, they will not be harmed." Lumeria's eyes darkened and her lips formed a moue. He went on. "But, if they resist..." She perked up, and her gaze flickered up from the small pouch to meet his own in anticipation. His gut soured, but the words poured out smoothly, nonetheless. "If they resist, we will burn them all to the ground. Every. Last. One."

He turned the pouch over in his hand and three small objects slipped out into his palm – a bone, a vial, and a carefully rolled piece of cloth. He touched the bone with his fingertip.

"The bone of a Mihalan Warrior, killed by my own hand."

He picked up the vial and flicked the stopper off with his thumb before pouring the contents over the bone.

"The blood of a Shendri, blessed by Luxeos, goddess of the sun."

He carefully removed the bit of cloth from the final item, and the jagged sliver of caeruleum core that fell out all but blinded them with its brilliance.

"The heart of the mountain, gifted by Lunares, goddess of the moon."

He paused, lips clamped shut as he resisted saying the dreaded words that would release the Buried Witch upon the world. The creature sneered at his feeble resistance, assuming control of his body as it hissed the final incantation in his stead.

"Escartum deLotus. Let her chains be broken."

His hand closed over the items, crushing them in his fist as the barrier started to fall. The ground shook, and Lumeria's laughter filled the underground cavern as light burst out of every inch of her skin. Stones fell from the ceiling, but they couldn't touch the two demigods as they stood, encircled in her golden light.

Lumeria grabbed his hand as she lifted the other toward the ceiling, sending a beam of blue light upwards through the rock, tunneling its way to the surface above. She squeezed his hand as their fingers interlaced.

"I'm finally going to see the sun again," she breathed, looking euphoric.

"I hate to be the one to tell you this, but it's the middle of the night. You're going to have to wait a few more hours."

"That's okay." A tear glistened on her cheek as she stared up at the patch of starlit sky that had appeared above them. "I've waited five hundred years. What's a few hours more?" Her grip tightened as she whispered a few words in the dark, and then they were rising, with nothing but the wind beneath their feet.

"It's ours now, Bade. All we need to do is take it."

Chapter Two

The dungeon at Hildegarde

"Tonight's the night. I can feel it."

Cashel's lips twitched in an almost smile. They couldn't quite seem to form the real thing anymore, though Edmund's eternal optimism, despite the months they'd spent wasting away in a dank, underground dungeon, made him try. It was either that or scream, and he'd already done enough of that to last a lifetime. The last had been when they'd taken Damek. He'd yelled and attacked the bars like a crazed animal, but all it had gained him was a raw throat and a sound beating.

Screaming would get him nowhere.

Hope, however...

"What makes you say that?" His voice was hushed as he leaned against the wall separating him from Edmund. It was hard to believe his only ally at the moment was a Lowlander knight of all people, but, given his current situation, he could hardly afford to be picky. And Edmund had proven to be a solid guy. There were worse allies to be had.

"Something's changed... it's been quieter than usual the last few days."

There *had* been fewer guards checking on them lately. Still. "How does that help us? Seems to me we're more likely to be forgotten and starve to death than break out of here."

"Ah, but I have a plan."

Of course, he did. Edmund always had a plan. Too bad none of them actually panned out. Then again, what did he have to lose? "I'm listening."

"The guard who brought us dinner... I think his name was

Gerald... or was it Harold?"

Cashel sighed. "Does it matter?"

"Guess not." There was a pause, and Cashel could tell Edmund was still trying to come up with the guard's name.

"So this guard..." he prompted.

"The guard, right. So, the one who brings us dinner is usually the same one that makes the late night rounds, and I don't know if you've noticed, but he's quite the chatter. Always talking it up with the guards posted at the door."

"What about it?"

"Tonight when he brought our food, he didn't say anything. Not a word."

Cashel furrowed his brow. "So...?"

"So, that must mean there *aren't* any guards at the door tonight. It's just him!"

Edmund sounded so triumphant that Cashel hated to say anything, but really... "You think he's alone just because he didn't feel like talking tonight? Maybe he's just having an off day."

"No, he's alone. I'm certain of it."

He certainly *sounded* certain, Cashel had to give him that. "Okay, so let's say it is just the one guard, and he's due to come back soon to check on things. How does that help us when we're in here?"

Edmund let out a calculated chuckle. "Because there's a good chance he doesn't know about your, uh, special ability. You know, the shifting thing. You haven't used it since we attacked the mine, as far as I know. And I doubt we left any witnesses."

He wasn't wrong. However, "I'm sure Bade knows about the Mihalans' ability to skin shift. He may have warned the guards to watch out for it."

"Maybe." Edmund sounded unconcerned. "But even if he did, hearing about it isn't the same as seeing it for yourself. I'm pretty sure we can use it to catch him off guard."

Cashel stood up and started pacing the cell as excited energy coursed through his system. "Okay... so, the guard comes down to make his rounds..."

"Alfie!"

Cashel stopped to stare at the wall of Edmund's cell in confusion. "What?"

"The guard – his name is Alfie, not Harold. Man, was I off."

Cashel groaned. If there wasn't a wall separating the two of them, he'd reach over and slap Edmund in the back of the head. Gods, he was as bad as Berg.

Berg. Had his twin made it back to Mihala? Was he safe? Or was he...

"... and then you tackle him from behind, knock him out and take the keys! And voila! We're outta here."

Shit. He'd spaced out and missed half the plan. "Run that by me one more time?"

This time it was Edmund's turn to sigh. "When Alfie comes through the door, you'll be pressed against the wall with your skin shifted to blend in. Given how dark it is in here, he's not likely to notice your outline. When he sees your empty cell, he'll open it up to investigate, and that's when you get the jump on him. Assuming there aren't any guards at the door tonight, there shouldn't be anyone to hear him shout for help."

"I don't know..."

The clanking of keys outside the dungeon door prevented him from expressing his doubts further, and with Edmund hissing "hurry" through the wall, he quickly slunk back against the darkest wall and laid his hands on the cool stone, soaking in its color and texture as the guard came shuffling into the room.

"Can't believe I'm stuck babysittin' a coupla of caged rats while everyone else is off enjoying themselves," the old guard grumbled as he made his way down the hall between cells. The light from his lantern flickered across the walls as he gave a careless glance into each one. When he got to Cashel's, he paused.

"What the... thought that big guy was in here. Don't 'spose they moved him...?"

Cashel held his breath as he waited for the guard to open the cell door and take a closer look, but to his chagrin, he simply moved on to Edmund's cell, muttering something about "no one telling him anything".

So much for that plan.

He held his shift until the light faded and he heard the door slam shut. Then he let himself slump down onto the floor of his cell in defeat.

"Damn. I thought that would work," Edmund grumbled, and Cashel heard him kick the bars of his cell. "Next time, I'll think of something fail proof."

Next time.

Right.

Cashel didn't even try to smile this time. The fact was, they were never getting out of this place unless Bade himself came down and released them. Which didn't seem too likely, given the length of their stay so far. No, there wouldn't be a next time. Just this. He thought about saying as much to Edmund, then decided against it. He'd probably realized it already, but his drive to return to Maya's side wouldn't let him acknowledge it out loud. Why shove it in his face?

"Did you hear something?"

Cashel attempted to shake off his dark thoughts as he replied. "No, what did it sound like?" A low rumble filled the dungeon, answering the question for him. "What the –" He jumped to his feet as the floor began to shake, sending bits of dirt and dust flying down from the ceiling. The sound grew louder as the shaking increased, and he ran to the door of his cell as a chunk of stone fell onto the ground beside his feet.

"Shit! The whole place is coming down!" Edmund yelled as more pieces of rubble began to fall. Cashel grabbed the stone that had fallen and began to smash it against the lock, each hit more desperate than the last.

If they didn't get out now, they'd be buried alive.

Chapter Three

The royal castle in Eldon

There was someone running toward her on the left. Heavy footfalls – this person was big, most likely a man. Either way, they weren't Shendri.

Fia waited until she felt them make a grab for her before sidestepping and twisting their arm behind their back. Sweep the leg, take them down. Brace yourself for the next attack.

Where the hell were the others?

Reach out with your mind – feel their presence. The Shendri are bonded by magic of the purest form. Embrace that bond, and you will never be alone.

Pretty words if only it were true. Fia grimaced as someone's palm smacked against her skin. A direct hit to the arm. Damn.

Thank gods they weren't using real weapons.

The rough fabric of the blindfold scratched her face, and she scowled as someone's arm wrapped around the back of her neck, pulling her into a headlock. Shit. There were moves she was supposed to use to counter just this thing, but right now – blind, exhausted, and drenched with sweat as she was – it was almost impossible to conjure them.

Tuck the neck, protect your windpipes... drive your hand into the back of his knee, pushing it down, and then... nothing. A total blank.

Just like her.

"Time!"

Luxeos's voice was a welcome relief as she brought the training drill to an end. The person holding Fia in place released their grip, and she let herself drop to her knees on the hard ground.

She ripped the uncomfortable blindfold off and blinked against the sun's glare as she looked around the arena, seeking out the others.

Well, that figures.

Standing back to back in perfect defensive formation were all three of her Shendri sisters – Josselyn, Lily, and Maya were completely in tune with each other. She was the only one who couldn't seem to connect.

Small wonder, seeing as how her bond had come dangerously close to being severed back when... well, she didn't want to think about that day. Thinking of it always led to thinking about him, and those were thoughts best left for when she was alone.

"You alright?"

The person hovering above her – Berg, the seemingly carefree Mihalan prince with a penchant for making her uncomfortable with his constant smiling – offered her his hand. "I didn't hurt you, did I?"

"Not at all." She stood up, ignoring the proffered hand as she dusted off the front of her brown, leather pants. "I'm just tired. Long morning."

"I bet." Berg shook his head, chuckling. "That Luxeos doesn't fool around. She's had you ladies running around from sun-up to sun-down for as long as I've been here. And you do it all, no complaints. Consider me impressed."

Fia shifted her weight from side-to-side as she glanced around the busy arena, looking for an out. She didn't want to talk about training. Not with Berg, not with anyone. Talking about it would only lead to the obvious conclusion – that despite their months of training, Fia had failed to regain her previous power.

She couldn't sense her sister Shendri. Her hand-to-hand combat was pathetic, and her weapons training was worse. Her stamina was okay, but nowhere near the others' capacities. And then, of course, there was Artemis.

The once great dragon who was now more akin to a lovable lizard companion.

At least I didn't lose him altogether.

While she might not be soaring through the skies on his back again anytime soon – if ever – at least she was still able to summon a miniature version of him. And, surprisingly enough, she seemed to be able to keep him out for as long as she wished without tiring. Whether that was due to his diminished size or the proximity of the other Shendri, she couldn't say. Either way, she was grateful. Artemis was the only thing keeping her going most days.

"Hello? You still in there?"

Fia jerked her head up in surprise as Berg tapped her on the shoulder, and he grinned. "There you are. Thought I might of lost ya." He tilted his chin toward the wide, double doors leading out of the arena. "Everyone's heading back to the castle to grab some lunch. You coming?"

"Oh." Fia looked around, startled by the lack of people. Apparently, she'd been lost in thought longer than she realized, as only her sister Shendri remained, hovering near the doorway. Waiting for her, most like. "I, um, yeah. I think I'll just, uh, stretch a bit first. You go ahead."

Berg gave her a concerned look. "You sure?"

She forced a thin smile. "Of course. I'll be along shortly."

"Well... alright." Berg hesitated, and she thought he might offer to wait, but he just shrugged and turned toward the doors. "See you in the dining hall, then."

"See you." She managed a half-hearted wave, then called out to the trio still lingering by the entrance, "I'll meet you guys in a bit. Gonna stretch first." She made a shooing motion and sighed with relief when they acquiesced, leaving her alone.

Wispy smoke pooled around her legs and rose higher, swirling around her body until it solidified into her now pocket-sized, black and green dragon. Perching atop her shoulder, he pressed his forehead against her own in what had become their routine greeting.

"You did well today, Shendri," he said, his voice filling her mind.

Fia snorted. "Ha! That might be more believable if you didn't say it after every training session, particularly ones like today. I failed, Artemis. Miserably."

"Just because you haven't been able to regain your former strength doesn't mean you haven't done well. You're trembling with fatigue and soaked in sweat. You look absolutely dreadful."

"Thanks?"

The tiny dragon let out a puff of smoke. "What I'm trying to say is that you've worked hard. As hard as you could. And that, Shendri, is why I can say with all sincerity that you've done well today."

She smiled – a real smile this time, not one of the forced ones she was always trying to summon around the others. "Shall we eat? I'm famished."

"You know I don't require food."

She laughed. "All the more for me, then." They exited the arena and were headed toward the castle when a series of shouts drew their attention to the front. Fia paused mid-stride and glanced down at Artemis.

"Do you think we should...?"

"See what all the commotion's about? I'll confess, I'm rather interested."

Fia's stomach rumbled, protesting the idea of delayed food. "It's probably nothing. An overturned cart or something like that." Even as she said the words, she felt her body gravitating toward the courtyard. "Ah hell, let's go." Having committed to the course, she fell into an easy jog as she made her way around the side of the huge, stone building. As they neared the front, she could hear the noise escalating as excited voices all clamored at once. Though she couldn't make out what they were saying, she took comfort in the fact that whatever was going on didn't seem unwelcome.

She swung around the corner and took in the gathered crowd. They seemed to be surrounding a small group of men on horseback. Three of the men appeared to be Eldorian soldiers, given that they wore the same uniform she'd seen every day since her arrival. The other two were more familiar. The taller one was clearly Mihalan, with a trail of blue markings tattooed across the dark skin of his bare chest, and he bore a striking resemblance to Berg. *He must be Berg's twin brother, Cashel.* The shorter one had a classically handsome face, despite being a bit gaunt, and a head full of shaggy, light brown hair. She was certain she'd met him before, but she couldn't seem to place him.

"Edmund!"

Maya's voice rose over the crowd as the wolf Shendri came flying through the open entrance doors. The crowd parted as the man swung down off his horse and tossed the reins to the nearest bystander, his steady gaze on the young woman barreling toward him. The weariness that hung from his frame just moments before vanished as his face lit up brighter than any sunrise she'd ever seen. He caught Maya in his arms, half laughing, half crying as he covered her face with kisses.

Fia felt her cheeks heat and quickly looked away from the romantic scene. Edmund. He and Cashel had been two of the prisoners left behind in Antos. Bade's prisoners. She wondered briefly if Bade had set them free. She doubted it.

She slunk away from the crowd before anyone noticed her standing there. Seeing as how the last time these men had seen her, she'd been protecting the very person who'd imprisoned them, she doubted hers was a face they'd want to see first.

If ever.

Chapter Four

Cashel gave the castle gardens a cursory look as he stepped outside. The afternoon sun bathed the grounds in golden light, and white and yellow butterflies flitted here and there above the vibrant flowers that lined the stone path. Birds chirped noisily from nests hidden deep in the grove of cherry trees that separated the gardens from the back wall.

It was beautiful, but, more importantly, it was empty.

Settling onto a stone bench near the back, Cashel tucked into the bowl of soup he'd smuggled out of the dining room.

"Damn, that's good."

He groaned in satisfaction as he swallowed another mouthful. Who knew cold duck soup could taste so good? Granted, just about anything would taste good after weeks of scavenging off the land as he and Edmund had crept their way across Antos. They hadn't eaten a solid meal until reaching the border, where they'd been fortunate enough to run across Edmund's old regime. Even then it'd only been soldier rations.

Seasoning had not been a priority.

He stretched his legs out, soaking in the sun's warmth as he savored this long awaited moment of peace. It'd probably been rude of him to sneak off, given how excited everyone was to hear about their escape, but he just couldn't handle answering any more questions. Berg must have realized how close he'd been to losing it, as it'd been his idea for Cashel to slip out. He'd even been kind enough to create a diversion, for which Cashel was grateful.

The bystanders who'd been splattered with duck soup? Probably less so.

He finished his soup and set the bowl to the side as he stared out over a row of rosebushes. There was just enough of a breeze for him to pick up a whiff of their fragrant scent. He took a deep breath, drinking it all in.

That was when he spotted it.

Something was moving near the base of one of the rosebushes. He leaned forward. It looked like some kind of lizard. He watched the creature dart from one bush to another. A lizard with... wings? What the hell?

He was getting up from the bench to take a closer look when he heard a hissing sound come from over in the trees. It almost sounded like a woman's voice.

"...get back here..."

Okay, that was definitely a woman's voice. It sounded like she was whispering at the weird, lizard creature. But why was she whispering? And what reason did she have for skulking in the cherry trees?

He crossed his arms over his chest as he faced the trees. "You might as well come out. I know you're in there."

There was a long pause, and he was starting to wonder if he should go into the grove himself when a hand appeared, wrapping around the trunk of one of the trees. It was soon followed by a face peeking out from the side. Then, after a slight hesitation, she stepped out fully into the light.

Cashel forgot how to breathe.

She was beautiful in that vulnerable, delicate way that made him want to scale mountains and fight off invading hordes single-handed, anything to keep this porcelain angel from breaking. Her long, red hair fell all the way to her waist, framing a face that stared back at him with round, fearful eyes. He softened his stance as he gave her an encouraging smile.

"Don't worry. I'm not going to bite." He gestured toward his discarded bowl. "I already ate." Her eyes darted toward the bowl, and he thought he saw her lips twitch. "I'm Cashel, by the way."

"I know."

He raised his eyebrows in surprise. "You do?"

She ducked her head. "I mean, I'd heard of your arrival and... and you look so much like Berg, I just assumed..."

"Ah. You know Berg." He sighed. "Why doesn't that surprise me? Please tell me my twin hasn't been making a nuisance of himself."

She looked up, and Cashel found himself studying her wide, flustered eyes. Were they brown? Or hazel? And why did he want to know so badly?

"Oh, no, not at all. He's shown me nothing but kindness, really."

"But..." He drew the word out as he gave her a knowing look.

Some of the nervousness eased from her face as she huffed a short laugh. "But he can be a bit... overwhelming, at times." She shrugged. "He means well. Truly."

Cashel opened his mouth to say just what he thought of his brother's 'well meant intentions' with the ladies when he noticed the strange, winged lizard from earlier pop out of the bushes and dart toward them. It ran straight toward the woman's legs, and Cashel made to grab it before it could reach them.

"Oh! Please don't."

The woman dropped to her knees and held her arms out to the strange creature. "He's my friend." She scooped it up, nuzzling it against her chest as she stood. In turn, the creature let out a puff of smoke as it eyed Cashel in a way that could only be described as smug. Could lizards be smug?

"What is that thing?"

"*Artemis* is a dragon." His face must have looked as dubious as he felt, as she added, "He used to be much larger."

"A miniature dragon. That's crazy." He shook his head. "Would you believe I've actually seen a full-size one before, close up?" He studied the dragon in her arms. "In fact, it looked an awful lot like that one, only huge." Her last statement sank in, and he lifted his gaze in surprise. "Wait – did you say he used to be bigger?" She nodded, the fearfulness returning to her face as she watched him work it out in his head. And work it out he did, as memories of that fateful day returned.

A humongous dragon. Bade, the demigod so powerful he was able to pin Cashel to the ground with a single word. And the woman who'd sacrificed her life for him. Or would have, if Maya hadn't delivered her to the phoenix Shendri in time.

"You're the dragon Shendri."

"My name is Fia Brendarrow." Her voice trembled as she all but whispered the name. "It's an honor to make your acquaintance."

"You were at Hildegarde. With Bade."

She flinched at the harshness in his tone, and he immediately felt like a jerk for snapping. Bade was known to have great powers of persuasion. Real power, not just an affinity for words. For all he knew, this poor girl had been just as much a captive as he had.

"Sorry. I've haven't been around people much lately." He gave her a rueful grin. "I'm glad to see Maya was able to get you here in time, before, uh... things got worse." He paused, wondering how much he should say. His best bet would be to just shut up and leave the poor girl alone, but there was something in the way her body curled in on itself that made him want to say something, anything, to reassure her. If only he knew what.

"Was it bad?"

She frowned, and he mentally kicked himself. *Wrong words, dummy.*

"Was what bad?"

"Being at Hildegarde. Was he... did he..." He swallowed. *Way to dig a hole, idiot.* "Did he hurt you? I know firsthand how hard it is to resist that voice of his, and I was only under its thrall for a short time. I can't even imagine living with that day after day."

"You think I was under his thrall?"

From the incredulous look on her face, she'd never even considered the possibility. He shrugged. "It would make sense. Why else would you stand by someone so blatantly evil?"

Oh, that got her. Gone was the trembling miss ready to bolt at any moment. In her place was an indignant warrior with fire in her eyes. *Dragon fire.*

"I understand you have reason to dislike him –"

"That's putting it mildly."

She glowered at his interruption. "*But,* I'll have you know he has never once used his power to manipulate me. He was..." Her voice cracked, and the fire that had burned so brightly a moment before faded until it was nothing more than dull ash. "He was *kind* to me."

She looked away, hiding her face behind a curtain of hair. He thought she might have said something else, but it was lost in the rustling of leaves. Blown away as easily as the fight he'd seen spark in her eyes. He reached a hand out to comfort her but stopped halfway when he saw her shoulders tense.

Note to self – she doesn't like to be touched.

"Look. I'm sorry if I offended you, I just..." He sighed. "Obviously I'm not seeing the whole picture. You're here now, and you seem to have recovered from your injuries. I don't know if you're planning to join the other Shendri in the fight against Bade or not, but, either way, I hope we can become friends." He paused as he watched the breeze play with a strand of hair covering her hidden face. "I can be kind, too, when I try."

She looked up at that, and he smiled."What do you say, Fia Brendarrow? Wanna be my friend?"

"I..." She swallowed. "I'd like that. Cashel."

His smile grew into a grin. "Excellent." He nodded at the creature she still held cradled in her arms. "So, this is Artemis?"

She stoked the top of the creature's scaly head. "That's right. My celestial beast and very best friend."

"I still can't believe this is the same dragon I saw in Antos."

"I'm afraid so." She gave him a sad smile. "The enchantments that had been worked into Maya's caeruleum arrow, well... let's just say Artemis and I are both lucky to be alive after being struck by something so potent. Luxeos says it must have damaged our bond severely. This is the only form Artemis can manage now, and I..." She clenched her fists. "I can barely fight at all. It's like all of the instincts that came naturally to me before are gone, and I'm a complete beginner again. It's pretty sad to watch, really."

"That's rough."

"It's not much fun, that's for sure." She lifted her chin. "But I'm training with the others every day. I'm sure it'll start to come back soon."

Is she a fragile flower or a stubborn warrior? He shook his head. *She's something, at any rate.*

She bit her lower lip, worrying the flesh as her gaze dropped to her lap. "I'm sorry, by the way – about your imprisonment. Everyone here has been worried sick about you all, Maya and Berg especially. In fact, Maya tried to sneak out and go after you so many times that Luxeos was forced to place a barrier around the castle, preventing her from leaving."

Cashel snorted. "I'm sure that went over well."

"There were words," Fia admitted, a soft smile tugging at her lips. "Some rather heated words."

"I bet," Cashel chuckled.

"It's not that Luxeos didn't want to see you rescued, of course," Fia hurried to add. "But the Mihalans were already forming a team to go after you, and with the Shendri all together for the first time... the risk..."

"Was too great," Cashel finished with a sigh. "I get it, really. And Berg told me about the team who'd been sent to retrieve us. Apparently Hildegarde was encased in such a strong barrier there wasn't the slightest hope of slipping through."

"I'd heard that," Fia admitted, looking at him curiously. "However did you manage to escape it?"

"Honestly? I'm still not entirely sure what happened out there," he replied. "There was an earthquake. We would have been buried alive in the dungeons if we hadn't gotten out when we did, but fortunately my cell door was weakened during the fall. I was able to get the both of us out before the ceiling collapsed altogether. And as for the barrier..." He shrugged. "Whatever caused the earthquake must have wiped it out. Either way, it wasn't in place when we fled."

"That must have been terrifying," Fia murmured. "But you said both of you... weren't there three of you being held prisoner?"

It was Cashel's turn to avert his gaze as the image of Damek's stricken face as they dragged him away floated through his mind. "There was," he replied, his tone clearly stating he didn't care to elaborate.

"Oh." She glanced nervously toward the castle. "I, um, should probably head back in. We're supposed to return to our training after lunch, and I don't want to keep the others waiting." She started to walk toward the castle, then paused and looked shyly over her shoulder. "It really was nice to meet you, Cashel. I hope to see more of you in the future." She gave him one last, tentative smile and left. It wasn't until she'd disappeared through the castle doors that he realized he hadn't said anything in return.

"I look forward to seeing more of you, too." He gazed at the closed door and grinned. "A lot more."

Chapter Five

He wanted to be her friend? Even knowing what side of the line she'd stood on before being brought, unconscious, to this place? To say she had doubts would be putting it mildly, and yet...

For some reason she couldn't explain, Fia hoped he meant it.

He was different from the others. Comforting, despite his initial bite. He may be the identical copy of his brother Berg on the outside, but inside... Fia could tell he ran far deeper. And he wanted to be friends.

Well, why not? It's not like I have a surplus of them at the moment.

She glanced around the small circle of women she sat cross-legged with in the dark forest. A fire crackled away in the center of their tight ring, sending orange sparks up into the night air. It lent an eerie glow to the women's faces – the faces of her sister Shendri.

To her immediate left was Maya, the skin-shifting wolf Shendri. Her first friend among the Shendri, Maya was also the one who'd delivered the near-deadly shot to Fia's chest. Not that it'd been meant for her or anything, but still... it did tend to complicate things. Sure, they talked as if everything that had happened – the Haven, Fia's injury – was all water under the bridge, but if they were being honest with each other, the closeness they'd once felt was gone.

On Maya's other side was Lily, the phoenix Shendri. A fair-haired nymph of a woman, Lily was probably Fia's favorite of all the sisters. She was just so soft. So kind. Not only had she healed Fia's chest wound as best she could after Maya had shot her, she'd also been the one to search her out in Roshka. Back when she'd been enslaved by the baron.

Fia shuddered as she let her gaze slide past Lily's delicate face. The last thing she wanted to do was think about the baron and all those nights she'd spent chained to the wall of that dark, windowless cell.

She had enough nightmares as it was.

Her gaze settled on Josselyn, the hellcat Shendri. Her green eyes were focused on the fire, her face set in an expression of steely determination. She wasn't their leader, per se, but she was the reigning queen of Eldour, which lent her an air of authority that she held even now, sitting in the dark with her sisters. Fia found it surprising that one of the celestial beasts was a hellcat, but she had to admit the two seemed to suit. Neither was afraid to use her claws when necessary.

Last, but not least, was the woman sitting to Fia's right – Luxeos, the former goddess of the sun. The creator of the original Shendri, she'd used the power of her own celestial robes to pull the beasts down from the heavens and instill them inside four young women of exceptional character and strong will. Her answer to Bade's destruction, some two hundred years ago. It'd been successful at the time, but now, here they were. Sitting in the woods, in the dark, as they tried to regain the strength they'd need to stave him off for good.

Assuming that's what had to be done.

Fia's head understood it to be necessary, but her heart... well, that was another story. One she couldn't afford to dwell on at this moment. For now, she needed to concentrate.

"Josselyn, tell me what you see." Luxeos' soothing voice filled the silence as the four Shendri focused on their meditation. Or attempted to, in Fia's case.

"I see Kella. She's lounging on the low branch of a tree, deep in the jungle."

"Very good," Luxeos murmured. "Now tell me, what do you feel when you look at her?"

"I feel... strength." There was a pause, and Fia cracked one eye open to see Josselyn's face lit with wonder. "It's emanating from her form. It's like I can actually *feel* it rolling off of her and into my own body." Josselyn flexed her hand. "It makes me wish I had my sword. Something to channel all of this power into."

"The hellcat is a natural fighter, as are you," Luxeos concurred. "With your sister Shendri at your side, you should have access to more power than you've ever had before. Use it wisely. Control is everything."

"I will," Josselyn responded confidently.

"Good." Luxeos turned to Maya, and Fia quickly squeezed her eyes shut, not wanting to get caught in her distraction. "Maya?" the older woman prompted. "How about you? What are you seeing and feeling at this moment?"

"I'm in a forest," the wolf Shendri replied. "Kitsune is here, running circles through the trees." She laughed. "I can hardly see her, she's so fast. Like a white blur."

"And how does that make you feel?" Luxeos prompted.

"Like I could run to Myr and back without stopping. I'd cut straight through Antos, and they wouldn't even realize I was there until it was too late," Maya bragged.

Luxeos hummed. "A *bit* over the top, but I like your confidence. And you're right. The celestial wolf gives you speed unlike any mortal you'll find here. Channel that ability into your archery and the Antoski won't know what hit them."

"Excellent," Maya gloated.

"Indeed," Luxeos murmured dryly. "And you, Lily? What do you see?"

Her question was met with silence, and Fia peeked through her lashes at the phoenix Shendri. Lily sat cross-legged, with her arms resting loosely on her knees. There was a look of intense concentration on her face, and she startled a bit when Luxeos repeated her name.

"Lily?"

"Oh! Sorry, it's just…" She paused, taking a breath and relaxing her shoulders before continuing. "Suzaku's home, it's so beautiful."

"Tell us," Luxeos urged. "What do you see?"

"An open sky, the bottom half of which is streaked with a permanent pink and orange sunset. Above that is a glorious display of stars, the like of which I've never seen before. It's absolutely breathtaking." She smiled, eyes still closed in concentration. "There's a lone tree standing amid a field of endless grass, and Suzaku's nest is in its branches."

"Is the phoenix there? Can you see her?"

"She is," Lily replied. "She's perched at the top of the tree, staring up at the stars."

"And what do you feel when you look at her?"

"I feel peaceful but also oddly protective." Lily wrinkled her nose. "Not of Suzaku so much, but of everyone else. Like I'd do anything to keep Lehi safe, even if I have to throw myself in front of an army to do so. Does that make sense?"

"Actually, it does," Luxeos replied. "You already know the phoenix has the power to heal. You were able to tap into that power before the Shendri were completely united, which is rather remarkable. Although, I suspect the dragon had something to do with that, but I digress. Now that you're all together, you should be able to hone your other abilities, not the least of which is the ability to shield."

"What do you mean?"

"I mean, you should be able to create a contained barrier, a protective bubble of sorts. If done correctly, it will be able to repel both magical and physical attacks. An incredibly valuable asset to have when going into battle."

"And you can teach me how to use it?" Lily asked.

"I believe I can," Luxeos confirmed. "We'll start training with it first thing tomorrow."

"Thank you," Lily exclaimed.

"You're welcome," Luxeos murmured, already turning her focus toward Fia. She quickly squeezed her eyes shut again, mentally cursing herself for not focusing on her own inner sanctum or whatever Luxeos had called it earlier.

"And you, Fia?" Luxeos asked. "What do you see?"

A whole lot of nothing, thanks for asking.

"I see... Artemis?" Fia wrinkled her brow, trying desperately to pick something out of the oblivion. *I don't suppose you could help me out here, Artemis?* Her plea was met with silence, and she gritted her teeth in frustration. *Thanks a lot, partner.*

"The Shendri are responsible for maintaining the bond, not the beasts," Artemis replied at last, his deep voice echoing through her mind. "There's nothing I can do that you cannot do for yourself

Great.

"What else do you see?" Luxoes asked, interrupting Fia's fuming.

"I see..." Fia took a deep breath, deliberating over her answer. Or, if she were being completely honest, stalling. She sighed. "Nothing. I see nothing."

"Nothing," Luxeos repeated. "Are you certain?"

"I'm afraid so."

"I see." It was Luxeos's turn to sigh. "I know this past year hasn't been the easiest, Fia, but you really must try. Lehi is depending on you."

"No pressure or anything," Fia muttered.

"I heard that," Luxeos retorted. "And yes, I do realize how much pressure the four of you are under right now. And I'm sorry for that. But what Bade is attempting to do to our world right now is unpardonable, and the four of you are the only ones strong enough to put a stop to it. So, I need you to put aside your past and focus on the present. Focus on regaining control. Your power is critical to the Shendri's success."

"My power?" Fia opened her eyes, not even pretending to meditate any more. "Don't you mean Artemis's power? Aside from partnering with a dragon – which I'll admit is pretty badass – I've never really had any true powers of my own. Not like the others, anyway."

"Oh, you have powers," Luxeos insisted. "You just haven't tapped into them yet."

"Okay, so what are they?"

Luxeos tilted her head to the side, studying her, and Fia tried not to squirm under the scrutiny. Around the circle, the others abandoned their own mediation as they leaned forward curiously. All eyes were on Luxeos as she spoke. "That's for you to discover yourself, I'm afraid. If you can't feel the connection, you won't be able to use them." She held up a finger as Fia's face twisted in disappointment. "I can tell you one thing, however."

Fia's ears perked up, and she held her breath as she waited for Luxeos to continue. The former goddess looked around the circle, meeting each of the Shendri's eyes before speaking. "The dragon has always been at the head of the celestial beasts. Which makes his host the leader of the Shendri. You, Fia, are the natural leader of this group."

I'm the leader of the Shendri? Seriously?

"Are you serious? *She's* our leader?" Josselyn gave Fia a dubious look, and Fia tried not to be insulted. After all, she'd been thinking the same thing.

"I thought Joss was our leader," Maya added. She looked at Fia and shrugged. "No offense, it's just confusing."

"It's true that Josselyn is the queen of Eldour, and in that manner she is your leader," Luxeos agreed. "But that doesn't necessarily make her the leader of the Shendri. The dragon is the beast that binds you together. I suspect it was his power that allowed Lily to tap into her healing abilities, back in Roshka. The leader has the ability to amplify or diminish the others' powers, depending on the situation. Fia, as his host, should be able to do so as well."

"So she can make us stronger?" Lily asked, giving Fia an encouraging look. "That's wonderful!"

"Or weaker," Josselyn muttered under her breath. Fia pursed her lips in annoyance. That'd definitely been an insult.

"She won't be able to do either without more training," Luxeos replied. "So I suggest we all head in and get some sleep. We'll be meeting in the training arena at the break of dawn."

There were a few grumbles as they all climbed to their feet and worked to put out the fire before leaving. As they trudged back toward the castle, Josselyn fell into step beside Luxeos. "We can't stay holed up here training much longer, you know. Not if we want to have any chance of helping the Roshkans fend off Bade's attack."

"I know," Luxeos agreed with a sigh. "But I can't send you out there until Lily can at least manage a basic shield. Once she's gotten the feel for it, you can go."

"I hope you're a fast learner, Lils," Josseyln called back. "'Cause we are dangerously short on time."

"Gee, thanks, Joss," Lily replied. "Nothing like a little pressure to make the training go smoother."

"I'm serious." Josseyln stopped walking in order to turn and face them all. "The Antoski army is already pressing in on Roshka. If we don't join forces with them soon, they'll take the kingdom completely. Which will leave only us and the Eastern Islands unclaimed. And I'll give you one guess as to who they'll be focusing on next." She gave them a pointed look. "We can't afford to wait and see any longer. We need to fight back."

"You say that like it's a problem." Maya smirked. "I've never felt stronger, and you've gotten downright terrifying with that sword of yours. Throw Kella and Kitsune into the mix, and we'll wipe the floor with those Antoski jerks."

"Ahem." Lily raised her eyebrows, giving Maya a look.

"And Lily," Maya amended. "She's the one who's going to keep us all in one piece, which I for one appreciate greatly."

Lily grinned. "Thank you." She turned to meet Fia's eyes. "And you'll be with us, making us more powerful than ever."

Fia managed a half-hearted smile but refrained from comment.

"Let's not forget we'll have both the Eldorian army as well as the Mihalan Guard backing us up, as well," Josselyn reminded them.

"Don't forget the Dirt Mercs!" Maya added. "The Mercs are always down for a good fight."

"That's right!" Josselyn grinned. "Bade may have the numbers, but we have some serious power."

He also has firearms and a voice that can control an entire crowd of people, but sure... let's focus on the positive, Fia thought to herself wryly. Out loud, she asked, "What about Eldour? How do we know Bade won't switch tactics and attack the Eldourian border once all of our forces have moved into Roshka?"

"Why? Does he have spies informing him of our movements?" Josselyn's eyes narrowed suspiciously. "You were his right-hand for over a year. How do we know you aren't communicating with him even now?"

"I'm not," Fia ground out. "I'm just pointing out the *obvious* fact that we'll be leaving the border unprotected, *Your Majesty*."

"She's right," Maya added calmly. "We need a plan in place in case he changes direction."

"I know." Josselyn blew out a gust of air. "And I do. Or rather, Luxeos does. I'm sorry, I just..." She threw Fia an apologetic look. "I'm having a hard time accepting the fact that you're on our side now. I want to believe you are, but, I mean, it's not like you chose to come here yourself. You were dragged here on the brink of death. I guess I'm still working on the whole trust thing."

"I get it." Fia dropped her head. "And you're right – I may never have come if he hadn't told Maya to take me. I was blind to everything then." Her stomach twisted as she thought of all the lies he'd told. Not just about the Haven but about his vision. She'd been convinced he had only the best of intentions. Now, with a little distance and the proof of all the damage he'd caused, the lives he'd felt justified in destroying... now she could see him for who he really was. And she didn't care for what she saw.

Funny how you could hate someone so much yet still long for them to hold you one last time.

The group fell silent, leaving a heavy feeling of discomfort to seep into air until Lily finally broke it. "You said you have a plan? For Eldour?"

Josselyn visibly relaxed. "That's right, we do." She turned to Luxeos, the only one who seemed unaffected by all the tension. "Luxeos? Would you like to explain to everyone?"

"I'd be happy to," the older woman replied, clasping her

hands together. "When the four of you leave for Roshka, I'll create and maintain a barrier around the kingdom that should keep any Antoski soldiers from crossing over and attacking while you're gone."

"You can do that?" Maya asked, looking more interested than surprised. Personally, Fia thought the idea was pretty shocking. A barrier around the entire kingdom? Who had that kind of power?

"With the help of your father and few of his more powerful caeruleum workers," Luxeos replied. She hesitated then added, "And a piece of my robes."

Josselyn turned on her. "You didn't tell me you were going to use your celestial robes. Luxeos, that's crazy! You'll wither away if you use too much."

"Pish posh. I'll be fine." Luxeos waved a hand in the air. "It won't take more than a few strips."

"But why use it at all?" Maya asked. "The Mihalans created a barrier around the mountains with just caeruleum – why can't they make something similar around Eldour?"

Luxeos tensed, the first sign of discomfort Fia had seen from her all night,and there was a long pause before she responded. "We have reason to believe that Bade has broken down the mountain barrier. There have been reports... several people, Edmund and Cashel included, have witnessed a number of earthquakes around the base of the mountains, particularly near the border of Antos and Myr. They've been quite severe, and both King Malachite and I agree that they are likely a result of the barrier's destruction."

"What about Mihala?!" Maya exclaimed. "Do you think he's attacked the city? Are the people safe?"

"Mihala has other measures in place to keep outsiders away," Luxeos replied, though her voice was less than reassuring. "We must hope they keep any invaders at bay until we can strike from the south. Hopefully, our presence there will draw Bade's attention away from the mountain city."

"Right." Lily smiled ruefully. "So in other words, I need to ace this shield training and fast."

"Pretty much, yeah," Josselyn confirmed. "But don't worry – we'll be right there with you. Between the four of us, you'll be throwing up shields in no time."

Chapter Six

The road to Roshka

The slow grind of wagon wheels, the steady clip-clop of horses' hooves. The heavy fall of booted feet marching in perfect rhythm. The air practically vibrated with the sound of impending battle.

Battle.

The word echoed in Cashel's mind as his horse lumbered down the Southern Road toward Devon. *Not a surprise skirmish, like in Antos. We had the jump on them then. We had a plan.* He tightened his grip on the reins. *This time, they'll know we're coming.*

His eyes darted toward Berg, who rode beside him on a spirited-looking stallion. Too spirited, in his opinion. Mihalans weren't exactly known for their horsemanship. His stomach clenched at the thought of Berg riding the beast into battle.

I won't be able to keep him out of it this time.

"You can wipe that look off your face right now, Cash."

Cashel coughed. "What look?"

"You know what look," Berg retorted. "The one you get when you're worrying over me like an old, mother hen."

"Oh. Right. That look."

Berg chuckled. "What's got your protective vibes all fired up this time?"

Cashel shot his twin a look. "Oh, I don't know. Maybe the fact that we're traveling to Roshka with the entire Eldorian army, not to mention a significant portion of the Mihalan Guard, in order to join the armies already gathered at the front lines? I don't suppose that would be considered a good reason for feeling protective of the people you care about."

"Cash. Breathe."

"I *am* breathing," Cashel growled.

Berg snorted. "Then breathe deeper. Whatever you gotta do to calm down. If you wind yourself up any tighter, you're gonna snap."

Cashel huffed out a sharp breath. "There. Happy?"

"As a matter of fact, I am."

He did look happy. Which seemed crazy, given the fact that they might very well be riding off to their deaths. He glanced around at the slow-moving convoy, taking in the mix of faces. Most were strangers, but many still were not. They were family, friends.

Loved ones.

"Why?"

The question came out sounding as incredulous as he felt, and he could see Berg's lips turning up in an amused smirk as soon as he finished asking it.

"Oh, I don't know," Berg countered, stealing Cashel's earlier phrase. "Maybe because my twin brother, whose life I worried after for months, is healthy and whole and at my side?" He lifted his chin toward the group of riders just ahead of them. "Or maybe because our father has finally been able to reunite with the love of his life after years of loneliness? Not to mention the fact that we have an awesome new sister who could kick all of our asses combined?" He turned to meet Cashel's eyes, and the fervency Cashel saw in his twin's gaze was startling.

"Or maybe, just maybe, it's because we're on our way to take down the asshole who not only imprisoned you and Edmund for months but killed one of my best friends."

"We don't know that Damek is dead for sure," Cashel replied woodenly.

"Yeah, we do."

Yeah. We do. Even if he hadn't witnessed it, there was no other reason for them to remove the guard from the dungeons when they did. No other reason than ridding themselves of one more mouth to feed. Not that they were fed well, anyway. *Bastards.*

"And, of course, there are the countless lives he's taken throughout Myr and now Roshka," Berg continued. "So yeah, I'm happy. Happy I'm finally gonna get a chance to kill the son of a bitch once and for all."

That did sound kind of nice. Though Cashel would prefer to keep his brother away from the action, and let one of the other qualified warriors do the honors, instead. He thought of the squadron of Eldorian knights riding up at the front, Edmund included. Any of them would do fine. And, of course, the Mihalan Guard, who rode among them, were apt fighters, as well.

The real odds, however, were on one of the Shendri taking him out. He hadn't been able to watch much of their training, but what he had seen had been impressive. More than impressive, really. The Eldorian queen, Josselyn, had been awe-inspiring with the way she wielded her sword, and her hellcat Kella?

Downright terrifying.

He'd known from experience that Maya was talented when it came to archery, but even his memory of her tearing through the field in Antos paled to what she could do now. She and Kitsu were a well-oiled machine, and he pitied anyone who crossed their path in battle.

The phoenix Shendri, Lily, wasn't to be discounted, either. While he wouldn't put money on her being the one to take out Bade herself, she was the shield that would allow the other two to succeed. Literally. He'd seen the shimmering wall she'd erected during their last training session, and he'd bet anything it'd block more than physical attacks. And here he'd thought she was just a healer. Ha. The three of them were growing more powerful by the day, and he, for one, was grateful to be on the same side.

And then there was Fia.

His eyes sought her out as if by instinct. She was on the outskirts of the group following the knights and Guard, which didn't surprise him. She always seemed to be hovering on the fringes. Lily and her fiancé, Draven, rode beside her, the only pair in the entire group riding double. He wondered if it was because Lily lacked experience as a rider, or if they simply didn't want to be separated. From the way Draven's arm wrapped possessively around her slender waist, he'd guess the latter.

Lily was chattering away about something, to which Fia responded with an occasional word or two, or sometimes just a slight nod. She seemed to be listening intently, however, and Cashel wondered if she was shy or just naturally quiet.

I wonder what her laugh sounds like.

"She's something else, isn't she?"

He snapped his head around to find Berg grinning at him like the cheeky bastard he was. He scowled at his twin, but Berg prattled on as if he didn't notice.

"She's a tough nut to crack, though. Stingy with her words and even more so with her smiles." He let out an exaggerated sigh. "But the goddesses help me when she does. Pure loveliness."

"Please tell me you haven't been forcing your so-called charms on her," Cashel groaned.

"Hardly!" Berg protested. "I've been nothing but a perfect gentleman."

Cashel raised an eyebrow, giving his twin a look of supreme doubt.

"Okay, so I've been a *friendly* gentleman," Berg amended. "But I never push her, if that's what you're worried about. I'm not some heavy-handed jerk who can't read the signs right in front of my face. She's nervous around men, and I respect that. I just can't help wanting to show her we're not all monsters, you know?"

Cashel made a noise of concession, but his mind was already replaying Berg's words. *She's nervous around men?* He wondered about that. Sure, she seemed kind of shy, but he wouldn't say she'd seemed overly nervous the other day.

Maybe she's different with me. The thought instantly made him feel like an arrogant fool. *Yeah, right. 'Cause you're so smooth and all. How could she resist?*

He chuckled to himself, more than willing to laugh at his own absurdity. Still, he found his gaze wandering in her direction more often than not as they pushed forward, inching their way toward the Roshkan border.

Chapter Seven

"I don't think I can take another day in the saddle," Lily groaned, rubbing her backside. "It's been three days, and I already feel like my butt's going to fall off."

"If you're worried, I'd be more than happy to hold it in place for you."

Fia averted her eyes as Draven wrapped his arms around the golden-haired phoenix Shendri, who lifted her face with a laughing smile as he bent his own down to meet her. After riding beside the pair for three straight days, she'd seen more kissing and flirting than one should ever have to be subjected to in a lifetime.

Assuming, of course, you weren't the one being kissed.

"I'm going to go set up my bedroll," she murmured, grabbing her pack off the ground and scooting around the couple, who she was fairly certain had forgotten her existence entirely. She picked her way across the busy encampment, heading to the outer edge. Several campfires had already been lit, with large pots of stew filling the air with a heavenly aroma. Her stomach rumbled in response, reminding her that it'd been hours since she'd last eaten anything.

I'll just find a nice, secluded spot to sleep, and then food, she promised herself, eyeing a group of Dirt Mercs as they hefted a large, wooden barrel off one of the wagons. *And maybe just one pint of rock fruit cider,* she added. *Seeing as how they went through all the trouble to bring it.* She noted the location of the Mercs' fire before moving on. *Maybe it'll help me sleep for once. Wouldn't that be something.*

Reaching the edge of the encampment at last, she looked around for a good spot to lay out her bedding. It wouldn't do to stray too far from the group, but set up too close and someone might hear her. She was willing to risk her safety a bit if it meant keeping her nightmares to herself.

I don't need any more of their pity.

She dropped her bundle onto the ground and knelt beside it, spreading it out across the soft grass. She took her time smoothing the blanket on top, as if it mattered. Really, she was just stalling. Hungry though she was, her stomach felt almost leaden as she thought of all the wary glances that had been cast her way since arriving in Eldour, a broken and useless traitor.

For that's what they thought of her as, really.

A traitor.

"Love makes fools of us all," she muttered, partly to herself and partly to Artemis, whose warmth she could feel even now, deep within her chest. But it wasn't Artemis who answered.

"Indeed it does, Miss Brendarrow."

She turned to find one of the Mihalan princes watching her from a careful distance. *Cashel,* she thought. *Berg would never sound so polite.*

"Sorry." He gave her an apologetic smile. "I didn't mean to sneak up on you. Thought you would've heard me coming." He shifted on his feet, looking uncertain. "I can go, if you want to be alone..." He started to turn away, and she scrambled to find her voice.

"No!"

He paused, and she hurried to put her thoughts in order before she caused yet another person to think she was some kind of broken freak. "It's fine. If you wanna stay, I mean." She winced at the eagerness in her voice. Must she sound so desperate? She stood, taking a breath as she did to steady herself. "I... I could use a, uh, change in company."

He raised his eyebrows.

"Lily," she hurried to add. "I've been riding with her and Draven for the past three days and, uh..."

"And they're a bit much to take?"

"Just a bit."

He chuckled. "Say no more. I've had my fill of moon-eyed lovers, myself, between Edmund and my sister, not to mention whatever poor female my brother is pursuing at any given moment. Ridiculous, the lot of 'em."

"They really are." She twisted her hands together, at a loss for anything else to say. Luckily, Cashel didn't seem to share her problem.

"I was just going to get some dinner when I saw you setting up over here." He gave her bedroll a curious look. "Kinda far away, isn't it?"

"Oh, um, yeah." She picked at a loose thread at the bottom of her tunic, avoiding his eyes. "I guess it is, a bit." She shrugged, hoping he'd leave it at that. He didn't.

"Why so far away?" He lowered his voice. "Do you snore?"

She let out a surprised laugh, then covered her mouth with her hand as Cashel's eyes grew wide. Her cheeks flushed under his fascinated stare, and he gave his head a shake.

"Sorry. I'm not trying to make you uncomfortable, I swear," he assured her, looking contrite. "You just surprised me. I don't think I've ever heard you laugh before."

Her cheeks burned even brighter.

"It's not that surprising," she protested. "We've barely spoken." *Despite your promise of friendship,* she added to herself. After their conversation in the garden, she'd expected him to seek her out sooner. Had actually hoped he would.

"True." He grinned. "But that doesn't mean I haven't been paying attention. When the most beautiful woman I've ever seen laughs, I notice."

"Okay, *Berg.*"

He laughed. "That bad, huh?"

She smirked. "Worse."

"Noted." He rubbed the back of his head, grinning ruefully. "I've never been good at flirting. Probably due to lack of practice."

"If it makes you feel any better, I've never been comfortable being flirted *with.* Usually it has me looking for the closest exit. At least when you do it, it's simply amusing."

"How is hearing that my pathetic attempts at flirtation are amusing supposed to make me feel better? That just sounds sad on my part."

"But amusing is a good thing," Fia argued. "It means I'm comfortable with you." She tucked a strand of hair behind her ear, feeling suddenly shy. "There aren't many people I can say that about. It's a compliment."

When he didn't say anything, she ventured a peek at his face, and the look she saw there nearly made her cry, it was so tender. When was the last time anyone had ever looked at her like that?

Shh, love. I'm here. I'll always be here.

She swallowed, brushing the memory away. It had no place out here in the sunlight, in the presence of a desperately needed new friend.

"So, uh, you wanna grab some food with me?" She attempted a smile, but it was weak and, from the curiosity she saw reflected in Cashel's gaze, obviously forced. He didn't question it, however. Much to her relief.

"Only if we can steal a pint of that rock fruit cider I saw the Mercs passing around earlier to go with it," he said. "Maya claims it's better than the stuff we make up in Mihala, but I suspect she's biased."

"She might be biased, but she's probably also right. Although, I'm more than happy to help you test that theory."

"What are we waiting for, then? Research awaits!"

Fia grinned. "Lead the way."

Two pints of cider and a bowl of stew later, Fia found herself feeling almost happy for the first time in months. Artemis was out and curled up in a ball on her lap. He made soft sounds of contentment as she stroked the scales along the ridge of his spine. The rest of the Shendri were seated around the fire with their respective partners (minus Alex, who'd reluctantly agreed to stay and run things in Eldour), and Lily's voice filled the night air with the sweet sounds of an unfamiliar love song.

And, of course, there was Cashel.

He sat sprawled out in the grass beside her, looking completely at home in the informal setting. His head was tilted back and his eyes were closed as he listened to Lily's singing, but they popped open and swung her way, as if he could feel the weight of her gaze upon him. His lips curved into a smile as their eyes met.

"I had no idea the phoenix Shendri was such a talented singer," he whispered, shifting his body closer in order to be heard.

"Oh, yes," Fia agreed. "Lily has the most beautiful voice I've ever heard. It's almost as sweet as she is."

"The two of you are friends, then?"

"I guess you could say that. She's certainly been kind to me, despite everything." She hesitated. "And, of course, she risked a lot to help me, back before I knew about all this." She looked down at the tiny dragon asleep in her lap. "Before I discovered Artemis and learned what it felt like to fly."

"That must have been pretty amazing, riding a dragon like that."

"It's alright," Fia teased.

Cashel grinned. "Just alright, huh?"

"Okay, okay, you're right. It was beyond amazing. Once I got over the initial terror of being that high off the ground, anyway. Thank goodness Bade was sitting behind me, or I might have fainted..." She trailed off as she saw Cashel's shoulders stiffen.

Why did I have to go and mention Bade? Gods, I ruin everything.

Cashel was quiet for a moment, but she could feel his eyes on her as he contemplated whatever it was that had him looking so pensive.

Please, don't ask me about Bade.

He cleared his throat, and she braced herself for the inevitable.

"You said Lily helped you before. What'd she help you with?"

Shit. I take it back. Ask me about Bade. I'd much rather talk about him than that... monster.

"It's a long story."

"Okay."

She narrowed her eyes. "And it's getting late."

He reached over and touched her arm lightly. "If you don't want to talk about it, just say so. I won't push you."

"I'm just tired, is all."

"Then I'll walk you back to your bedroll." He stood up and offered her his hand before she could protest. Reluctantly accepting it, she was surprised at the way her body seemed to relax the moment his large hand covered her own. As if it were the most natural thing in the world to be holding this man's hand.

"How do you do that?" she asked, looking up at him in wonder.

He laced his fingers through hers, keeping hold of her hand even after she was solidly on her feet. "Do what?"

"Make me feel so... safe."

"I make you feel safe?" He grinned, looking pleased.

She blushed. "Well... yeah. Somehow. I can't really explain it."

"No need, I get it." He winked. "I'm an impressive specimen of a man, after all."

"Now you sound like Berg again."

"Damn it. And here I was trying to sound smooth."

"Hmm."

"And what's that supposed to mean, Little Miss Hmm?"

She smirked. "Maybe just stick with comfortable. Smooth doesn't really seem like your thing."

"Ouch." He flinched. "You wound me."

"Well, I am a warrior, or so they tell me." She made a face. "Me and my tiny dragon."

His expression grew serious. "He might be tiny now, but keep working at it, and who knows. You could be flying above us all before you know it."

She shrugged, not willing to admit her doubts out loud. She'd busted her butt during those last few days of training, trying to amplify the others' power somehow, but the whole concept still seemed rather murky and confusing. Then there'd been the hours of meditation spent seeking Artemis's sanctum and the key to her own powers, all in vain. She was still as clueless as ever.

They stopped at the foot of her solitary bedroll, and Cashel threw a concerned look back at the encampment, the edge of which was a good fifteen feet away.

"Are you sure you don't want to sleep with the other Shendri?"

"I'm good here."

"You're not worried? There could be wolves out here, or, uh... I don't know, snakes."

"I'll be fine," Fia insisted. "I sleep better without anyone near me." *Liar. You sleep better when Bade's with you.*

"I see." Cashel seemed to consider this. "How about this?" He dropped down onto the grass and stretched out on his back, folding his arms behind his head. Fia felt the heat rising to her face yet again as she tried not to stare at his sculpted – and very bare – abdomen, but was soon distracted by something far more fascinating.

His skin was turning green.

She blinked. Not just green. It was as if the very texture was changing before her eyes. *Like grass.*

"Wow."

The word slipped out of her breathless lips before she could stop it, and a set of white teeth flashed in a wide grin from the Cashel-shaped patch at her feet. "I'm Mihalan, remember? We can skin-shift."

"Right. I knew that." Fia shook her head in disbelief. "I've just never seen a full shift like that. It's incredible."

"It's a handy skill to have. And," he added. "It makes me practically invisible. You won't even notice me."

"Wait —" She gaped at him. "You're not suggesting you

should sleep like that? Here?"

"Why not? I'm perfectly comfortable, and this way I'll know you're safe."

"But, um..." She swallowed. "Won't you get cold without any blankets or, um, a shirt?"

"Nah. Mihalans never get cold. Another perk of my impressive lineage."

"And the ego? Is that an inherited trait or is it just you?"

He chuckled. "Quiet down, would you? I'm trying to sleep over here."

"You're not serious."

"I'm always serious. Now, go to sleep already. I'm tired." He let out a loud yawn, and she couldn't resist sending a little kick into the side of his leg, which he ignored. Her stomach sank as she realized he had every intention of staying. And no doubt if she moved, he'd simply follow.

Maybe I won't have any nightmares tonight. She reluctantly settled into her bedroll, casting one last look at Cashel's grass-covered form. It was strange, but, much like Cashel himself, oddly comforting. Briefly, she wondered what it would feel like to be wrapped in those same, strange arms.

Would they feel like His?

Chapter Eight

The Royal Palace in Garish, Antos.

The moon was hiding tonight.

His mother's moon.

Bade's fingers tapped restlessly against the crystal tumbler he held as he gazed out across the blanketed darkness from the study's window. A wrinkled piece of parchment hung loosely from his other hand.

So, the Eldorians are finally making their move. His fingers tightened around the parchment, crumpling it. *An entire army marches down to join the Roshkan front. No doubt led by the Shendri.*

He waited for the creature to chastise him, reminding him once again that he should never have allowed the wolf and dragon Shendri to slip from his grasp, but there was nothing. Only blessed silence. He took a slow sip of wine, savoring the moment.

If only there was a way to quiet it forever – that insidious creature who'd taken root inside his mind, bending him to its will. Turning him into a monster.

He'd considered killing himself, ending it all before he could do any more harm, but the creature inside him would always stop him before he could follow through. As if it knew even before he did what he was going to try.

Perhaps it did.

It certainly seemed to know everything else about him.

Not everything, he reminded himself. *Not when it comes to her. If it knew how much she meant to me, it would have never let her leave here alive.* How he had managed to hide it, he couldn't say.

He was simply grateful she'd been allowed to escape.

Grateful, indeed. He shook his head before downing the rest of his drink. *You've been miserable every moment she's been gone. Why lie to yourself?*

A brisk knock sounded at the door just before it opened behind him. He smothered a sigh of irritation. *Why bother knocking at all, if you're just going to barge in?*

"It's late," Lumeria complained in a petulant voice. "How long are you planning to keep me waiting up there?" She swept into the room, and he inwardly cringed when he turned and saw she was clad only in a thin, white nightgown. And a rather translucent one, at that.

"I didn't realize I was. My apologies."

She walked over to his desk and traced a finger along the edge as she made a show of looking over the papers there. "You say that every night," she grumbled. "So, what's your excuse this time? More urgent plans?"

"As a matter of fact, yes." He held up the crumpled piece of parchment. "I've just received a report that the Eldorians are marching south down to Roshka. From their location, I would guess they'll arrive at the capital in a few days."

"And?"

"*And*, we'll need to be prepared. Our army alone may not be enough to hold the territory we've already secured. Not with the two kingdoms working together."

"But our men have firearms. Surely that must count for something."

"Something, yes. But not enough. Not until I can finish my newer designs. The ones we're using right now are powerful, but limited. The reloading is far too time consuming for my liking."

"So what do you propose, then?"

"I propose we join them." He watched as her eyes flared with a mixture of excitement and suspicion.

"You want to travel to the front lines. The two of us," she stated, watching him carefully. He dipped his chin in a nod.

"The Eldorians will be helpless against our combined

powers. You'll cage them in, and I'll soothe them into submission. As easy as that."

"And neat," she added, narrowing her eyes. "Not a single drop of blood spilled, I suppose."

He shrugged. "Why kill when you can reform? Wouldn't you rather claim their people for our own?"

"Not particularly." She sniffed. "I'd much rather dance across a blood-soaked battlefield. Your methods aren't nearly as much fun."

"The goal of this war is to create a better life for those who need it. To lift up the poor and weak while tempering the power of those who consider themselves elite. If we can achieve that without bloodshed, then all the better."

"Says you," Lumeria groaned. She moved around the desk, closing the distance between them. "A bit hypocritical, don't you think?" Resisting the urge to back away, Bade gave the witch a cool look as she trailed a hand up his arm until her fingers brushed the hair on the back of his neck.

"And why is that?"

"Oh, I don't know." She rolled her eyes. "Maybe because you have no qualms about linking your name with ruthless mercenaries like the Sea Snakes and the Dredgers, and yet you still claim to want a bloodless revolution."

"I've never ordered them to do anything overly violent." *At least, not by own will,* he thought bitterly. The creature, on the other hand, had a definite taste for blood.

She snorted. "And yet, how many villages have the Dredgers razed in your name? How many ships have found themselves at the bottom of the sea after a surprise attack from the Sea Snakes?"

"I didn't ask them to do those things."

"The orders may not have come from you directly, but you are just as responsible for the outcomes. You're their leader, after all."

He glared at her, wanting to contradict her words. If only they weren't quite so true.

"And let's not forget Mihala," she added with a sly smirk. "Or what's left of it, anyway."

His stomach soured at the reminder, and he turned his gaze away, focusing instead on the dark window.

"If you use nothing but sweet words to turn the people's minds, you'll find them turning back again in the long run," Lumeria continued, oblivious to his distress. She grinned, her fingers digging into the back of his neck. "But if you show them blood, they will learn to fear you." She pulled his face down, capturing his mouth in a rough kiss that ended with her teeth sinking into the soft flesh of his lower lip. "They'll learn to fear *us*," she added in a husky whisper.

An ache built in his temples as the creature began to stir. No doubt awoken by the blood lust in Lumeria's voice. The two of them seemed to have that in common. His hand trembled as he fought to retain control.

"I don't wish to be feared," he managed to whisper. "I want to be respected."

Lumeria's lips pursed in disapproval. "Now that is foolish indeed, my love." She patted his cheek. "It's a good thing you came back for me. I can see you're going to need my help if you wish to see this through."

She started to turn toward the door, but his hand shot out, grasping her arm tightly as he stopped her. Pulling her into his chest, he lowered his head, claiming her lips in a passionate kiss – the creature was fully awake now. It shoved him aside as it took control, using his lips to lay a trail of kisses down Lumeria's face. Hungrily, it moved to her neck, sucking at the smooth flesh with a roughness Bade would never have dreamed of using himself.

"The Eldorians," Lumeria murmured, tilting her head to the side as she allowed him access. "They'll be led by your old enemy, the Shendri, will they not?"

"Most likely," he murmured distractedly, nipping at her earlobe.

"That woman... the one with the dragon who I've been told used to follow you around everywhere before turning traitor...

she's one of them, yes?"

His mouth stilled, his consciousness pushing through the creature's control. "She is."

"Good." Lumeria turned her face so that they were eye to eye, and her sun-rimmed pupils flashed bright gold. "I look forward to killing her."

Red, hot anger burned in his gut at the thought of Fia dying at the witch's hand. It forced the creature into a rare submission, and he barely managed to hold his anger in check for the few seconds it took her to sweep out the door. There was a shattering of glass as the crystal tumbler burst into pieces in his grip, and he closed his hand over the remaining shards, seeking control in the pain. He waited until the anger abated, then opened his fist and examined the damage there. Blood oozed from ripped skin, and he ran his thumb over the slick, wet flesh as he contemplated the inevitable.

What am I going to do?

Chapter Nine

The road to Roshka

After that night, Cashel became a permanent fixture at Fia's side, and given her blessedly dreamless sleep, she wasn't complaining. Being fully rested for once made everything so much easier.

In the mornings before they broke camp, she worked with Lily and the other Shendri as they trained. Her physical prowess was definitely improving, though she still couldn't seem to find any control over the others' powers. If she were honest, she wasn't even sure how to begin trying. Luxeos had been more than a little vague about the whole thing, the frustrating goddess.

The camaraderie among the Shendri had grown, as well, and Fia attributed a good deal of that to Cashel. She simply felt more relaxed when he was nearby, though she couldn't for the life of her say why. Regardless of the reason, it helped her converse with the others as they traveled, and she could see Josselyn warming up to her more each day.

It was nice.

Of course, there were the speculative looks and hushed whispers that seemed to come with the Mihalan prince's sudden attachment, but Fia did her best to ignore them. People would talk. If they wanted to gossip, there was little she could do to stop them. Even if the very idea of a romantic attachment was ridiculous.

Cashel was her friend.

"He just about killed himself doing it, too, the idiot," Cashel laughed. He'd been regaling Fia with stories of his and Berg's childhood for most of the morning's ride, and each one added to the picturesque setting she imagined them in. She smiled, picturing tiny versions of Cashel and Berg running amok in the fantastical tree-city he'd described. *What would it have been like to grow up that way? To have a sibling as your constant companion and confidant? To have a father who adored you and an entire village of people watching out for you?*

"What about you?"

She shifted in her saddle. "What about me?"

"Were you a wild child when you were little, like Berg? Or were you always this level-headed?"

"You think I'm level-headed?" Fia asked, avoiding the real question.

"Most of the time." Cashel moved his horse closer, so that they're legs were almost touching. "So, what were you like as a kid? I wanna hear one of your stories this time."

Her stomach sank. "You don't want to hear about my childhood. It'd only depress you."

"Why do you say that?"

Her fingers tightened around the reins. "It was rather... bleak, is all."

He was silent for a moment, but she could feel his gaze on her, even as she studiously kept her own fastened to her horse. When he did speak, his voice was soft. Tender, even.

"I'd still like to hear about it. If you don't mind the telling, that is."

Did she? Usually, she avoided the topic at all costs. Feared the nightmares that might come with dredged up memories. The ones she already had were bad enough. *But, maybe... with Cashel...*

"I grew up in the Eastern Islands, or, more specifically, on the island of Kreá." She paused as the memories flooded in, one after another. As if simply stating the island's name was enough to release them. She licked her suddenly dry lips.

"That's the main island, if I'm remembering correctly?" Cashel interjected.

She nodded. "It's quite large, really, for an island. The royal family lives there, of course, but there's also a substantial amount of farmland in the east, with several small villages sprinkled in here and there."

"Is that where you grew up? In the country? Or were you a city girl?"

She swallowed. "I'm told I was born to a couple living in the capital, but I spent my childhood years in the northeast." Her stomach twisted. "In an asylum for orphaned children," she added in a whisper.

"I'm sorry. My own mother died giving birth to us twins, and I know how keenly I've felt that loss growing up. I can't even imagine losing my father, as well."

"I didn't lose them," Fia whispered. Bitter tears stung the corners of her eyes, but she refused to let them fall. "They left me there." She steeled herself as she turned to look at Cashel. "They saw the black flames marking my side and cursed me for a changeling. They claimed a demon had stolen their baby during the birth and replaced her with me. They were too cowardly to kill me themselves, so they abandoned me to the asylum, where the staff made sure to remind me of my deformity every day until they sent me away."

She waited as Cashel processed this glimpse into her past, his expression shifting from shocked to thunderous as the weight of it sank in. When he spoke, his voice was rough with controlled anger.

"How old were you? When you left the asylum?"

"Just shy of sixteen."

"Where did they send you?"

"We were sent on a ship to Roshka, and from there I was taken to Antos, to the home of a wealthy earl and his wife."

"We?"

"There were four of us. All girls who were getting too old for the system. We were supposed to be set up with apprenticeships on the mainland, or so they told us." She scoffed. "In reality, they were selling us off to work as slaves. Ridding themselves of a few extra mouths and making a small sum on top of that."

"That's despicable."

She shrugged. "That's life. Once we reached Roshka, the other girls were sent to a workhouse that made a habit of purchasing cheap labor. I was different. My markings made me unique. A beautiful oddity the man called me when he delivered me to the earl. Apparently, the earl and his wife were eccentrics. Their entire staff could have gone on tour as a traveling circus and no one would have thought twice about it."

"Were you a maid there?"

"Of sorts." She made a face. "Mostly I had to walk around in ridiculous costumes that highlighted the markings on my side. I'd dust, polish silver, that sort of thing. They never had me do any of the grunt work. Altogether, it wasn't that bad, aside from the fact that I was basically an unpaid prisoner in their home." She hesitated. "That, and the parties."

Cashel raised an eyebrow. "Parties?"

She flushed. "The earl and his wife enjoyed having..." She lowered her voice. "*Scandalous* parties, if you know what I mean."

"I think I have an idea," he grit out, his expression darkening. "They didn't... you didn't have to..." The muscles in his jaw twitched.

"No," she replied quickly. "No one was ever allowed to lay a finger on me. I was purely ornamental." *An ornament who had to witness things no young girl should even be aware of.*

Cashel hissed a curse under his breath. "Is that where you were when Lily came looking for you? Working for the earl?"

Not with the earl. With him...

"What is this? Some kind of interrogation?" Fia forced out a laugh. "Must you have my entire life story before you'll be satisfied, Sir Asks a Lot?"

"Sorry." Cashel grimaced. "I know it's none of my business, it's just... I want to know where you come from, what you've been through. I want to know who you are." He shook his head. "But I'm being pushy. You're right. I can stop."

Does he have to look quite so much like a kicked dog when he says that?

Bloody hell.

We're doing this.

"When I was eighteen, one of the earl's guests took a particular interest in me. A man named Miles Tennyson, or, more formally, the Baron Dunlop. Despite being a mere baron, he was wealthier and more well-liked than any of the earl's usual guests. Having him in attendance at one of their parties was considered quite the accomplishment. So, when he told the earl he just had to have me on his staff, the earl turned me over without batting a lash. I returned to Roshka with the baron at the end of the party, and it was at his estate that Lily eventually found me."

"How *did* she find you, anyway?"

"Dreams, I guess. Or visions. Honestly, I'm not entirely sure. I've only heard bits and pieces of her side of the story, since I left with... well, I left the baron's estate without really speaking to her. I was the first person she used her healing powers on, though. I can tell you that much."

Cashel pulled back on his mount's reins, slowing it down to a walk, and Fia followed suit. She watched as the distance between them and the other riders in their group increased. A glance over her shoulder proved that the wagons, driven by the Dirt Mercs, were still a fair distance behind.

"I know what you're doing," she murmured.

Cashel blinked innocently. "I'm doing something?"

"Falling back from the group? Keeping us out of earshot?" She gave him a look. "Have you always been the protective type, or is it just with me?"

He laughed. "Always, I'm afraid. Being Berg's twin made it a necessity." He shook his head. "Sorry, am I making you uncomfortable? We can catch up with the others. I just thought you might like a little privacy. You looked... agitated."

"Agitated?" She wrinkled her nose. "How so?"

"Well, for one thing, you've been gripping your reins so tightly I think your knuckles have turned a permanent shade of white."

She glanced down at her hands and blushed. He wasn't wrong.

"I guess I'm a little nervous. All that stuff with the baron... it's not something I like to talk about. Ever."

"And you don't have to, not if you don't want to." His voice softened. "But if you ever decide that you do, just know that I'd be happy to listen. When you're ready."

She swallowed. "Thank you. Really. Someday I may just take you up on that."

"But not today, right?"

"Not today."

"Fair enough." Cashel grinned. "I guess that means it's my turn to hold up the conversation again. Have I told you about the time Berg tried to go cord jumping off the wall in the royal gardens? I thought for sure he was going to get himself killed that time. For one thing, he didn't have nearly enough cord, and –"

He broke off mid-sentence as a shout from the front of the line brought the entire convoy grinding to a halt. They looked at each other in surprise.

"Should we go...?" Cashel tilted his chin toward the front.

Fia's mouth settled into a hard line as she nodded.

"I wanna see this."

Chapter Ten

The shouts came from one of their scouts, who'd ridden ahead to Merin to assess the situation. Judging by his wide eyes and profuse sweating, Fia could only assume it wasn't good.

"Something's not right, Your Majesty," the scout said nervously after presenting himself to Josselyn. "The whole place is sealed up tight and quiet as a tomb." His face paled. "Might just be a tomb, now I think of it. Didn't see anyone outside the gate, and there wasn't any response to my shouting."

"What about the area surrounding it?" Josselyn asked. "Did you see any signs of an army?"

"Not that I noticed, but it's hard to say for certain. None in sight, anyway."

"They could be inside," Draven suggested. "If we're too late, and the Antoski already succeeded in overturning the capital, they could be lying in wait to trap us." He grimaced. "It's just the kind of dirty trick an Antoski would try."

"And you didn't hear anything, anything at all?" Josselyn asked, watching the scout carefully. "No voices, no one moving around?"

"Dead silent, Your Majesty," the scout replied.

"Well, then." Josselyn looked thoughtful. "I suppose we'd better check it out." She glanced over at Lily. "Think you could send Suzaku over for a bit of reconnaissance? See what she sees over the wall?"

Lily nodded, closing her eyes briefly. Soon a bright light emanated from her skin, swirling around until it formed the shape of the great phoenix. With a final burst, Suzaku arose, red and gold feathers shining gloriously in the sun with just a hint of flame flickering off her wings.

"Subtle," Cashel remarked beneath his breath, just loud enough for Fia to hear. She smothered a grin as she watched the phoenix fly off, heading for Merin.

"Let's keep moving," Josselyn called. "We'll ride to the outskirts of the capital while we wait for Suzaku's report."

There was a chorus of agreement as riders urged their mounts back into motion. The wagons picked up more slowly, with the foot soldiers marching along behind them. Fia took up position with the rest of the Shendri, knowing that they would need to consolidate their power. Who knew what they might be facing when they arrived.

Or whom.

Her traitorous heart skipped a beat as she pictured the face of one man in particular. She shouldn't want Bade to be there. His presence would mean that the Roshkans had been defeated, which wouldn't bode well for their own army. And it was true that he'd gone too far, pushed too hard. Killed too many. He had to be stopped.

If only her heart could see that as plainly as her head.

"They're asleep."

Lily's eyes were wide as she stared out over the grass field that lay between them and Merin, and her statement was met with silence as everyone tried to catch a glimpse of some sort of human life along the city's wall.

"Who's asleep, love?" Draven asked, and everyone turned their gaze to rest on Lily. She waved a hand at the city.

"Everyone. The guards on the wall, the people in the streets, everyone Suzaku was able to set eyes on. They were all just... sleeping. As if they all fell asleep in the midst of whatever they were doing."

"An enchantment," Maya stated, her face darkening.

Lily nodded. "It would seem so. It's nothing natural, anyway."

"I'll have my man Trekklin summoned," King Malachite stated. Both he and Jade, Maya's mother and the leader of the Dirt Mercs, had joined the group of Shendri, along with General Townsend. "He's the best we have when it comes to sorting out enchantments. We should have him take a look at the place before we decide how to precede."

"I'll get him," Cashel offered. "I'm pretty sure I saw him riding in one of the Merc wagons with that Builder guy." He turned toward the wagons, and Fia's stomach twisted as she watched him disappear into the throng of soldiers. It was silly, really, but something about this place was making her skin crawl just looking at it. The need for Cashel's strange security was strong.

"Did Suzaku see any signs that might indicate there was an Antoski army hiding inside somewhere?" General Townsad asked, and Fia tamped down her nerves as she tried to focus on the impromptu strategy meeting going on around her.

Lily shook her head. "As far as she could see, it was only the usual Roshkans inside. She wasn't able to get inside all of the buildings, but there were only Roshkan soldiers inside the barracks, and most of the houses were empty. If they are there, they're most likely bottled up inside the castle, although Suzaku didn't see any large gatherings from the windows."

"Why would they need to hide their army, anyway?" Josselyn mused. "If they've already breached the city, why tuck themselves away out of sight?"

"Because they want us to go in," the general stated.

"But still – how would that give them the advantage?" Josselyn countered. "If we're expecting them to attack, we'd be on the defensive from the get go. Plus, we'd already be past the wall. Doesn't seem like a very effective trap."

"Maybe the enchantment works on anyone who enters the city?" Lily suggested. "And they're hoping to catch us sleeping."

"If that's their plan, they'll be sorely disappointed." Maya smirked. "There's no way Trekklin would let us wander into something like that. He's too good."

"I hope you're right," Lily replied, watching the wall with a worried look. Draven wrapped a hand around her waist, pulling her into his side.

"Looks like we're going to find out," he muttered, nodding toward a lanky figure with a bulging pack on his back making his way through the crowd beside Cashel. "'Cause here he comes now."

The young, Mihalan man grinned as he made his way over, eyes gleaming with interest. He rubbed his hands together as he looked around the group. "Cashel says you have an enchantment you'd like me to examine?"

"Something's happened to the people inside Merin, an enchantment of some sort that's made everyone fall asleep," King Malachite explained. "We'd like you to check it out before we attempt to enter the city."

"A sleeping enchantment." Trekklin's grin seemed to grow even wider, if that was possible. "Excellent."

Cashel cleared his throat, and Trekklin managed a somewhat more sober expression. "I'll, uh, check it out right away, Your Majesty."

"Thank you." King Malachite's lips twitched as he nodded toward the city wall. "Have at it, then."

The young man started off across the field, his long-legged stride moving so quickly he might as well have been jogging. He hadn't gone far, however, before Josselyn called after him, halting him in his steps.

"Wait!"

He turned to look at them with a quizzical expression, and Josselyn stepped forward, unsheathing her sword. Dark shadows poured from her chest as Kella took shape beside her, her massive frame looking just as terrifying as it always did.

"We'll come with you," she stated. "Lily, Maya, Fia? You in?"

There was a burst of silver shadows as Maya, already mounted astride Kitsune's back, called out, "I'm in." She drew an arrow from the quiver strapped across her back and nocked it into place on her bow as she aimed at the wall. "And ready for anything."

"We'll set up a shield," Lily added as Suzaku made her appearance once again. The phoenix began to circle them, leaving a trail of golden light in her wake that soon created a shimmering sphere of protection around the five of them – Draven had yet to release his hold on her waist. When he did, it was only to draw his sword.

"You know I'm coming, too," he said as the others turned to stare at him. "I may not be a Shendri, but I'll be damned if I'm going to hang back watching while Lily puts herself in danger."

"There may not be any danger," Lily pointed out. "This is just a precaution."

"Then you won't mind me tagging along, then, will you?"

"Fine." Lily sighed, rolling her eyes heavenward. "Worry wart."

"I'm coming, too, then," Edmund declared, stepping forward.

"Actually, Edmund, you're not." Josselyn gave him an apologetic look. "I need you to stay with your men. The general, as well. The two of you will need to lead them should anything happen while we're checking things out."

Edmund's face grew tight, and Fia was sure he wanted to argue. Seeing as how his orders were coming from the queen, however, he bit his tongue and stepped back, throwing Maya a look that made Fia blush from the sheer intensity of it. Feeling like a voyeur, she cleared her throat.

"I guess that leaves Artemis and me." Smoke pooled around her ankles as the tiny dragon emerged. He flew up and perched atop her shoulder, his amber eyes looking the others over critically. Fia drew her twin daggers and nodded. "Ready."

Josselyn gave her an approving look, then turned back to face the wall. "Alright, Trekklin. Let's go."

"And me."

She stopped as a seventh person strode forward, inserting

himself into their sphere. Fia beamed with pleasure as Cashel came to stand beside her, his own sword drawn. Josselyn simply sighed.

"Fine," she grunted. "But no more. This shield will only cover so many. Now let's go see what's going on with this place."

"Yes, Your Majesty," Cashel replied. His eyes slid sideways toward Fia, and she met his gaze with a small smile of her own. He winked, then turned his attention to the front as the group began to press forward across the field. Fia felt her cheeks grow pink, but she couldn't help but feel relieved.

Cashel will keep me steady, even if He's near. Her heart flipped over at the thought. He very well might be. In fact, she was almost certain he was.

Chapter Eleven

"Ooh, they're bringing their little pets to scout things out." Lumeria smirked. "How utterly adorable." Her eyes fluttered open, and the smirk twisted into a grimace as she shifted her weight around in the straight-backed throne.

"Good goddess, what were the Roshkan's thinking when they commissioned these torture devices? You'd think they could have added a little padding. They are meant for royalty, after all."

"The throne is supposed to be uncomfortable," Bade remarked dryly. "Great power is not to be taken lightly."

Lumeria snorted. "If you say so."

Bade bit back a retort. Lecturing Lumeria on the importance of responsibility would be a waste of his breath. The witch seemed to care for nothing but power and praise, with the latter being heaped upon herself. It grated that the creature had insisted they needed her by their side.

I wouldn't need her if I just ended it all. A sip of poison would do the job nicely.

"And just what would your mother think of such a cowardly plan, hmm?" the creature in his head hissed its disapproval. "Does she not deserve vengeance?"

My progenitor has been dead for almost two centuries. What kind of vengeance can I take now?

"You can weed out his kind," the creature hissed back. "Tear down the greedy and depraved and replace them with those of virtue and compassion. A righteous task if ever there was."

By killing hundreds of innocent people? How is that righteous?

"Those who resist change are as guilty as their worst

offenders," the creature snapped, and Bade winced as pain seeped into his head, causing his thoughts to grow fuzzy and disjointed.

That... that doesn't make sense? He shook his head, attempting to clear it.

"Are you questioning my judgment?" The creature became eerily calm, and Bade felt a sliver of dread slip down his spine. When he failed to respond, the creature spoke again, sharper this time. "Perhaps I've given you too much freedom. I only wished to guide you, as I would have your mother when she wore me all those years ago, but now... now I wonder if that's enough. If I can't trust you to do what's needed, then perhaps I should be the one in control. *All* the time."

Bade stiffened – this was no idle threat. The creature would happily shove his consciousness back into the recesses of his mind forever.

I'll do what is necessary, you needn't worry on that count.

"We'll see about that," the creature replied. "You've been known to go rogue where that woman is involved."

What woman? Bade asked, even as his blood turned to ice in his veins. He knew very well which woman the creature referred to. There was only one, living woman who mattered, after all. A single woman out of the dozens who'd surrounded him, hoping to gain his favor.His brave yet fragile warrior and sole owner of his heart.

Fia.

"Don't play dumb with me," the creature scoffed. "I'm a part of you, after all. I know you better than anyone. Which is why I worry about this little confrontation Lumeria has planned. If you push the witch too far, she may decide to turn on us, and I cannot allow that to happen, understand?"

Of course.

"You won't do anything stupid?"

I never do anything stupid.

"We'll see about that, won't we?" The creature sounded unconvinced, but the pain in his head blessedly dispersed, leaving him only slightly dizzy as he struggled to retain his outward calm.

Lumeria leaned over the side of her throne and rested a hand on his bicep. "It won't be long now." She grinned wickedly, her sun-rimmed pupils glowing bright with anticipation. "I so look forward to greeting our guests."

"Soon," he replied, forcing his lips into an answering smile.

Too soon.

Chapter Twelve

"I'm not so sure about this..."

"Don't worry. He knows what he's doing."

"Are you sure? I mean, look at him... what is he even doing over there?"

"Well, obviously, he's, uh... you know..."

Maya scratched the shaved side of her head as she watched Trekklin tap his finger against the wall, then step back and stare at it through a pair of ridiculous looking goggles he'd taken out of his travel sack.

Josselyn looked dubious. "Nothing about what I'm seeing is obvious."

Maya sighed. "Okay, yes. It does look kind of odd, but I promise you, Trekklin knows what he's doing. He was the one who freed me from Bade's enchantment, after all, and that was no simple magic. Trust me, he's got this."

Trekklin turned to look over his shoulder at them. "Actually, I don't."

"What do you mean?" Josselyn demanded. "Can't you break the enchantment?"

"Maybe I could, if there was an enchantment in place." He shrugged. "But there's nothing."

"Are you sure?" Maya took a step forward, peering at the wall.

"Positive," Trekklin replied, looking perplexed. "I've checked everything, and there isn't a single magical trace to be found anywhere near this wall."

"So... what does that mean?" Josselyn asked. "How is everyone inside magically asleep if there's no magic happening around them?"

"I would think that obvious, Your Majesty," Trekklin replied.

"Careful, Trek," Cashel muttered. "She is a queen, you know."

Trekklin's eyes widened, and he looked over at Josselyn in surprise. "No disrespect, Your Majesty."

Josselyn waved a hand. "You're fine. Please, explain."

"All I'm saying is, if the magic isn't happening around them, it goes without saying that it must be happening inside them."

Josselyn nodded. "That makes sense. An enchantment placed on each person individually, not on the area itself. Which means..."

"That it should be safe to go inside," Maya finished, striding over to the heavy, wooden gate. "That said, how do we get in?" She gave the doors a push. "These things are solid, and that wall is awfully high."

Josseyln grinned. "Simple. We break it down."

"I suppose we could make some sort of battering ram," Draven mused, looking around. "One of those trees over there might do, if we can get it chopped down. Might take a bit of doing. Not sure what kind of tools we brought."

"Don't need to make a battering ram," Josselyn called over her shoulder as she moved to stand in front of the gate. Kella prowled along beside her, all sleek, black fur and rippling muscles. "Kella and I can take it down just fine."

"*You're* going to break this thing down? By yourself?" Draven didn't even bother to hide his disbelief as he gaped at the pair of them. "That's insane."

"Does seem a bit ambitious, Your Majesty," Cashel added.

Josselyn smirked. "Never underestimate the power of a female feline. You ready, Kella?"

The hellcat growled her approval, squaring off to the gate and crouching low on her haunches. A second later they were moving, charging the gate in perfect tandem. Josselyn's shoulder struck just as Kella's head butted.

Craaaaack.

Fia yelped as shards of wood went flying every which way as the gate burst into pieces. She threw a hand up over her face as several flew her way, but they stopped short of hitting her as a shimmering shield slid into place in front of her.

"Thanks, Lily."

"You're welcome," Lily panted. "Took a bit more out of me than anticipated," she added, trying to catch her breath. "I've never put up a shield on such short notice before."

"Well, we can get in now, anyway." Maya raised her bow and nudged Kitsu toward the broken door. Josselyn and Kella were already inside, waiting. "Nice muscles, Joss," she teased as she joined the two of them. "I can hardly tell which of you is the beast anymore."

"Says the girl who can make herself look like a tree," Josselyn shot back. "You're one to talk."

Maya shrugged. "You're right. We're both awesome."

"So, what now?" Fia asked, looking around the city. Houses lined the road ahead of them, which led down to a second, lower wall. The royal palace loomed tall and opulent in the center, looking far more grand than either the Eldorian or Antoski castles. Clearly, the Roshkans liked nice things. "Do we look around the city or head straight for the palace?"

"I'd like to examine some of the townsfolk before we go any further," Trekklin stated. "It's possible I'll be able to glean something through closer inspection. Perhaps even wake them up."

"Then that's what we'll do," Josselyn replied. She pointed toward a guard who sat slumped against the inside of the wall a few feet from the broken gate. "You can start with him."

"Alright." Trekklin pulled his travel sack off and began rummaging around inside of it. "Just need a few things," he muttered to himself. "Now, where did I put that..."

Fia shivered as a cool breeze picked up, sending a chill through her body. She rubbed her arms as she watched Trekklin crouch down on the ground, his head buried inside his overstuffed bag.

The wind grew stronger, and she made a startled noise as she felt herself stumbling to the side. A strong hand reached out to steady her, and she looked up to see Cashel staring at the gate with a concerned expression. He looked like he was about to say something, but any words he might have spoken were whisked away as the wind turned into a full-on gale. There was a series of muffled shouts as all seven of them found themselves being pushed down the street. Cashel pulled Fia into his chest as he braced his feet against the ground in a failed attempt to keep them from moving. Even Josselyn and Kella, the strongest of them all, seemed to be struggling to find purchase. Ultimately, they too failed, and were swept down the road in a swirl of fur and limbs.

The wind brought them straight to the palace gate, which opened a split second before they flattened themselves on it. Without slowing, the wind tossed them up into the air and blew them inside the palace itself, whose doors stood open as if expecting them. As soon as they were inside, however, they closed with an abrupt *slam*.

And then, at last, it stilled, and they found themselves unceremoniously dumped onto the floor of the palace's entrance hall. There was silence for a moment as everyone recovered their wits.

"*That* was not the work of an enchantment," Trekklin said, breaking the silence. He looked around at the others, his goggles slightly askew. "In case anyone was wondering."

"Then what the bloody hell was it?" Draven muttered, picking himself off the floor before reaching a hand down for Lily.

Fia tried to stand as well but found her legs were more than a bit wobbly. Fortunately, Cashel was quick to catch her under the elbow before she ended up back on the floor.

"You okay?"

His voice was soft as he bent down, his lips almost brushing her ear. The sensitive flesh tingled in response, and Fia felt herself flush at the unexpected reaction.

That strange wind has seriously thrown me off-balance. Yeesh.

"I'm alright." She straightened to her full height, grateful that she didn't wobble this time. "Just a bit winded, heh."

He chuckled. "Look at you, making jokes in the face of danger. Nice."

She managed a tremulous smile. "I'm tougher than I look."

"I never doubted you were."

They shared a look which was interrupted by the sound of Kella's low growl, and a voice filled Fia's head, its silky tone painfully familiar.

"Welcome, Shendri. Please, join us. Your companions, as well, of course."

From the look on the others' faces, she wasn't the only one hearing something. They looked at each other uneasily, then turned their gazes as one to the arched doors at the far end of the hall as they swung open.

Apparently, they were being invited in.

"Together," Josselyn commanded, lifting her sword and facing the doors with Kella beside her. Fia followed the other two as they fell into position behind her. Artemis flew up to her shoulder and perched there, little puffs of smoke wafting from his nostrils as he glared at the open doors in front of them. Draven and Cashel raised their swords, as well, placing them besides Lily and Fia, respectively. Trekklin lingered at the back, watching everything with interest.

"Do you have a weapon you can draw?" Cashel glanced back at him, looking concerned, but Trekklin just grinned. Holding up his hands, he showed them the two round objects he was holding. They sparkled with a strange, blue light.

"I've got a few tricks ready, should I need them."

"In we go, then," Josselyn said, striding forward. They followed close behind, and soon found themselves standing inside the throne room. A handful of guards lay asleep on the floor, but it was the pair sitting casually on the two thrones that demanded Fia's attention.

One was a stunning woman with dark skin and wavy, golden hair. Her ethereal beauty was only marred by the disdainful twist of her lips as she glared down at the lot of them, but Fia easily ignored her as she focused on the man sitting beside her. Tall, dark, and sinfully handsome, his silvery-blue eyes locked onto hers.

Fia's heart took off at a gallop.

How many months has it been? How long since those eyes met mine? Since those lips crooned me to sleep? Since those arms pulled me close? Since...

He blinked and looked away, letting his gaze roam over the others standing poised for a fight, and her stomach fell, weighted down by a million stones.

"What've you done to these people?" Josselyn's voice, loud and demanding, jolted Fia back to the present. The warrior queen strode across the room, her hellcat prowling along beside her, teeth bared. "Well? What do you have to say for yourself, *Bade*?" She spoke his name like a curse, and Kella underscored it with a low growl that seemed to fill every corner of the room. She may as well have purred for all that the pair sitting before them were affected.

"I've done nothing untoward, I assure you." Bade rose slowly from his throne and shoved his hands into the pockets of his black trousers as he regarded them with an expression of disinterest. "Simply whispered a few, lulling words into their ears is all. Shall I do the same for you? You do look a bit... frayed around the edges."

"I'll fray your edges," Josselyn snarled, charging forward.

"Reilentah."

The word was whisper soft, and yet Fia could feel its familiar weight binding her limbs into place. Josselyn froze mid-stride, her sword poised to strike.

The sound of a giggle set Fia's teeth on edge. The woman lounging on a throne behind Bade clapped her hands together.

"Well done, my love! A single word and the famed warriors are reduced to statues." Her face split into a malicious grin. "I love it." She stood. "Let me play with them, won't you?" Her eyes settled on Fia. "You know how much I've been looking forward to this."

She started to glide toward them, eyes gleaming.

Those eyes... I've seen those eyes before...

"No!"

The woman stopped, her expression darkening as she turned to glare at Bade. "Why ever not? They came here to kill you, after all."

"They're resisting my power – look there." He gestured toward Josselyn, who had in fact begun to shift slightly. Squeezing her eyes shut tight, Fia dug deep, attempting to regain control of her limbs. Her foot slid to the right.

She opened her eyes and saw Maya's arm moving, her bow already equipped with an arrow. The woman's eyes widened as it flew straight for her face. It was quick, but she was quicker as she threw a hand out to the side. Wind blew from her fingers, blocking the arrow and trapping them all in place as it created a shimmering sphere around them.

"Nice try, wolf girl." The woman sneered at Maya. "But I'm not limited by some blasted, Mihalan curse any more. So you and your mutt are going to have to do a little better than that this time, if you think to beat me."

"What is she talking about?" Josselyn shouted, bracing her feet as she struggled to maintain her fighting pose amid the swirling wind.

"I haven't the foggiest," Maya shouted back. "Lady's crazy if you ask me."

"Crazy strong," Draven yelled. "What's the plan, Your Majesty?"

Josselyn's knuckles were white as she gripped her sword with two-hands, her face a mask of determination. "I'm going to gut them both," she growled. "How's that for a plan?"

"Sounds like a good one to me," he replied. "Can you do it?"

"Watch me."

She burst forward with a feral yell and charged headfirst into the barrier of wind. Blue light streaked down the blade of her sword, and there was a shower of sparks as it sliced through the wind, creating just enough space for Josselyn to slip through. Without missing a beat, she continued to move forward, her steely gaze focused on the man who'd started it all – Bade.

She's going to kill him.

The realization hit Fia like a fist in the gut, and she felt the breath leave her lungs as panic swelled inside her.

He's going to die.

Bade.

My savior.

My soul.

My love.

She was on fire. There was no other explanation for the searing heat, the flames licking their way up her chest and into her throat. Her lips parted, making way for the inferno that so desperately needed to be released.

"Stop!"

The glowing, blue blade froze, inches from Bade's chest. His impassive gaze flicked from the tip of his would-be death to Fia, sliding past the now frozen Josselyn without so much as a cursory glance.

"Run."

What is he saying, run? More importantly, what did I just do?

Bade took a step back as the woman beside him lifted her hands. Golden orbs of light materialized above her palms, and she grinned maliciously as she drew her hand back, Josselyn's frozen form her target.

Oh, shit.

"Josselyn, move!"

Josselyn stumbled forward, falling to her knees. A ball of crackling light flew toward her, and Fia vaguely registered the sound of someone screaming as a streak of black fur launched itself into the line of fire.

"Get her out of there!"

Arrows flew one after another through the gap in the wind barrier, pushing Bade and the woman back as a bloody Kella nudged Josselyn onto her feet. She complied, looking dazed, and, with another push from Kella, started running back toward the barrier. Shadows trailed after her as Kella returned, too injured to remain on the outside. A second later the barrier disappeared, releasing them all, and there was an outraged shriek from the woman. She shot Bade a suspicious glare before returning her focus to the group scrambling around on the floor below her.

"Enditreum Pradieta!"

The ground beneath their feet began to shake, and there was a series of loud *cracks* as the marble floor began to split.

"Retreat!" Josselyn yelled, waving them toward the door. "Retreat!"

They turned and ran, with Maya keeping a steady stream of arrows flying behind them. They never quite seemed to make it to their targets, however, but instead fell harmlessly onto the floor in front of them, as if hitting an invisible wall. The cover seemed to prevent the pair from following them, and Fia felt a measure of relief as she heard the doors slam closed behind her.

Still, they didn't stop. They ran straight through the palace and into the courtyard, through the gate and down through the surrounding city.

"What about them?" Lily yelled, pointing toward the sleeping villagers.

"They'll have to wait," Josselyn yelled back. "We need to get back to the army, first. Once we've got backup, we can get them out."

"You mean that army?" Cashel asked as they passed through the broken gate on the outer wall.

And onto a battlefield.

Chapter Thirteen

"Berg!"

Cashel fought his way through the carnage, one eye on his twin, the other watching for incoming attacks. Taking a hasty step to the left, he narrowly avoided being impaled by an Antoski sword. With a roar worthy of a Mihalan, he swung his own sword around, decapitating his attacker in a single swipe.

There truly was nothing finer than Mihalan steel.

Except perhaps, Mihalan strength.

Hop-stepping over the fallen bodies – gods, there were so many – he finally managed to throw himself into the pack of Mihalans fighting back-to-back, Berg included. Without missing a beat, he joined them, picking off a soldier near the outer edge of the fray.

"What happened?" he shouted.

Berg grunted as a blade nicked him in the side. "Came outta nowhere," he gasped, knocking the soldier back. "Shot us up to hell before we even realized what was happening. Now this."

Cashel chanced a look around. It didn't look good. Their numbers must have been severely depleted during the initial attack. "We can rally. We've got the Shendri on the field now."

As if to prove his point, an arrow came whistling past and lodged itself into an attacking Antoski's neck – precisely placed in the only bit of flesh not covered in armor.

"Damn, our sister's good." Berg grinned, looking slightly manic. The spray of blood across his chest didn't help. He let out a yell as he threw himself back into the fight with renewed vigor.

Cashel started to do the same when the scenery around him abruptly changed and he was swinging his sword into... nothing.

Fog rose from the ground as Cashel stumbled backward in the now-dark field. And then he heard it. A voice – *Bade's* voice. It whispered in his ear, nailing him to the ground.

"There's no need for such violence, my friends. All you need do is accept the inevitable. Accept *me*."

There was a pause, and Cashel struggled to regain control of his limbs. No luck.

"I do not wish to be your enemy. I only wish to see Lehi thrive. And it will thrive, once I am in control."

"We're doing just fine without you, asshole," Cashel yelled into the darkness. The voice ignored him.

"Surrender now, and no one will be harmed."

"And spend the rest of my life back in your dungeon? Like hell I will!"

Cashel growled as he jerked one leg free of its paralysis, but it was heavy and numb. *Damn it. I can't go back. Can't let them take Berg.* He heaved himself forward. One step. Two steps. *Fia... can't let them hurt Fia...*

A streak of light and flames lit the sky above his head, and he looked up in time to see Suzaku screeching past, the darkness shattering in her wake.

"Everyone to me!"

Lily's voice, he was certain, and yet it was grittier than usual. Sharper.

He twisted around, eyes squinting in the sudden brightness, and spied the shimmering sphere of Lily's shield. Grabbing Berg by the arm, he pulled him toward it. "Get in the shield! Now!" The remaining Mihalans ran as one toward the protective barrier, with a handful of bloodied Dirt Mercs and ragged knights falling in beside them. Nearing the sphere, he stopped and turned to face the pursuing soldiers, determined to provide cover for the remaining Eldorians still struggling to reach safety. A glimpse of white fur told him he wasn't alone as Maya and Kitsune raced through the crowd. His gut told him the queen was probably still fighting, as well.

Where's Fia?

He scanned the field, searching for a glimpse of red hair, and finally spotted her off to the side. She had both her daggers out and was struggling to fight off an attacking soldier as Artemis pelted the man from above with tiny bursts of flame. *What is she doing out there?* He clenched his teeth in aggravation as he sprinted across the field. *She isn't like the others. She should be in the shield, protected.*

He slammed into her attacker just as she stumbled backward onto the ground. With a furious roar, he gripped the man's face, dislodging his helmet, and smashed his head into the ground with every bit of pent-up rage he had. Again and again, he pulled his arm back and struck, until his fingers slipped on the gore and his frenzied brain registered the fact that the man was already dead.

Get Fia to the phoenix, now!

Bade's voice broke through the chaos of his mind, making him jump. Jerking his head around to face the city, he spied Bade standing on top of the outer wall.

"The hell?!"

She's coming after her. You need to move, now!

"Who's coming after her – oh, shit!"

Gliding across the bloody field like an angel of death was the woman from the palace. Her golden eyes were blazing as they stared Fia down, lightning crackling from the tips of her fingers. He stepped in front of Fia, blocking her from the woman's view.

"Get up and run to the shield," he ordered in a surprisingly calm tone. "We're retreating."

Fia scrambled to her feet. "But what about her? I can't let you face her alone."

"You can, and you will," he growled. "Now go!"

"No." Her voice shook on the simple refusal, but she held firm as she assumed a fighting position, daggers raised. "I'm one of the Shendri. You go."

"Damn it, Fia." The woman was drawing closer, and he could see a wicked grin spread across her face as a ball of light formed in the palm of her hand. He swore as she pulled her arm back, taking aim. "Fine," he snapped, scooping Fia up into his arms, daggers and all. "We'll both go."

His long legs flew across the ground as he zig-zagged his way back toward the shield. Laughter followed him, and a ball of light narrowly missed his shoulder. He pushed harder.

"Almost there. Hold on."

Another narrow miss as he dodged right.

"We've got this. It's going to be okay."

The shield was only a few steps away now. His pulse quickened at the welcome sight. The phoenix's power would block anyone and anything it chose. They'd be safe there.

And then it struck.

At first, the pain was so intense, so sudden, that he almost didn't register the fact that he'd been hit. But then he toppled forward, and all he felt was fire.

"Cashel! No!"

Fia's hands were under his arms, dragging him across the ground. *Leave me,* he thought blearily as the pain screamed its way up his body. *I'm already dead.*

"Lily! Someone get Lily! He's hurt!"

"She's holding the shield – there's no way she can stop now."

"He needs help!"

"Someone get me some bandages!"

"Oh gods, his leg."

"We've got to stop the bleeding."

"We've got to get the hell out of here! She'll kill us all!"

The voices blurred together in a frantic, garbled mess as the pain intensified.

And then, blessed silence.

Chapter Fourteen

"Is she going to be okay?"

Fia stared at Lily's pale face, resting against Draven's chest as he held her cradled in his arms. Every now and then his hand would reach up to brush back a stray piece of golden hair as it fell across the sleeping Shendri's face. The two of them were huddled at the back of the wagon lumbering along slowly in front of her.

At least they still had the wagons.

"She'll be alright," Josselyn replied. "She just needs some rest. Holding a shield that size for as long as she did... I can't even imagine the strain that must have been. And trying to heal people on top of that? Small wonder she passed out when she did."

"She's the strongest of us all, if you ask me," Maya stated. "Me being a close second, mind you.

"Ha!" Josselyn leaned forward on her horse, peering around Fia as she shot Maya a look. "That's not how it looked to me. I was kicking some serious ass back there." She sobered. "Little too late, though." She sighed and looked around at the smattering of mounted soldiers clustered around the few wagons they'd managed to retrieve during their escape. "This is so not how I pictured us returning to Eldour."

"We're lucky to be returning at all." Maya grimaced. "If it weren't for Lily, we might all be dead." There was a heavy silence as they let her words sink in. Maya nudged her horse forward. "Think I'll just check on things in front quick."

Josselyn smiled wryly. "I'm sure Edmund's doing fine. It was just a few scratches."

"Scratches don't require stitches," Maya shot back over her

shoulder.

"Can you check on Cashel while you're at it, too?" Fia called after her.

"Will do," Maya called back, riding to the front.

"Thank you," Fia whispered, knowing Maya wouldn't be able to hear her but needing to say the words anyway. *Please, let him be okay.* The image of him lying on the ground flashed through her mind, and she gagged on the sudden bile rushing up her throat. She'd seen a lot of dark things in her life, felt a lot of pain, but never had anything compared to the sight of his leg after being struck by that woman's magic. Or rather, what was left of his leg... *What am I thinking, hoping he's okay? Of course he's not okay. He may never walk again, and for what? For me?* She balled her hands into fists, squeezing the reins. *Such a waste.*

"He'll come around."

Fia turned to find Josselyn watching her with what looked like pity.

More pity. Great.

"He lost half his leg, Joss. His *leg*. That's not something you just *come around* from."

"True." Josseyln shrugged. "But he's alive, isn't he? And his family? They're all alive, too. I'd say he's doing alright, considering."

"Maybe, but..." She swallowed, looking down at her hands. "He could have had all that and his leg if..." Her voice dropped to a whisper as shame crept up the back of her neck and heated her cheeks. "If it weren't for me. You'd all be better off if it weren't for me."

Josselyn didn't respond, and after a moment Fia chanced a peek in her direction. The queen's face was grim as she met her gaze.

"What happened back there?" she asked. "In the palace, when I was going after Bade... I was about to kill him, but you yelled for me to stop and..." She shook her head. "My body just *stopped*, all on its own. Like someone had chained it to the floor." She narrowed her eyes. "It was you, wasn't it?"

Fia squirmed in her saddle. "I, uh... may have accidentally used my power on you..." She flinched. "I swear I didn't mean to. I mean, I didn't even know I *could* use it until it happened... the power of the dragon."

"The natural leader," Josselyn deadpanned.

"It wasn't intentional, truly," Fia repeated, feeling miserable.

"Maybe not," Josselyn mused. "But tell me this, Fia. Would you do it again? If the moment repeated itself, would you be able to sit back and watch me kill him? Or would you intervene?"

"I..." Fia hung her head, feeling every bit like the traitor she was. "I don't know. Maybe."

Josselyn sighed. "And that right there is the problem. The not knowing. When it comes to battle, we have to know with every fiber of our being that our sisters have our backs. Otherwise, we're destined to fail."

"I'm sorry," Fia whispered. "I wish I could be more certain, but I... I just can't. He meant too much to me."

"I know he did." There was a pause, and then she lifted her mouth in a crooked grin. "We'll figure something out. Luxeos will know what to do. Let's just worry about getting these guys back safely for now. Strategy can come later."

"Yeah?"

"Yeah." Josselyn tipped her chin toward the front. "Now cheer up, cause I can see Maya on her way back now, and goodness knows I don't want to get into all of this with her until I've had at least one good night's sleep in my own bed."

Fia pasted a smile on her face. "Better?"

"Not really, but it'll have to do." Josselyn lifted her voice as Maya approached. "Still alive, is he?"

"Edmund is recovering nicely, thank you," Maya retorted dryly. "I'm sure he'd be touched by your obvious concern."

"He knows better than to beg sympathy off of me. I know him too well." Josselyn smirked. "Although I'm sure he's eating up all the attention *you're* giving him, the big lout."

"And Cashel?" Fia interrupted, seeing Maya's eyes snap. "How was he doing?"

Maya sobered. "He's doing as well as can be, all things considered. Lily was able to heal what was left of his leg, so I don't think he's in too much physical pain. Just overwhelmed, you know? It's a big change. Berg's with him, though, so he's in good hands. I'm sure he'll pick up once he's had a chance to wrap his head around the whole thing."

"I hope you're right," Fia whispered.

The trio fell silent after that, and Fia felt the guilt that had begun gnawing at her stomach grow with each step their horses took toward home.

What have I done?

Chapter Fifteen

The duke's castle in Devon, Eldour

If I could just live in the sea, everything would be so much simpler.

Cashel closed his eyes, reveling in the warm touch of the sun on his face as he rose up and down atop the gentle waves. It was a familiar feeling, floating weightless in the water. It was comfortable.

Unlike walking.

The thought of his recent deformity broke the calming spell of the sea, and he rolled over onto his stomach, salt stinging his eyes as he swam back toward shore. Berg sat lounging in the sand, watching him, as he crawled his way onto the beach. Cashel ignored him, reaching for the newly made prosthetic Trekklin had presented him with earlier that day. It was a well-made wooden leg, if a bit simple, and Cashel couldn't help being impressed at the speed in which it'd been crafted. Which was basically the only positive feeling he could muster for the thing.

He strapped the prosthetic in place, fitting it securely against the stump of his leg and grimacing. Not that it hurt – Lily had made sure of that. She'd healed his leg to the best of her ability, saving him from a lifetime of residual pain. And he was grateful to her for it. That didn't change the fact that he'd never be the man he'd been before.

He was a cripple, plain and simple.

"How's the leg feel? Getting used to it yet?"

Trust Berg to be direct. Cashel gritted his teeth as he tightened the last strap and pushed himself up. He immediately stumbled forward, catching himself just before he fell face first in the sand. Righting himself, he grunted his annoyance.

"It's great," he snapped. "I'll be running races any moment now, watch out."

"That good, huh?"

Cashel shot his twin a withering look. Which silenced him for a whole two seconds.

"You missed the meeting."

I meant to.

"Dad was pretty miffed. You've never missed a meeting in your life."

Yeah, well, I've never had to hobble around on one leg before, either. People change.

"Fia asked about you. Even went out of her way to talk to me, which never happens." Berg quirked an eyebrow. "She seemed awfully concerned about your sorry ass... anything you care to share?"

An image of Fia's horrified face as he fell to the ground flashed across his mind, and he clenched his hands into tight fists, wishing for all the world he had something to punch. *I don't need her pity.* His stomach twisted as he limped his way across the beach. *I don't want her pity.*

"I'm going inside," he growled, not bothering to see if his brother followed him or not. He did, of course. Berg was nothing if not persistent.

"It was kind of a big deal. The meeting, I mean."

"Aren't they all?" Cashel eyed the ground in front of him, watching for anything that might trip him up. He'd rather not fall on his ass in front of Berg if he could help it.

"Not like this." Berg paused. "The sun goddess, Luxeos, was there."

He'd heard something about the king arriving late last night, having ridden down from Eldon to meet them at the duke's castle in Devon, where they'd taken refuge after crossing the border into Eldour. He hadn't heard anything about the goddess being with him, however.

"I thought she had to stay in Eldon to maintain the barrier

around Eldour."

"I guess she can manage it from here, as well. Might even be easier, since the Shendri are all here. They seem to feed off each other somehow."

Cashel grunted. "So she's here. Huzzah. Are we done?"

"Aren't you a ray of sunshine today," Berg muttered. "And no, we're not done. They covered quite a bit at the meeting – which you'd know, by the way, had you bothered to attend. Some of it even pertains to you."

That stopped Cashel in his tracks. "Me?"

"Ready to listen, are we?"

"Shut up and talk."

"Bit tricky to do both, but whatever," Berg huffed. "Here's the gist. Luxeos starts the meeting all fired up to regroup and head back into Roshka, with her in attendance this time. She wouldn't be able to maintain the barrier around Edlour, but the Shendri would be stronger, and therefore have a better chance of ending things once and for all. An all-in sort of approach."

"They're going back?" Cashel cringed, recalling the searing pain of the strange woman's magic. Combined with Bade's ability to manipulate people's minds, it made further attacks seem borderline suicidal.

"That was her initial plan, yes. But then Josselyn told her about what happened in the palace, about the woman with the crazy powers, and she just froze on the spot. Seriously. It took her a full five minutes to regain any kind of cohesive speech. And when she did, she was fidgety and weird. She agreed we should stay here and hold down the fort for now." Berg paused, looking pensive. "If you ask me, she's hiding something. Luxeos, I mean. I think she knows more about that woman than she's willing to admit."

Cashel nodded slowly. "Now that you mention it, the woman did seem kind of familiar. I didn't make the connection before, but now that I think about it, she kind of reminds me of Luxeos. Golden hair, dark skin, and those eyes... they burned like the sun when she was on the attack."

"Coincidence?" Berg asked. "Or something deeper?"

"Hard to say, but it's worth looking into." Cashel scratched his chin. "So, how did I fit into the agenda?"

Berg toed the sand, avoiding Cashel's eyes. "Along with keeping Eldour secure, they've decided it'd be a good idea to send an emissary to the Eastern Islands, specifically the main island of Kreá."

"Don't tell me they've chosen me for the role?"

"Not exactly."

"What do you mean, not exactly? Who're they sending?"

"Fia."

"Fia?!" Cashel reared his head back, incredulous. "But she barely has any power left. They can't just send her off to a foreign land on her own like that."

"Technically, it's not a foreign land to her. Remember, Fia was born in the islands. As a native citizen, she makes for an appealing choice. Not to mention..."

Cashel narrowed his eyes at his twin. "Not to mention what?"

Berg shrugged, looking apologetic. "I know you've taken a liking to her and all, but the fact is she nearly got us all killed. Josselyn explained what happened in the palace, how Fia stopped her from killing Bade. Something about her being the 'natural leader' and having the ability to control the other Shendri." He held up his hands as Cashel's expression turned murderous. "No one's blaming her. We know it was unintentional. But the fact remains that she's a liability. Sending her to Kreá will allow her to be helpful without endangering the others. It just makes sense."

Cashel sighed. "Fine. But please tell me they aren't shipping her off by herself."

"Oh, they're not."

"Who're they sending with her, then?"

Berg smirked. "Isn't it obvious?"

Cashel's stomach sank as he realized just what Berg was implying. As much as he enjoyed Fia's company, he doubted she'd be too thrilled by the prospect of a one-legged companion slow-ing her down. "It's me, isn't it?"

Chapter Sixteen

"Remember, when you get to Kreá you're to go straight to the palace and present them with the introduction I wrote for you. Eldour has always been on good terms with them, so I'm sure King Gregor will invite you to stay there."

Fia stepped to the side as two burly sailors passed by, carrying a large crate up the gangplank of *Juniper's Folly*, the cargo ship Draven had secured passage on for her and Cashel. Josselyn, Maya, and Lily stood grouped together at the bottom, determined to see her off.

"And if he doesn't?" Fia asked.

"He will," Josseln replied confidently. "But if something comes up and it doesn't work out, use the funds I'm sending along to get yourself a room somewhere nearby. I'd prefer to have you there as a sanctioned ambassador, but we need a presence in the islands no matter what. If only to alert them of the danger Bade poses on us all."

"You'd think they'd be well aware of it by now."

"Islanders tend to think they live in their own, private world," Lily explained. "They don't pay much attention to the goings on of the mainland, aside from trade. At least, that's been my experience. Was it different where you're from?"

Fia shrugged. "I couldn't tell you. I wasn't allowed outside of the asylum. It's true that I don't remember any of the mesdames discussing the mainland at all."

Lily's face fell, and Fia immediately felt bad for putting such a crestfallen look on her sweet friend's face. Forcing a grin, she gestured up the gangplank. "Whelp, I'd better get up there before they decide to leave me behind. Adventure awaits!"

Lily's eyes misted over, and Fia soon found herself wrapped in a surprisingly tight hug. Two more pairs of arms enfolded her from the sides, as Josselyn and Maya joined in.

"I'm sorry about this," Josselyn whispered. "It's not that we don't want you with us."

"It's fine, really," Fia replied in a muffled voice. "I just hope I can make a difference over there. I hate feeling useless."

"You're gonna do great," Maya said, releasing her hold. The others followed suit, and Fia took a step back as she wiped a stray tear that'd found its way out of the corner of her eye.

"Thank you."

Their goodbyes were cut off as a loud bell began clanging aboard the ship.

"Pretty sure that means I need to get my ass on board." Fia bit her lip as she looked her sister Shendri over one last time. "I'll see you all when this is over, right?"

"Of course," Josselyn replied.

Lily nodded emphatically, looking too choked up to manage a verbal response.

Maya grinned. "You couldn't keep us away if you tried."

"Alright then." Fia started up the gangplank backwards. "I'm off."

She turned and walked the rest of the way up, making a conscious effort to keep her chin up. There was no reason to let on how much she dreaded returning to the islands. She couldn't stay in Eldour, that much had been made very clear. So she'd do her duty and take on this 'mission' she'd been given, no matter how doubtful it was she'd make a difference.

At least she wasn't likely to hurt anyone there.

"Quit yer bawlin' and shet ep already. Yer givin' me a headache with all that racket yer makin'."

Fia wrapped her hands around the bars of her crate, gripping them tight. "Please, let us out," she begged. "There's been a mistake. We're supposed to be passengers, not prisoners."

"That so?" The pair of men sitting across the room chuckled, one of them tossing his cards down onto the table and standing up. He adjusted his considerable girth as he moved closer, his beady eyes glinting viciously in the lantern light. The other girls whimpered in their crates as he approached, but Fia only gripped the bars tighter, steeling herself.

"Madame Germaine said we were to be assigned apprenticeships on the mainland, training to help us get started on our own. Not be sold like cattle."

The ugly man smirked. "Seems to me yer Madame lied. The only trainin' chits like you need is on yer backs." He fiddled with the buckle of his pants, his smirk turning to a leer. "Now, if ya really wanna get outta that there crate, my friend and I would be more'n happy to give ya some lessons. Whaddya say?"

"I'd rather bite off my tongue," Fia hissed.

"Be my guest, bitch," the man snarled, his booted foot striking the bars where her fingers were curled. Pain shot through the tender digits, and she felt a surge of hate as she glared up at her captor. The feeling heated her skin, until she felt as if she might burst into flames at any moment. Opening her mouth, she heard a voice that wasn't her own commanding the man to kneel. Seconds after he complied, she erupted, the flames pouring out of her mouth and burning the man's doughy flesh.

His screams were as sweet as an angel's song.

Fia stared up at the ceiling of her cabin. The lack of windows in the tiny room made it impossible to tell whether it was morning or night, but she knew she was done sleeping, regardless.

That was new, she thought, turning the dream over in her mind. Usually her nightmares were about the baron or Mistress

Han, his resident taskmaster. *Must be the ship. It triggered memories from the last time I crossed this god-forsaken sea.* She felt the ghost of a smile on her lips. *Although, that trip didn't have nearly as lovely an ending.*

It'd been years later, after recounting the story to Bade during one of their many late night conversations, that she'd finally had her fiery revenge. Bade had surprised her by hunting the man down and bringing him back to Hildegarde so she might mete out her justice. She probably should've been horrified at the prospect, but watching the man burn under Artemis's flames had been one of the single greatest pleasures of her life.

Right after Bade killing the baron and awakening her dragon.

Who am I kidding, pretending to be some kind of hero Shendri? I'm nothing more than a villain, the perfect match for Bade's darkness. Trying to be anything else just ends up hurting more people.

With a heavy heart, she crawled out of bed and threw on a shawl, not bothering to change out of her nightgown. It's not like she was trying to impress anyone, anyway. Shuffling up the steps to the deck, she pushed the door open to find a blanket of stars blinking their lights above her.

Still night, then. She pulled her shawl closer, shivering. Picking her way around the stacks of wooden boxes and barrels, she made her way over to the ship's rail. The water was almost black except for the slivers of moonlight streaking across its surface. *The moon's beautiful tonight. Bade would have loved it.* She pictured the wrathful beauty who'd usurped her position at the demigod's side and jealousy twisted around her heart, digging its sharp talons into the sensitive organ. *Or maybe he's enjoying it right now, in the arms of his new lover. A vast improvement on my pathetic existence, I'm sure.*

She leaned over the railing until it dug into her abdomen, entranced by the darkness below. *It's almost... inviting.*

"Careful, Fia."

The *thud* of wood tapping against the deck floor had her spinning around with a gasp of surprise. Cashel's scowling face stared back at her, almost completely hidden in the shadows. He took another awkward step forward, and moonlight illuminated his tall frame. He struck a contradictory picture, both strong and fragile at the same time, and Fia's stomach sank under the added weight of guilt as her eyes flickered down to his wooden leg.

My fault. It's my fault.

He cleared his throat, and she jerked her gaze upwards, flushing.

"You shouldn't be out here so late. It's not safe."

"You're out here," she countered, feeling her back stiffen under his angry scowl. *He must hate me now. And why not? I deserve it.*

"Yeah, well, I'm not the one leaning over the railing of a ship in the middle of the night like a foolish child," he snapped. "What if the boat lurched and you fell overboard? No one would even know what happened to you."

What if, indeed.

"I'm not a child," she retorted, pushing back the image of enticing, black waves.

"You could have fooled me. Traipsing around half-naked in the dead of night, hanging over railings."

"You're one to talk," she grumbled. "When was the last time you bothered putting a shirt on?"

There was a pause, and for a minute she thought he might be fighting a smile. A trickle of light broke through her gloom at the sight of it, and she opened her mouth to tease him further when the boat suddenly lurched, sending her stumbling backwards. Cashel jerked forward, making to grab her arm, but his wooden leg slipped out from under him instead, causing him to fall forward onto his hands and knees. Steadying herself, Fia moved to offer him a hand up, but he snapped the minute she came close.

"I've got it."

She froze, hand halfway extended. "R-right. Sorry."

His hand clenched into a fist, and he hit the floorboards with a frustrated growl. "Stupid leg," he muttered as he pushed himself back onto his feet.

"Are... are you okay?"

"I'm fine." He glowered at her. "Stay away from the edge, alright? I'm going to bed."

"Oh... okay." She blinked back the tears that were threatening to spill. The last thing she wanted to do was start crying in front of the poor man. She'd caused him enough misery as it was. "Goodnight."

He hesitated, his eyes narrowing in on her own, but then he turned and hobbled inside without another word. Leaving her alone. Again.

My parents were right. I am cursed. Destined to ruin everyone and everything around me. I'd leave me, too, if I could.

"I haven't left you."

Fia touched her chest, feeling Artemis's familiar warmth as his deep voice filled her mind. *Could you if you tried?*

There was a pause. "I suppose not."

So, basically, you're stuck with me.

"Perhaps, but I am happy to be with you, nevertheless."

Even though you've been reduced to a mere fraction of your size? Because of me? She shook her head. *I've been a lousy host, admit it.*

"The world has been unkind to you, but you've born it all with your head held high. I've never been anything but proud of you."

Even when I was with Bade?

A pause. "I can't say I was thrilled, but I understood your attraction."

Hmm. She grinned wryly. *He was rather irresistible, wasn't he? I wonder what that's like.*

"What *what's* like?"

She sighed and walked back to the railing, letting her gaze fall once again to the moon-brushed darkness below. "Being wanted."

The words slipped out of her mouth on a whisper as she leaned forward, unresistant to the strange pull that tugged at her chest. The dark water called to her, answering her whispers with one of its own – an invitation to escape it all.

Hey, Artemis...

"Yes, Shendri?"

What happens to you if I die? Do you die, too?

"If you die before passing me on? I suppose I'd return to the heavens. Reform the great dragon in the stars. That's where Luxeos pulled me from before attaching me to Aoi, my original host."

Would you like that? Being part of the heavens again?

"I always found it agreeable before. But..."

But?

"But I would miss being with you. More than I care to admit... Fia."

There was silence as Fia let his words wash over her, caressing her soul. A single tear fell unchecked down her cheek, and she swallowed over the sudden lump in her throat. She braced her arms, pushing herself up until she was able to swing a leg over the railing, then two. Facing the sea, she gripped the railing behind her back as she took a final breath in.

Artemis?

"Yes?"

I'll miss you, too.

She exhaled and let go.

Chapter Seventeen

The cold hit first, shocking her body and causing her muscles to clench. Fia sank deeper into the frigid depths as the air slowly depleted from her lungs. The sensitive organs burned with a pain that only increased with each passing second, and panic swelled as reality sank in.

What am I doing?

She kicked her legs, eyes locked on the thin stream of moonlight shining through the surface. *I don't wanna die.* She kicked harder. *I'm not ready. I...*

She gasped as her face broke the surface, only to be smacked back down by a crashing wave. Again, she pushed through, surfacing just long enough to see *Juniper's Folly* disappear into the distant darkness. Regret hardened in her stomach like lead, pulling her back under as her limbs gave way, weakened by the ever shifting waves.

Do you remember what it felt like to fly, Artemis?

There was no answer as she sank down, still watching the moonlight despite the fiery sting of salt in her eyes.

Flying with Bade, his arms wrapped around my waist... was there ever a more wonderful feeling than that?

She started to close her eyes, giving in to the inevitable, when suddenly the moonlight brightened, wrapping around her until she was cocooned in its glowing light. The pressure on her lungs increased, and she sucked in a breath despite herself. But rather than the burning pain of water filling her lungs, there was something like... air.

She sucked in another gulp, then released it in a startled gasp as the figure of a woman formed in the moonlight, mere inches in front of her face. The watery figure stared back at her, ink-black hair swirling around a hauntingly beautiful face. It reached out a hand, and Fia flinched as icy fingers brushed against the skin of her cheek.

But only for a moment.

After the initial chill, warmth soon followed, wrapping around Fia's body like the softest of quilts. Emboldened by the warmth, Fia whispered, "Are you... a ghost?" She swallowed. "Am I dead?"

"I am not a ghost, and you are still very much alive." The woman looked at her curiously. "Does that disappoint you? I know you jumped, but were you truly hoping to end things?"

Shamefaced, Fia lowered her gaze. "I... I don't know. I guess I thought it'd be better this way... for everyone."

The woman frowned. "Not everyone."

Fia looked up in surprise.

"Not for my son," the woman continued. "He needs you, Fia. More than he knows."

"How do you...?" She shook her head. "Your son?"

The woman's mouth tilted up in a tender smile. "He loves you, you know."

"No one has ever loved me," Fia replied, feeling suddenly tired. "Not even my own parents. You must be mistaken... whoever you are." She glanced around at the strange, moonlit bubble they were floating inside and added, "*Whatever* you are."

The woman's smile turned knowing. "While it's true I've been mistaken about such things in the past – particularly when it came to myself – I'm more than certain about this. I know my son. I know what he thinks, what he feels." She paused. "How he suffers." She touched Fia's face again, and this time Fia couldn't help but press her cheek against the cool, porcelain skin. "He needs you, Fia. You're the only one who can save him."

Fia gazed at the woman in open wonder. "Who are you?"

"Who do you think I am?"

Moonlight, a mysterious figure in the sea, that face... there's something familiar about that face. Fia's eyes widened. "You can't be... Lunares? The moon goddess?"

"Clever girl. I can see why my son is so taken with you."

"Your son," Fia repeated. "He's Bade? *My* Bade?"

"I'd prefer to think of him as *our* Bade," Lunares countered. "After all, I did sacrifice my mortal shell giving birth to him. I believe that entitles me to at least a small claim."

"But... how? I mean, I thought you died...?"

"When my body ceased to function, my spirit attached itself to the sea." Lunares's expression grew wistful. "I used my power to bind my soul to Bade's, so that, no matter where he went or who he became, I'd always be able to feel his presence close to my heart. I wanted so much to see him grow."

"You must have really loved him." Fia's chest ached at the thought. *What would it be like to be loved like that?*

"I do," Lunares replied. "Which is why I called you here."

"I'm sorry?" Fia wrinkled her brow. "I don't remember anyone forcing me to throw myself into the sea. As misguided as it may have been, that was all me."

"Was it?"

"Well, yeah..." Fia hesitated. "Wasn't it?"

"Yes and no," Lunares replied. "It's true you were feeling particularly vulnerable. I may have just... pushed you over the edge a bit, so to speak."

"You can do that?"

Lunares arched a brow. "I am a goddess, after all. Even without my celestial robes, I am not completely incompetent."

"I guess that explains where Bade gets his silver-tongue from," Fia muttered.

Lunares's face hardened. "He may have inherited his charisma from me, but the rest of it... the power to control people's minds, to bind their bodies... *that* power comes from the hagrüs."

"What do you mean, the hagrüs?"

A chill ran down Fia's spine as soon as the strange word slipped past her lips, and she wished she could recall it, if for no other reason than the inexplicable sense of unease upon hearing it.

"The hagrüs is a parasite that has attached itself to my son's soul, twisting his mind and forcing him to do unspeakable things." Lunares's face darkened with rage, her ethereal features twisting with hate. "It's eating away at him, bit by bit. For two hundred and thirty years my sweet boy has suffered the monster's torture, finding relief only at night, when the power of the moon increases and Bade's true self gains greater control."

"But that... that's awful," Fia cried. "Does he know? He never said anything."

"He knows," Lunares replied. "He's known ever since the thing took root. It speaks to him. Whispered lies meant to warp his mind." Her face twisted. "Lies about me, about what I'd supposedly wish for him." She snarled. "Rubbish, all of it. As if I'd wish to see him sully his soul like this."

Fia was quiet for a moment, letting the goddess's words sink in. She pictured Bade during the daylight hours – his face set in an implacable mask, never letting even the slightest emotion make its way to the surface. He was always so... controlled. He'd spoken to her, of course, but never with the warmth she'd felt at night, when he'd lie in bed beside her, warding off the nightmares. When they'd hold whispered conversations about anything and everything. When she'd think that maybe – just maybe – he cared about *her*, not just her dragon.

When she first realized she'd fallen in love with him.

"How did it happen?" She reached out, taking Lunares hands and holding them tightly. "How did this thing get inside him?"

Lunares sighed. "It was my robes. I'd wrapped him in my ruined celestial robes, selfishly wishing for him to someday learn who his mother was. I thought the robes would connect us. Instead, they ended up being his ruin." She squeezed her eyes shut. "He was such a remarkable young man, my Bade. He saw the darkness that Antos had fallen under, saw the corruption in the hearts of those in power, and he tried to change it. But his ideals made him desperate, and he used dark magic to draw power from my robes. That was when the hagrüs was born, and Bade went from being a champion to being a villian."

"But he's not the villain," Fia said slowly. "The hagrüs is."

All of those villages razed.

The unnecessary deaths.

Bade didn't choose to do those things, the hagrüs did.

She squeezed Lunares's hands. "You said he needed me. What did you mean by that? What does he need me to do?"

Lunares brightened, and the smile that lit up her face was nothing short of radiant.

"He needs you to save him, of course."

Chapter Eighteen

You can be a real asshole, you know that?

Cashel cursed as he wrestled with the straps holding his wooden leg in place. The hammock he'd been assigned shifted beneath his weight, making the process more difficult. He stilled, his eyes staring blankly down at the leather straps in his hands.

I shouldn't have snapped at her like that. It's not her fault I'm so pathetic.

He groaned.

Bad enough to be pathetic, but to be a pathetic asshole who loses his temper on unsuspecting women? Gods, I'm the worst.

He stared at the leather strap.

I should apologize in the morning.

Grasping the leather ends, he pulled them tight, securing them in place.

Or maybe I'll just see if she's still out there. What is it Berg always says? Why put off what you can make right, right now?

He struggled to his feet, stumbling at first before finding his balance. Glancing around the dark room, he was grateful to see none of the sleeping crew members had been awakened by his bumbling. Moving as quietly as possible, he crept out of the bunk and into the hallway. The stairs leading up to the deck were a bit more challenging, and he had to bite his tongue to keep from swearing with each awkward movement.

By the time he stepped out onto the deck, he was sweating and feeling just as grumpy as he had been earlier, when he'd made Fia cry. Not a great start.

This isn't about you, it's about Fia. So relax, already, before you say something even worse and she writes you off for good.

He rolled his shoulders in an attempt to release some of the tension there, then hobbled out across the deck, looking for Fia.

Who, it would seem, had left.

Damn it.

And she's gone. Of course she is.

He balled his hands into fists at his side, feeling irrationally annoyed with her for not being there. Why she should be expected to hang around the deck in the middle of the night, he wasn't sure, but he was annoyed with her absence all the same. He had just started to turn back when a flash of light off the side of the boat caught his eye. Limping his way over to the railing, his hand sought out the knife he kept strapped to his belt.

The belt he wasn't wearing.

He cursed.

The light flashed again, and he realized it was coming from the water itself. A stream of silvery light was racing across the water, heading straight toward the boat. He stumbled backward as it approached, its trajectory aimed almost directly at the spot he was standing. Tripping over his wooden leg, his backside hit the deck just as a tower of water shot up and over the side. It curved down toward him, and he realized with a start that the head of the water was shaped like a dragon.

A dragon who's jaws were opened wide, as if to swallow him whole.

He stared up at it, slack-jawed. Knowing he should try to move out of the way.

Why wasn't he moving?

The water struck, pushing him back against the floor and pinning him there. Something solid landed on his stomach and he let out an *oomph* as the air was forced out of him. He started to thrust his hands out, trying to free himself of the offending weight, when a shock of familiar red hair appeared above his head in the midst of the cascading water.

It stopped as quickly as it began, and he found himself staring up at a sopping wet Fia. Her hands pressed against the deck on either side of his head, arms braced as she hovered above him. Droplets of water clung to the ends of her hair, intermittently dripping onto his face. He hardly noticed.

"Fia?"

It shouldn't have been a question, because who else would it be, and yet the woman staring down at him had such an intense look of determination he hardly recognized her. And her eyes! Those hazel eyes that always seemed to be edged with sadness were now gleaming with excitement.

She broke into a radiant grin that set his heart pounding, and it was all he could do to breathe as she hovered above him.

"There's been a change of plans," she exclaimed breathlessly, beaming down at him.

"A change of plans?" he repeated, struggling to set his confused mind to rights.

She nodded. "When we reach Kreá, we need to head straight for Nimrey."

"Nimrey?" He cast around in his memory for any recollection of the place, but came up empty. "But... the king..."

"Won't give a fig whether we show up or not," Fia stated. "It's not like he was going to listen to us, anyway. Trust me."

I am so confused.

He started to sit up, then realized Fia was actually on top of him, straddling his chest. He cleared his throat, feeling suddenly warm. She must have noticed their awkward position at the same time, because she sat up quickly, her back ramrod straight. Which inadvertently drew attention to the fact that her nightgown was soaked through, making it practically translucent. He swallowed. Translucent and clingy.

He bit back a groan.

"S-sorry," she stammered, wiggling her hips down toward his waist as she attempted to work her way off of him. This time he really did groan, and she toppled off to the side and scooted away as if he were made of molten lava.

Which, considering how hot he was suddenly feeling, may not have been far off. He threw an arm over his face as he lay there, prone and overheated, his voice coming out in a strangled squeak as he asked, "Why Nimrey?" He paused, letting his arm drop as he pushed himself up on his elbow. "And did you just shoot up out of the sea?"

"There's something there I need to find, something important." Her face lit up again, all traces of awkwardness gone as the excitement returned. "And yes. Yes, I did."

He waited for her to expound, but she simply sat there, grinning.

"That's it? You're not going to tell me what the hell is going on?" He sat up, gesturing wildly toward the side of the ship. "You literally just shot out of the bloody sea in some sort of crazy water dragon, and that's all you have to say about it? How? Why?" He pinched his arm. "Am I asleep right now? Damn it, I must be."

"You're not dreaming," Fia replied calmly. "And I'll tell you all about it. Just as soon as we get to Nimrey." He opened his mouth to protest, but she continued before he could get anything out. "I'm asking you to trust me on this." She paused. "Can you do that?" A hint of uncertainty crept into her voice. "Can you trust me?"

Gods, this woman is going to be my undoing.

He sighed. "Yeah, I can do that."

"Thank you." She stood up and leaned down, offering him a hand as he struggled to his feet. Or foot, as it were.

He took it, even though he knew he could manage without it. But it felt so right there, tucked into his own large hand, that he kept hold of it well after he was fully righted.

"Actually, I, uh... wanted to apologize," he said as they stood there holding hands and dripping onto the floorboards. "I shouldn't have snapped at you earlier. I'm sorry."

She glanced down at her toes. "And I'm sorry about your leg. If it weren't for me, you wouldn't have been hurt."

"It wasn't your fault!"

She shrugged, still avoiding his gaze. "Maybe not directly, but I'm sorry all the same." She looked up, and the moonlight danced across her face, illuminating the seriousness in her expression. "I can't change what happened, but I can do something to change this war." She paused. "And you're going to help me."

"Sure I won't slow you down too much?" he asked, tapping his wooden leg on the floor. She smirked.

"As if I'd let you off that easy."

Chapter Nineteen

The duke's castle in Devon

"She's so pale..."

"And thin. She's practically wasting away."

"What do you expect? She never eats, never sleeps. Just pours herself into the barrier, day in and day out. It's killing her."

Luxeos rolled her eyes heavenward as the hushed whispers floated through the conservatory door, which stood cracked open. For prying Shendri to spy on her through, apparently.

"I'm not deaf, girls. Merely old and out of practice with holding enchantments. Now, if the three of you could cease gawking for a moment, why don't you come in and have a seat? There's something I need to discuss with you."

The three Shendri filed into the room, Lily and Maya trailing behind Josselyn like recalcitrant children prepared for a scolding. Josselyn, however, leveled Luxeos with a stern look as she took a seat beside the potted gardenias. "Admit it. The barrier is too much for you to hold on your own."

No beating around the bush with that one.

Luxeos sighed.

"The barrier is getting to be a bit much." She pursed her lips in response to Josselyn's triumphant look. "Only because they're pushing back so hard, mind you. If they weren't so strong, I'd be fine."

"About that." Josselyn paused as Lily and Maya slunk past, finding seats of their own near the glass wall separating them from the gardens outside. "We've been discussing this mysterious ally Bade seems to have procured – the one with the ability to control the wind?"

"And lightning," Maya added. "Don't forget the great balls of lightning she conjured out of nowhere. I know I won't."

"Right. Which means this woman is a serious threat. Maybe even more of a threat than Bade himself." Josselyn scowled. "And we know next to nothing about her, aside from the fact that Maya think she looks *vaguely familiar*."

"I said *very* familiar," Maya interjected. "I know I've seen her somewhere before, I just can't seem to put my finger on where. It's as if every time I come close to placing her, my head gets all muddled. It's rather unpleasant, actually."

"That is peculiar," Luxeos murmured. Her gaze shifted to the side as she attempted to avoid making eye contact without being obvious about it. If any of them were to meet her gaze now, they would surely see the secrets hiding there. Shameful secrets that would inevitably come to light as this war they found themselves in ran its course. *Not yet. Not when I could still be wrong.* "Tell me again what she looked like? This new adversary of ours?"

"Tall, dark-skinned, golden hair," Maya recited, ticking off her fingers. She paused, her gaze suddenly intent. "Eyes that shone like the sun," she added, watching Luxeos carefully. "Kind of like yours."

Lumeria. It has to be. After all these years – centuries, even – she's been freed.

A thrill of anticipation ran up Luxeos's spine, even as her stomach twisted into knots at the thought of the coming confrontation. She forced her expression into one of neutral interest. "How curious."

"Curiosity isn't what we need right now. What we need are answers," Josselyn snapped. Lily shot her a reproving look, and she slumped forward. "Sorry. Everything's just so stressful right now, and with the barrier beginning to weaken... I just don't know what to do. As much as I want to fight back, realistically, I know we're not strong enough as we are now to beat them. If only Fia still had her full powers... and, you know, wasn't in love with the enemy..."

"There's nothing we can do about that now," Luxeos replied. "But there is something we can do about the barrier."

"There is?"

She nodded. "It's not ideal, but we'll have to evacuate the area, reduce the barrier size so it's easier to maintain. I'd suggest moving everyone toward Tallis. The cliffs there will help provide some natural protection against the sea."

"You want us to surrender the castles?" Josselyn asked, aghast. "But they're our best protection against attack."

"They're also an excellent place to starve to death once supplies run out and we've yet to come up with an attack of our own," Luxeos countered. "Besides, the barrier will be all the protection we need. Given a smaller radius and the presence of three Shendri, I should be able to fortify its strength nicely. Having the sea beside us will provide us with a food source we can count on to last. It's our best option at the moment."

"Our best option is to turn tail and run," Maya muttered. "Great."

"It won't be forever, just until we come up with a plan of attack." Lily patted Maya's hand. "Isn't that right?" she added, looking back and forth between Luxeos and Josselyn. Luxeos hesitated, not wanting to give the girl false hope. What plan could they possibly come up with that would defeat such an impossibly strong opponent? Josselyn, however, didn't seem to share her misgivings.

"No question," she declared, standing up and facing them all with grim determination. "Everyone has weaknesses, even demigods. We figure out what they are, and then we destroy them. Shendri style."

Maya pumped a fist into the air, grinning. "Now, there's some leadership I can get behind. Let's crush them!"

Luxeos pressed her lips together to keep from smiling. Someone needed to keep their cool in this group of hot heads, after all. "Yes, yes. Crush them all, but first – we make for Tallis."

"Right. I'll start spreading the word." Josselyn turned to go, with the other two falling in line behind her. She paused at the door, looking suddenly hopeful. "And hey – maybe Fia will have some luck with the islanders. Who knows, we could be seeing re-inforcements arrive before long."

Luxeos nodded, watching the girls leave, before sinking back into the cushions.

She'd have to be very lucky, indeed, to convince the islanders' king that there's a world worth saving outside of his little island bubble, but at least it'll keep her too busy to cause any more trouble.

Chapter Twenty

The village of Nimrey in Kreá

"This is as far as I go."

The old man they'd begged a lift off of back in Lochless slowed his wagon to a stop in front of a small, open air blacksmith shop, and Fia could feel the smithy's eyes taking the pair of them in as she and Cashel hopped out the back. Or rather, she hopped, and Cashel did a sort of awkward, one-legged dismount of his own. "If you're lookin' fer rooms, I'd try over at The Bent Penny. Rooms are a bit cramped, but ye won't find better grub this side of the island. Jest another coupla blocks down that a-way. Can't miss it."

"Sounds good," Cashel replied, pulling Fia's travel sack out of the wagon bed and passing it to her before reaching for his own. "I'll take good food over a fancy room any day."

"Definitely," Fia agreed. She smiled up at the old man. "Thanks so much for the ride! I was starting to think we'd have to walk all the way here."

The old man grunted. "We don't get a lot of visitors from the mainland 'round here. Most folks prefer the southern islands fer their holidays. An unusual couple like yourselves can be a bit... disconcertin', is all. Don't take it personal."

"Oh, we're not... that is..." Fia threw Cashel an embarrassed glance, but he seemed too preoccupied with their surroundings to notice. *Well, if he doesn't care if people think we're a couple, then neither do I. What difference does it make, anyway?* "Um, thanks. I'll, uh, keep that in mind." Hefting her travel sack over her shoulder, she started off down the road with a wave. "See you around!"

"Thet ye will," the old man replied. "And welcome to Nim-rey!"

She and Cashel walked the next few blocks in relative silence, taking in the rustic fishing village. Multi-level wattle and daub houses crowded together along the side of the rough cobble-stone street, with the occasional break for a granary or what appeared to be a shared village well. Several women in patched and faded work dresses bustled about, hands full and legs moving quickly as they hauled water from the well or baskets of laundry down toward the shore. Young children darted across the street, shouting and laughing and generally getting in the way. The women smiled indulgently when they crossed their path, but those same smiles turned to frowns when their gazes landed on Fia and Cashel. While they didn't say anything or even stop what they were doing, Fia could see the suspicion line their faces with each stolen glance.

"Seems we're popular already," Cashel muttered.

Fia cringed. "The old guy wasn't kidding. Guess they really don't get a lot of visitors around here."

"Particularly not ones that look as different as we do," Cashel added.

"Hey! Who're you calling different?"

"Um, us?"

"What's so different about the way we look?" Fia demanded.

"Oh, I don't know, maybe because I'm a six-and-a-half foot tall Mihalan with a wooden leg? And you, well, you'd stand out anywhere with those long legs and red hair. Face it, you're gorgeous."

"Flattery, huh? Are you sure you didn't trade places with Berg before you left?"

"Berg doesn't have exclusive rights to flirting, you know. I can be charming, too, when I wish."

"Okay, prince charming," Fia scoffed. "Keep your shirt on."

"Ugh, thanks for reminding me." Cashel tugged at the rough spun tunic he'd donned before disembarking that morning. "I don't know how you Lowlanders can stand wearing these things every day. They're torture."

"Yeah, well, if you think people are giving us strange looks now, I'd love to see how they'd react to you shirtless."

"I bet you would."

"I meant that facetiously."

"Sure you did."

"I don't remember you being quite so incorrigible before."

"Maybe I'm turning over a new leaf, spicing up my personality. Let's face it – I'm not going to be making the ladies swoon with my fancy footwork anymore."

"I liked you just fine before, you know, without the added spice. Although it is preferable to the grumpy, cold shoulder routine you were giving me on the boat."

Cashel cringed. "Yeah, I wasn't exactly at my best, was I? Sorry. I was feeling pretty awkward about this new leg of mine. Still am, if I'm honest, but I'm trying to leave off the sulking."

Fia stopped walking. "You have nothing to feel awkward about. You lost your leg saving my life. It doesn't get any more heroic than that. You should be proud of yourself." Her voice caught, and she willed the impending tears away. "I owe you my life, Cashel. You're my hero."

There was pause as Cashel stared down at her, his face inscrutable. After a moment, the corner of his mouth twitched and his eyes began to dance playfully.

"Your hero, huh? Would you say that I, oh I don't know, make you *swoon*?" His mouth stretched into a grin as she let out an exasperated huff. "Should I take my shirt off after all? 'Cause I will. Anything for my fans."

"Ha, ha. Very funny." Fia shifted her glare over his shoulder and pointed. "Oh, look. The Bent Penny. Excellent." She made a beeline for the door, fists clenching as the sound of Cashel's laughter followed close behind.

Once inside, they managed to secure two adjacent rooms from the hard-mouthed woman manning the taproom bar. Not the easiest of feats, given the way the woman kept hemming and hawing. Surprisingly enough, it was Cashel's teasing remark about being happy to share one that broke the woman's icy exterior. She had quite the chuckle watching Fia's face turn as red as her hair, and set them up with two keys and the promise of a hot meal later that evening.

"Already cleaned up the lunch dishes, ain't nothin' left but some hard rolls and maybe a bit o' meat and cheese. You're welcome to it, if ya like."

Fia laughed as Cashel's stomach let out a loud growl. "I think that's a yes, please."

Cashel shrugged. "What can I say? It's been a long morning."

The woman chuckled. "Big man like you hardly needs a reason to be hungry. I'll have the cook scrape something up for ya while you settle into your rooms."

"That would be wonderful," Fia replied. "Thank you so much."

"No problem at all, dear. Now, should I have that sent up to your rooms, or will you be coming back down for it?"

"Actually, would it be possible to have it wrapped up to go?" Fia asked. "I was hoping to walk down to Starlight Beach this afternoon, and I think we'd best head down soon if we want to be back in time for supper."

Cashel shot her a questioning look, but she ignored it, mentally promising to explain everything to him later. Something she wasn't entirely looking forward to.

The woman gave her a curious look. "How d'ya know about Starlight Beach? Thought for sure you were both mainlanders."

"We are," Fia put in quickly, before Cashel could say anything about her being a former islander. She was in no way prepared to answer the multitude of questions that were sure to follow. "Some of the sailors mentioned it on the way over. Said it was the prettiest stretch of beach on the island."

The woman nodded. "That it is, and then some. Alright, I suppose I can have that packed up for ya, easy enough." She gave Cashel a sly smile. "Wouldn't wanna stand in the way of a romantic, beach picnic. Not with two lovebirds such as yourselves."

"We're not –"

Fia's protests were cut off as Cashel threw an arm around her and pulled her into his side. "Thank you! That'd be wonderful."

"Alright. You two stop down here before ya go, and I'll be sure to have something wrapped up for ya. And if anyone in town gives you any trouble, you jest tell 'em you're staying with Maddie, and that'll shut 'em right up."

"Will do, Maddie," Cashel replied, ushering Fia toward the stairs, his arm still wrapped firmly around her shoulders. "And thanks again!"

He stopped at the stairs and gestured for Fia to go ahead, his eyes dancing with barely restrained mirth. She stuck her tongue out at him and started up the steps, only to stop at the sound of Maddie's voice calling after them.

"Be sure to stay out of the water while you're down there! It's not safe for swimming, you know."

Fia turned to look at the woman. "What do you mean? Are there a lot of strong undertows or something?"

"Worse than that," Maddie replied. "It's haunted."

Cashel and Fia exchanged surprised looks. "Haunted?"

Maddie nodded. "There's an evil spirit lives in there, everyone knows that. Lights up the water all strange like at night." She shivered. "I've seen it myself, once, back when I was a young thing, traipsing around the beach at night." She brushed her hands together. "Anyway, you'll be fine so long as you stay outta the water." And with that, she turned and disappeared into the kitchen.

"Evil spirits, huh?" Cashel looked down at Fia, amused. "This have anything to do with our sudden change in travel plans?"

"Possibly."

"Care to share?"

Fia hesitated, looking over Cashel's shoulder at the taproom below. "Yes, but not here. Think you can hold out till we get to the beach?"

"If I must."

"You must."

"And then you'll tell me everything? Every little last detail, no matter how insignificant it may seem?"

Fia bit her lip. "I'll tell you everything, so long as you promise to keep an open mind."

"Well, that sounds... foreboding," Cashel said, widening his eyes in an exaggerated fashion. When Fia refused to respond, he sighed. "Fine," he relented. "Consider my mind open. Now, let's get this stuff up to our rooms already. The sooner we're on our way, the sooner I prove just how open-minded I can be."

Fia managed a small smile before turning to head back up the stairs, but inside, her stomach was twisting into knots over the prospect of telling Cashel everything that had transpired in the sea that night. Would he understand?

Am I crazy to even be considering this, Artemis? Everyone hates Bade. Who's going to believe he's even remotely worth saving?

"You won't know how they'll react until you tell them, Shendri. The worst that happens is they chalk you up to a pathetic, lovesick fool with horrendous taste in men."

Wow. That's reassuring.

Fia shook her head as she let herself into her tiny room and dropped her travel sack onto the bed. *You can do this, Fia. With or without their help. Bade* is *worth saving, and you're going to be the one to save him.*

Chapter Twenty-One

"So, this is the infamous Starlight Beach."

Cashel looked down the expanse of white sand separating the sea from the increasingly steep cliffs of the island. Bright green vines, amassed with leaves and fluted, white flowers, hung over the tops of the cliffs, giving them an almost festive look. "Pretty."

Fia was already pulling off her shoes. Sinking her toes into the warm sand, she grinned. "As much as I hated this island, I have to admit I loved the beaches. Not that I was allowed to visit them often. The asylum wasn't exactly big on pleasure outings." She lifted her face to the sun as she let her eyes fall closed. "Can't stop me now, though, can they? Ha!"

She's so incredibly resilient, Cashel marveled, admiring her profile as she drank in the sun. *And here I've been, sulking over a flesh wound. That's nothing compared to a lifetime of mistreatment.*

She turned her head to the side, eyes fluttering open as if she could feel the weight of his gaze on her face. He smiled. "So? Are you ready to tell me why we're here?" He held up the rusty shovel he was carrying. "And what in Lehi you asked to borrow this for?"

She hesitated for a moment, then nodded. "I suppose it's time. Just promise you'll listen and be open-minded? At least until I'm done."

"Well, that's ominous."

"I'm serious."

"So am I." Cashel chuckled as she made a face at him. "I'll listen to every word, I promise."

"You'd better," Fia warned. "Alright, here goes." She took a deep breath. "That night on the boat – the one I didn't want to talk about?" she began.

"The one where you dropped down out of a water dragon and landed on my chest?"

"That's the one. Prior to that happening, I'd, uh... kind of, sort of, fallen into the sea."

"You fell overboard?!" He narrowed his eyes. "Wait, what do you mean 'kind of'? Either you did or you didn't. There's not a lot of gray area there."

She dropped her gaze. "I may have climbed over the railing and jumped in, but it wasn't entirely my fault. I was being compelled."

Cashel's stomach sank as he thought of Fia throwing herself into the dark, frigid water. Had she been hurting that much? *How could I have not realized she was suffering?* He searched his memory for signs but couldn't come up with more than a few hurt looks, a hint of wistfulness. "You said you were compelled? What do you mean?" *Please let there be a reason.*

Fia turned to face the water, twisting her hands together nervously as she did. "Remember what Maddie said about the sea being haunted by an evil spirit?"

"I do," he replied, dragging out the words slowly. *Where is she going with this?*

"Turns out she's half-right. There is a spirit living in the sea, only she isn't evil." She paused. "She's Lunares."

"Lunares," he deadpanned. "As in, the former goddess of the moon?"

"The one and only."

"Correct me if I'm wrong, but didn't Lunares die giving birth to Bade?"

"She did."

"And now you're saying her spirit is haunting the Valiant Sea?"

"I wouldn't say haunting so much as residing in, but yes. That's basically what I'm saying."

"That's what I thought." He sighed. "Continue."

"That night on the boat, it was Lunares who compelled me to jump."

"I thought you said she wasn't an evil spirit," Cashel snapped. "Luring people into the sea seems pretty evil to me."

"Calm down. She wasn't going to let me drown," Fia replied. "When her mortal body broke down, her spirit became tethered to the sea, but it still draws its power from the moon. So the only way she could speak with me was if I was submerged in the sea while the moonlight was reflecting off the surface. And she needed to speak to me, so... she compelled me to jump."

"Still not sold on her not being evil," he retorted dryly. "But go on. What did the nice moon spirit need so desperately to speak with you about? Updates on her son's brutal take over?"

Fia folded her arms across her chest, annoyed. "You said you'd be open-minded."

Cashel sighed. "Right, sorry. Go on."

She watched him skeptically for a moment before resuming. "The reason Lunares reached out to me was because she needs my help. According to her, Bade is being controlled by something, something evil. I think she called it a... a hagrüs."

Cashel stiffened. Though little was known on the subject, one thing was certain – a hagrüs wasn't something to be taken lightly. Once it sunk its fangs into someone, there was precious little hope of freeing them. The only way to kill a hagrüs was to kill its host, and pray that it didn't find someone else to latch onto before it shriveled away into nothingness. If it was controlling someone as powerful as Bade... he shuddered.

We're doomed.

"Are you certain she said it was a hagrüs?"

"Positive."

Bloody hell. "And it's infected Bade? How? When?" His legs ached with the need to pace across the sand, but his wooden leg held him stationary, mocking him for his uselessness all over again. *How am I supposed to fight a freaking hagrüs like this? I can't even pace properly anymore.*

"Lunares said it happened when Bade used the remains of

her celestial robes to create an enhancement potion. It was supposed to magnify his charisma and strength, which, technically, it did. A lot. The problem was the magic he used... it was an ancient spell created by the mountain witch. Dark magic. It warped the power of Lunares's tainted robes, creating a hagrüs in their place. It's been controlling Bade ever since."

Fia turned to face him fully, her eyes beseeching.

"Everything he's done – the war he waged two-hundred years ago, the villages he's destroyed, the people he's killed – none of that was his doing. It was the hagrüs."

Cashel winced at the desperate note in her voice. *She loves him so much she'd overlook it all.* He swallowed against the sudden lump in his throat. *Why does that hurt so much?*

"We can't know it was all the hagrüs's doing," he replied harshly. "From what I've read, Bade was pushing for a revolution well before he gained his new powers. Before he even took his new name. Who knows what lengths he would've gone to, to support his cause? Clearly, he wasn't above using dark magic. Who's to say he wouldn't have resorted to violence, as well?"

"He's not like that," Fia whispered, her voice barely audible as she turned back toward the water. She took a few steps toward the lapping waves, shoulders curling in as she hugged herself. Cashel clenched his fists, wanting to reach out and soothe the hurt he saw there, but knowing it wasn't his comfort she was wishing for.

"You can't know that." He cringed, feeling like a heel for what he was about to say, but, honestly, it was the truth. She needed to hear it. "You don't even know him. Like you said, he was being controlled by the hagrüs. That fact applies to your time together, as well."

"You're wrong." She lifted her chin, hands falling to her sides as her voice strengthened. Though she didn't look at him, her words struck him full in the face with their intensity. "I do know him. He's gentle and compassionate. There's no way he would have allowed himself to do those things if he had any other choice."

"That was the hagrüs – "

"It wasn't!" Her voice trembled slightly. "Not at night. Not when the moon was out. Then it was him, or at least as much of him as he could retain control of." She paused. "He was different at night. More... human." She shook her head. "I should have realized something was off sooner. It seems so obvious now."

She sniffed, and Cashel's heart broke to see how hard she was trying to hold it together.

"You're in love with him," he stated, unable to hold the words back any longer.

"That's irrelevant," she replied, dabbing hastily at the corners of her eyes.

That's not a denial. He sighed. "I wish that it were, but it isn't. Tell me, Fia, why are we here? What did Lunares ask you to do?"

"She asked me to save him."

Of course, she did. "And how does she expect you to do that?"

"By using her celestial robes. Or, a piece of them, anyway." Fia gestured down the beach. "This beach, Starlight Beach, is where Bade was conceived. About a mile or so down the coast we should find the cave where he was born. That's where we'll find what we need."

"I thought Bade corrupted the robes with dark magic. Isn't that what you said made the hagrüs in the first place?"

"Turns out he was missing the sash. Apparently, when Lunares's lover stole her robes, the sash slipped free and was left behind in the sand. Lunares found and saved it, hiding it in a wooden box and burying it in the cave she sheltered in during her pregnancy." She nodded toward the shovel. "Thus the need to borrow that. If we find the cave, we should be able to dig up the sash."

"Assuming it's still there," Cashel warned. "I wouldn't get your hopes up about finding the thing."

"But you'll help me look?" Fia asked, looking up at him hopefully.

As if I could say no to anything you asked of me while looking like that. He groaned. *Damn, I've got it bad.*

"Sure, why not? It's not like I have any other plans."

"Yes!" Fia pumped her fist in the air. "Come on, the cave should be down this way." She started off down the beach, shoes swinging in her hand as she danced across the fine, white sand. Cashel couldn't help the grin that crept onto his face as he followed.

"So, what are you supposed to do if you actually find this magical sash, anyway?" he asked as they hiked along the coastline.

"That's the best part!" Fia replied. "*When* we find it, we'll be able to use it to make a counter-potion, one that will purify the tainted robes' essence, therefore killing the hagrüs and freeing Bade."

"You know how to make potions?"

"Well, no," Fia admitted. "But Luxeos does. We'll have to bring it back to Eldour with us and convince her to help us make it."

"Good luck with that," Cashel chuckled.

"She'll do it," Fia insisted. "Freeing Bade from the hagrüs is in everyone's best interest. Save Bade, save Lehi. It's a win-win."

So is killing Bade, if you ask me.

"Don't forget, it's not just Bade anymore who poses a threat. There's still the matter of his new side-kick. You know, the one that blasted my leg off with her crazy lightning powers?"

"She'll be a challenge, but I'm confident the Shendri can take her. Especially once Bade is no longer working with her."

"Right. And how exactly are you planning to make that happen? Say we do find this sash *and* get it back to Eldour *and* Luxeos is able to make the counter-potion, how do you get Bade to drink it? I'm assuming he'll need to consume it in order for it to work."

Fia slowed her pace, and Cashel could see the determination creep into her face. "He'll drink it because deep down, he hates what the hagrüs is doing. He wants to be free. I just need to get it to him when the hagrüs's control over him is at its weakest."

"Which is..."

"On the night of a full moon."

Cashel swore. "That's, what? Two weeks from now? Or less?"

"Something like that," Fia agreed. "But isn't sooner better than later? Who knows how long Luxeos will be able to hold the barrier?"

"Still." Cashel shook his head. "It's gonna be tight. Unless we wait for the next cycle, but that'd be another six to seven weeks. And that's if we even find it."

"We'll find it," Fia insisted, picking up her pace once again. Cashel stumbled along behind her, only just managing to keep up as he maneuvered his wooden leg through the sand. He focused on Fia's back, drawing strength from her determined stride.

I hope you're right. 'Cause you're more alive now than I've ever seen you, and I'd do anything to keep you that way. Even if it means saving the enemy.

Chapter Twenty-Two

The opening to the cave was just as Lunares had described – low and wide, with moss and vines hanging over the entrance like a curtain. At five foot seven, Fia had to duck her head to avoid smacking it against the rough stone as she entered. She cringed to think how much trouble Cashel was probably having.

Not that he'd let on, the stubborn bastard.

Fortunately, the ceiling of the cave was significantly higher than the entrance, and they both took a moment to stretch their backs as they looked around the dimly lit space.

"Damn. We should've brought a lantern with us," Cashel remarked, squinting into the shadows. "It's gonna be hard to find anything in here, much less a scrap of fabric."

"No worries, I've got us covered." Fia grinned as she pulled two thin candles out of the pocket of her skirt. "What do you say, Artemis? Wanna come out and light these for us?"

Artemis grumbled inside her mind. "The once great dragon, now nothing more than a candle lighting lizard. How the mighty have fallen." He sighed, and Fia felt the flame-shaped marks on her side tingle as smoke poured out around her feet, forming Artemis's shape.

She let out a surprised "Oh!" as he solidified.

"Artemis! You've grown!"

Though he wasn't nearly as large as his former self (a good thing, really, given the cramped quarters they were currently standing in), neither was he the lizard-sized dragon he'd been the week prior. Now, his head rose up to Fia's navel as he stood on all fours before her. He stretched out his wings, looking smug.

"It's a small improvement, anyway," he murmured inside her

head, but Fia could see the gleam in his amber eyes that belied his aloofness.

"It's a *huge* improvement!" she exclaimed, moving around him slowly as she took in every little detail of his transformation. "How did you manage it?"

"As much as I'd like to take credit, I'm fairly certain it belongs to you. This time," he added.

"What? How?"

Cashel grunted in frustration, interrupting her questioning. "You two do know I can't hear what Artemis is saying, right?"

Fia waved him off with a shushing noise. "I'll fill you in later," she said distractedly. "Artemis? Explain, please?"

The dragon flared his nostrils in Cashel's direction, letting out a puff of smoke and curving his wide mouth in what Fia would swear was a smirk. "The beast is only as strong as his host. When you were shot with caeruleum and almost died, your body was severely weakened. But bodies heal, and so yours has. The caeruleum complicated things, however. It weakened our bond, as well as the one you share with your sister Shendri, and those sort of things aren't as easily healed. It takes spirit and determination to heal a damaged bond, and, until recently, those are two things you've lacked. Bade stripped you of them when he sent you away. Because of that, you lost hope."

"Until I met Lunares," Fia picked up. "She gave me something to fight for." Her eyes widened, excitement creeping into her chest and setting her nerves to humming. "Do you think you could be fully restored? Become a full-fledged dragon again?"

Artemis dipped his head. "Given this recent development, I'd say it's a definite possibility. But it won't come easy. You'll need to work for it."

"I can. I will!" She turned to Cashel, who was watching them with a mildly irritated expression. "I need to start training again. Will you help me?"

"Right now?" Cashel gave her an incredulous look. "Aren't we already in the middle of something? Something *you* insisted on doing?"

"Well, obviously not right this second," she replied. "But soon. Tonight!"

"I see." He hesitated. "Exactly what kind of training did you have in mind?"

"You know, *training* training. Scaling walls, throwing knives, sparring. That sort of thing."

"You do realize I only have one leg, right?"

"Please," she scoffed. "As if that would stop someone as skilled as you. Losing your leg didn't strip you of your experience, did it?"

"I guess not..."

"So, you'll modify. Whatever you need to do. I just need someone to push me. If there's any chance I can bring Artemis back to his full power, I have to take it."

"The training is to regain your powers? You think that's a possibility?"

"Well, yeah. I mean, isn't that what we were just talking about?"

"No. That's what you and Artemis were just talking about, apparently. I've been over here listening to a one-sided conversation and wondering when we're going to start digging for this supposed treasure."

"Oh. Right." She grimaced. "Sorry. Artemis? Would you mind?" She waved the candles she was holding, and the dragon grudgingly huffed out a stream of fire for her to light them in.

"Is that all?" he asked. "Or do you have some other mundane chores for me to do?"

"Just that," she replied. "Thank you."

"Good. I'm heading back in to nap in my own cave. Wake me when you're ready to train."

"I didn't know you slept in a cave. Is it comfortable?"

"Better than that – it's majestic. Unlike this crap hole." He sniffed, casting a disparaging look around the dark cave. "I'll see you later, Shendri," he added, dissolving back into a pool of smoke and returning to his home inside her chest.

To think there's an entire realm inside me, made just for him. Fia

135

shook her head in wonder. *It's simply mind-blowing.*

"Think I can get one of those?"

She looked up to see Cashel staring pointedly at the candles flickering away in her hands and hurried to pass one over. "According to Lunares, there should be a tunnel at the back of the cave that leads to a second, smaller room. She hid the sash inside a small wooden box and buried it there, right in the middle of the room." She moved deeper into the cave, eyes scanning the ground in front of her feet as she went. "If we can find the room, it shouldn't be too hard to dig up the box."

"Let's hope not," Cashel replied, hobbling along beside her as they crept through the dark cave. He stumbled a bit on the dark, uneven floor, his wooden leg catching clumsily in each little dip and divot along the way. "How far back does this thing go?" he grumbled.

"I think this is it," Fia said as the light from their candles illuminated the opening to a narrow tunnel. A very narrow tunnel. She glanced over at Cashel, eyeing his large frame uncertainly. "Think you can fit through here?"

"Only one way to find out." He slid sideways into the tight space, grunting as the rock pressed against both his back and front, wedging him in. "Like a glove."

Fia watched him awkwardly wriggle his way down the tunnel. "If that glove was three sizes too small, sure." She scooted in behind him. "You're not going to get stuck in here, are you?"

"I sincerely hope not," he grunted, inching his way along.

Several minutes and a bucket of sweat later, they finally stumbled out into the secondary room with matching gasps of relief. "See? Just as Lunares said it would be." Fia lifted her candle as she glanced around the room. Rocks of every shape and size crowded the edges, and one wall appeared to have caved in at some point, spreading rubble across the hard-packed dirt floor.

Cashel swore. "The center of the room, huh? I don't suppose you know if that was before or after a section of it caved in?"

Fia sighed. "I guess we'll just have to dig until we find it." She rolled her shoulders back, stretching her neck to the side. "Best get started. This might take awhile." She held her candle out to Cashel. "Pass me the shovel, will you?"

He raised an eyebrow at the waxy object. "And why are you trying to give me that?"

"So I can start digging, obviously."

"You expect me to stand here holding candles while you break your back digging?" he asked incredulously.

"Well, yeah."

"Like hell I will." He shoved his candle at her. "Here. You hold the candles, I'll dig."

"I'm perfectly capable of using a shovel, Cashel," Fia retorted.

"I'm sure you are," he replied. "However, I'm incapable of standing around and watching someone else do all the work."

"That's ridiculous, and you know it," Fia huffed, shoving her candle forward again. "Just take the candle already. I need the exercise for my training."

"You take the candle," Cashel growled. "I need the exercise for my sanity."

Fia opened her mouth to argue, but a third voice interjected before she could even begin.

"Oh, for crying out loud. *I'll* hold the damn candles if it'll get the two of you to shut up."

Chapter Twenty-Three

Fia froze, candle hovering midair, and her eyes met Cashel's own shocked gaze before whipping in the direction of the voice. A girl popped up from behind one of the larger rocks, looking exasperated. A younger boy stood up beside her, eyeing them suspiciously.

"Who...?" Fia gaped at the pair of them, unable to form coherent thoughts. Cashel stepped in, his voice calm despite his previous shock.

"Who are you, and what are you doing in here?"

The girl stuck out her chin. "Name's Nunya, and this here's my brother, Business. As in, none of ya business."

"Cute," Cashel muttered.

"Look, I'm offering to hold your stupid candles while you dig around for whatever it is you're looking for. Do you want my help or not?"

"What I want is to know what two little kids are doing skulking around in caves and eavesdropping on strangers," Cashel retorted.

"We aren't kids," the boy interjected. "I'm ten, and Rosie here is almost fourteen."

The girl jabbed her elbow into the boy's side, and he slapped a hand over his mouth, looking regretful.

"Rosie," Fia murmured, studying the girl's elf-like features, half-hidden under a greasy clump of brown hair. Smudges of dirt marked her cheeks and forehead, and her navy blue dress was equally grubby. Fia's eyes narrowed in on the familiar drab ensemble. "You're from the asylum, aren't you? Madame Germaine's Foundling Asylum?"

The girl took a step back. "What do you know about the asylum? You work there or something?"

Fia let out a humorless laugh. "Oh, I did plenty of work there, but not for pay. I was just one of the many ungrateful mouths to feed, or so I was told."

"Sounds like something Madame would say." The girl looked Fia over, still wary. "When were you at the asylum? You don't look familiar, and I never forget a face."

"Seems like a lifetime ago, but I suppose it's only been, what... three years or so? I was almost sixteen when they sent me to the mainland."

"You got an apprenticeship?" the girl asked, watching her carefully.

"An apprenticeship," Fia scoffed, laughing bitterly. "Are they still selling girls that line? Try slavery. That'd be a bit more accurate."

"See, Rosie? I told ya it smelled rotten!" The boy jerked his thumb at the girl beside him. "They tried to tell Rosie here they were gonna set her up all nice on the mainland, too, only we ran away 'fore they could send her off, on account of not wanting to be split up. I knew that cranky old witch was up to no good. I knew it!"

The girl paled. "I was supposed to set sail next week, but we took off as soon as we heard. Been hiding out in this cave ever since."

"You've been living in here?" Cashel asked, surprised. "By yourselves?"

"Better than living at the asylum," Fia countered, giving the siblings a knowing look. "But you know you can't live here forever, right? You'll freeze come winter, if you even make it that long."

The girl, Rosie, shrugged, looking uncomfortable. "It's not like we've got anywhere else to go. Madame Germaine confiscated all of our possessions when we were placed in the asylum. All we were able to get our hands on before running off was a few loaves of bread, and those are long gone."

"I managed to snag your locket from her office," the boy reminded her. He grinned up at Fia proudly. "Picked the lock and everything."

"Ten years old, and you already know how to pick locks?" Cashel eyed the boy incredulously. "Where the hell did you learn something like that?"

He shrugged. "My Uncle Jake taught me. He knew all sorts of neat tricks like that."

"He sounds like an... interesting man," Cashel commented.

Rosie snorted. "If you find pirates interesting, then sure. He's real interesting."

"Your uncle is a pirate?" Fia wrinkled her nose. "He isn't a Sea Snake, is he?"

Rosie shook her head. "Nah, he's not that crazy. Knows better than messing around with a bunch of enchantment junkies. He sailed off with Cap'n Deadeye's crew a couple years ago, headed for the western continent."

"He tried to sail to Tentalla?" Cashel asked in surprise. "But there are monstrous sea creatures living in the deep between here and there. Ships rarely attempt the voyage. It's just too dangerous."

"Uncle Jake claimed Deadeye knew a safe route to travel," Rosie replied. "Whether or not they made it..." She trailed off with awkward shrug. "Wasn't even a year later that Pa took ill, then Ma shortly after that. After they died, there wasn't anyone left to take us in, and we ended up at the asylum."

"And now you're here." Fia tilted her head, studying the pair of them. "Have you given any thought to Orphan Island? I've heard the woman who runs it, Ms. Fairway, is exceedingly kind. I'm sure she'd be happy to take you in."

"That sounds great and all, but..." Rosie's gaze dropped to the cave floor, and she kicked at some loose stones. "Like we said – "

"We ain't got any money," the boy interrupted. "And nobody wants a coupla orphans bunkin' a free ride on their boat, ya know? No money, no passage."

"Ah, I see." Fia looked over at Cashel and raised an eyebrow.

"Arranging two extra passages when we return to the port shouldn't take too long, would it?"

He thought for a moment. "I don't think it'd be too much of a setback."

"Excellent!" She grinned, turning back to the siblings who were watching them with barely concealed excitement. "Whaddya say? You up for an adventure?"

They gaped at her, wide eyed. "You'll help us? Really?"

"Of course. Us asylum kids have to stick together." Fia grinned. "Now that that's all sorted, how about we get to work, eh?" She gestured toward the shovel. "This floor isn't going to dig itself. Rosie – it is Rosie, isn't it?" She looked expectantly toward the girl, who nodded.

"Actually, it's Rosalind. Rosalind Haverdash, but everyone calls me Rosie." She tipped her head toward her brother. "And this is my brother, Cole."

"A pleasure to meet you, Rosalind and Cole Haverdash," Fia replied. "My name's Fia, and my friend here is Cashel." She leaned in and whispered, "We're on a top secret mission for the queen of Eldour. Very important stuff."

"Cool," the boy breathed, looking impressed.

His sister snorted. "The queen sent you all the way over here to dig in a cave?"

"We may have gone a bit rogue," Fia admitted. "But trust me. There's a very special treasure buried in this cave."

"If you say so."

"I do." Fia held her candle out. "Here. Why don't you and your brother hold the candles while Cashel and I take turns digging. How does that sound?"

The girl shrugged. "Fine, I guess."

"Finally!" Cashel exclaimed, all but shoving his candle into the girl's hands. He drove the shovel into the hard dirt, using nothing more than his upper body strength to drive the rusted metal down. It didn't go as deep as it might have with the help of his foot, but it worked well enough all the same. Fia bit her lip to keep from suggesting she try her hand at it first, knowing he felt the need to prove he was still capable. Instead, she rubbed her hands together in anticipation as she watched him work and grinned.

"Lehi's salvation is buried somewhere in this room. And we're gonna find it."

Chapter Twenty-Four

"I can't believe we didn't find it," Cashel groaned. "All those hours spent digging in the dark, missing dinner, and nothing. We even had the bloody kids taking turns at it, and for what? A fistful of blisters?" He leaned forward on the floor, stretching his leg out as he slowly worked the buckle of his prosthetic. After pulling it off and tossing it to the side, he leaned back on his forearms and turned to watch Fia as she braided her hair into a single, long plait. There was a slight hunch to her shoulders as she finished, and she didn't answer as she stared vacantly out the bedroom window.

"Fia? You okay?"

She glanced back at him, her lips twisting in a sad imitation of a smile. "Of course. Just a little disappointed is all. I... I really thought it would be there, you know? After everything Lunares said, I thought for sure, but... here we are. Back at the beginning, with nothing to show for it." She shrugged. "At least we tried, right?" she added, crossing the room and dropping onto the bed.

"Trying's good," Cashel agreed, eyeing her warily as she rolled onto her side and pulled her knees into her chest, hugging them tightly. "But so is succeeding. I know how much you wanted this, Fia. It's okay to be upset."

"I'm not upset, really."

"If you say so. Just don't go jumping off any more ships because of this, okay?"

"We're on solid ground, Cash. You don't need to worry."

He chuckled, lying back on the floor and crossing his arms behind his head. "You calling me Cash now?"

"It just kind of slipped out. Sorry."

"Don't be." He smiled to himself. "I like it." *I like you.*

There was silence for a moment, and he wondered if she'd fallen asleep. But then she spoke, her voice barely louder than a whisper. "Hey, Cashel?

"Yeah?"

"It was really nice of you to give up your room for those kids. I could have never fallen asleep tonight if I knew they were out there in that cave, all alone in the dark."

"It was no problem. You're the one forced into putting up with my snoring all night."

"True enough." She laughed. "We're still going to help them, right? Even though we won't be needing to secure passage to Tallis now?"

"Of course. A promise is a promise, and they certainly did their fair share of digging. We can take them there before heading to the capital."

"They did at that." She paused. "Do you really think meeting with the king will be worth it?"

"It's not like we have anything better to do," he replied. "Might as well follow through on Josselyn's orders, right?"

There was a pause before she answered, somewhat reluctantly, "I guess so." She pushed herself up and leaned over to blow out the candle. She hesitated just before extinguishing it, glancing down at his prone figure. Or, more specifically, his bare chest. He held back a satisfied smirk. Sort of.

"Are you sure you don't want a blanket?" she asked.

"Nah, I'm good. Mihalan, remember?"

"Ah, yes. How could I forget. You all run hot."

"I am pretty hot, aren't I?"

She blew out the candle, submersing them in darkness. "Goodnight, Cashel."

He chuckled softly. "Night, Fia. Sweet dreams."

"Please... please, I can't... I can't breathe..."

Cashel sat up with a jerk, heart-pounding as his eyes sought Fia's thrashing form in the darkened room. She tossed from side-to-side on the bed, blankets twisted around her legs as she cried out. Her delicate hands clutched the fabric of her nightgown, pulling it away from her throat. He jumped to his feet, only to realize a moment too late that that was no longer a possibility. Collapsing on the floor, he crawled his way over to the bed, urgency overcoming humiliation as Fia's voice grew more panicked by the moment.

"Fia! Fia, wake up! It's just a dream." He pulled himself onto the bed and reached out, one hand holding her in place as the other stroked her hair in an awkward attempt to soothe. "It's just a dream," he repeated. "It's not real. You're safe." The thrashing slowed, and he leaned in, pressing a gentle kiss against her forehead. "I've got you, Fia. I'm right here."

She stilled, her lips parting on a small sigh. "Bade?"

His gut clenched, but he continued to gently stroke her hair. "It's me, Cashel. I'm right here, Fia. It's okay."

Her eyes fluttered open, her gaze locking with his for a long moment before she finally spoke. "He strangled me," she whispered. Her hand slid toward her throat. "The baron. He strangled me over and over with that... that *thing*. An enchanted collar, he called it, but that never sat right. It was too whimsical a description given the torture he'd use it to inflict. And inflict it he did, again and again. Bringing me to the brink of suffocation and then relenting just enough..." Her voice cracked, and she squeezed her eyes shut as tears leaked out the sides. Cashel's chest tightened, and he lowered his hand to brush the moisture away. Her eyes opened at his touch, meeting his once more, and he felt the breath leave his lungs at the depth of pain he saw there.

"I was beaten before," she whispered. "Many times. But it was nothing compared to that. To not being able to catch more than the slightest breath. Getting just enough to keep struggling. It was the worst torture I've ever endured."

Cashel swallowed against the lump of agony and rage that had lodged itself in his throat. He wasn't sure what he wanted to do more – scoop her into his arms and never let go or run out and pick a fight with the first luckless soul he could find. The hand that supported his weight on the bed clenched, digging into the worn coverlet, and he forced himself to relax before he ended up scaring her.

Goddess knew she'd had enough of that for a lifetime.

"I'm so sorry, Fia," he choked out, cupping her cheek in his hand. She slid her own hand up to cover his, holding it there.

"I had nightmares every night after that." His heart twisted at the rawness in her voice. "Every night," she continued, "until one night when the nightmares became so intense I couldn't stop screaming in my sleep. I must have woken Bade up – we were at Hildegarde, and his room was just down the hall from mine – because he came in to check on me." She let out a shaky laugh. "I was so embarrassed. He was everything I wanted to be – cool, confident, powerful. And there I was, a damaged basket case with enough baggage to fill a castle, having nightmares like some sort of scared child. I was mortified. I thought for sure he'd come in to reprimand me for being too loud." Her lips curved into a watery smile. "But he didn't. He didn't say anything at all, not at first, anyway."

"He simply laid down on the bed beside me," she said, threading her fingers through Cashel's as she spoke. "Wrapped his arms around me," she continued in a whisper, pulling Cashel's arm across as she rolled over onto her side, settling her back against his chest. "And held me, like this, all night." She sighed, and Cashel's breath caught at the breathy sound. "Could you hold me, Cashel? Just for tonight?"

Cashel swallowed. "Of course," he whispered into her hair, pulling her closer as he tightened his arms around her. "I can do that." He held himself still as he listened to her breathing even out, growing heavier with sleep, then pressed a kiss against her hair as he closed his eyes and gave into his exhaustion.

"I would hold you like this forever," he murmured, as sleep

began pulling him under. "If only you'd let me."

Chapter Twenty-Five

"Do you ever wonder if you're making a mistake? That maybe you should have just let Lehi be and live your life in peace?"

"And do what? Take up farming?" Bade's chest rumbled with laughter, the vibrations sending a thrill up Fia's spine, nestled as she was in the ring of his arms. She smiled, interlacing her fingers with his own as she snuggled closer.

"Maybe," she whispered, not wanting to speak too loud and break the intimacy of the moment. "I could help. I certainly have enough experience with manual labor."

"A dragon Shendri, working the fields?" he scoffed. "Preposterous. You were meant for far greater things than that."

She let out a wry laugh. "Try telling my parents that. Or the mesdames at the asylum. I suspect they'd disagree."

"Idiots, the lot of them."

She smiled to herself, imagining Madame Germaine's face if she were ever to hear someone as powerful as Bade refer to her as an idiot. Gods, she'd be mortified.

"Madame Germaine always said I was worth less than a single dram, and a rusted one at that."

Bade's arms tightened, squeezing her gently, and she tried not to sigh in contentment. Tried being the operative word.

"As I said, your Madame Germaine was a moron, and if you'd let me, I'd hunt her down myself and let her know just how little I think of her opinion." He paused. "Besides, if you're only worth a single dram, then I must be worth even less, for you far outshine me in every way."

"Nah, you're worth almost as much as me," Fia teased. "If only just."

He chuckled. *"So we're just a pair of drams then, huh? Quite the treasure we've got here."*

"More like a single dram," Fia countered. *"We're just two sides of the same dram, tossed into the river with the hope of having our wishes come true."*

She felt Bade's lips curve into a smile as they pressed against the top of her head. "And are they?" he asked. "Coming true, that is?"

She closed her eyes, concentrating on the feel of his arms around her, his chest pressed against her back, his breath in her hair. "Almost," she whispered. "Almost."

∞ ∞ ∞

Fia blinked drowsily as sunlight filtered into the room from the window, urging her to wake. Not an easy feat, given just how comfortable and warm she was with Bade's arm around her, his hand clasped just below her breasts, holding her in place against his chest.

Wait. Bade's arm? That wasn't right.

Her eyes flew open as her groggy brain caught up with reality, and her gaze dropped to the dark, muscled arm wrapped possessively around her. Not Bade's, but Cashel's. Memories of the previous night flooded her brain, and she cringed to think how pathetic she must have appeared. And poor Cashel. She'd practically forced him into her bed, pulling his arms around her like some kind of needy child. How awkward he must have felt.

Speaking of awkward...

Her cheeks lit up brighter than Artemis's flames as she took note of the rather, ahem, insistent object prodding her backside. Wriggling her hips forward, she attempted to extricate herself from Cashel's hold, only to feel his arms tighten in response.

Damn.

She cleared her throat quietly. "Cashel?"

Nothing.

She raised her voice. "Um, Cashel?"

The infuriating dolt stirred, only to snuggle in closer. Her stomach did a funny little dance at the sensation, which only increased the heat in her cheeks. Mustering her courage, she yelled, "Cashel!"

"Mmm?" His hips shifted as he slowly regained consciousness, and she bit down on her lip to keep from making any embarrassing noises. Gods, why did that feel so good?

There was a momentary pause as he collected his bearings. She waited, frozen in place, for him to register the intimacy of their position. And register it he did.

"Oh, shit." He practically jumped backward in his haste to make some space between them. "I am... I am so sorry."

Feeling her face cool from the obvious embarrassment in his voice, Fia rolled over onto her back and flashed him a reassuring smile. "It's fine, really. I mean, it happens. Right?" The last part came out as more of a question than anything, as she honestly wasn't sure if such a reaction was normal or not. Gods knew it never happened to Bade when they slept together.

"I guess so." Cashel threw an arm over his face. "I am sorry. I swear I didn't... I mean, I wasn't trying to... shit."

"It's okay. Really." Fia rolled her head to the side, eyeing him curiously. "Have you? Um, you know... done that before? Back in Mihala?"

He lifted his arm enough to peek over at her. "That being...?"

She started to blush all over again, until she noticed the playful twinkle in his eyes. "You know very well what I mean," she huffed.

"Do I?" He was grinning now. Getting a kick out of her discomfiture, the jerk.

"Forget I asked," she grumbled, sitting up and swinging her legs over the side of the bed. She started to stand, but he caught her hand and pulled her back down.

"It's against the law."

She shifted her hips, twisting herself around as she gaped at him. "Mihala has a law against having sex?" she asked incredulously. "But how else do you have children?"

Cashel chuckled. "Mihalans have babies the same as everyone else. Sex isn't prohibited to the majority. Just us unmarried princes. And princesses," he added. "Should there be any."

"Why just you, though?"

"Because we have royal blood, and so will any of our children. Which means, no irresponsible spreading of seed that could lead to problems down the road."

"I see." Fia nodded. "I guess that makes sense, although I find it hard to believe Berg has been able to adhere to such a restriction."

"So do I," Cashel replied with a laugh. "But then, he's always been good at finding loopholes."

"Now that, I can believe." Fia grinned as she stood up, uninterrupted this time, and stretched her arms over her head. She heard the bed squeak behind her as Cashel moved over to the side.

"Mind passing me my leg?"

"Of course." She bent down to retrieve the wooden prosthetic. It felt oddly intimate in her hand, and she hurried to pass it over, scolding herself for being ridiculous. *It's just a piece of wood. What are you getting all worked up over?*

He accepted it with a resigned smile and leaned forward to strap it in place.

"What about you?" he asked, his voice low as he studiously worked the buckles.

"What about me?"

"Fair's fair," he replied, keeping his gaze on the prosthetic. Apparently, it required a great deal of focus. A very great deal. "Have you ever," he cleared his throat, "been with anyone?"

"I've been with lots of people," she teased, pulling her brush out of her travel bag and running it through her hair. "Why, I'm with you right now, aren't I?"

"Ha ha. You know what I mean," Cashel retorted.

"Now, where have I heard that before?" She tapped her chin with the brush, pretending to mull it over.

151

He stood up with a playful growl and crossed the room, scooping her up and tossing her over his shoulder. His fingers reached around, tickling her ribs, and she half-squealed, half-laughed as she smacked the brush against his backside in retaliation.

"Not so funny now, are ya?" he teased, fingers dancing up and down her side.

"I will so sic my dragon on you," she gasped between bouts of laughter. "Don't think that I won't."

He chuckled, his fingers finally relenting as he tossed her down on the bed. Propping his good knee on the edge, he braced an arm on either side of her head as he hovered above her, eyes bright with restrained mirth.

"You wouldn't dare."

"Sure about that?"

"No," he admitted. "But I'm sure about one thing."

"Oh yeah? And what's that?"

His grin slipped, giving way to a look so heated Fia felt her toes curl on instinct. "This," he whispered hoarsely, dropping onto his forearms as his face lowered toward hers. He hesitated for a split second, his lips close enough to hers that she could have darted her tongue out and tasted them. A thought that made her breath catch with a lusty gasp before her brain could even make sense of it, and then it was too late for sensible thinking, as his mouth claimed hers in the softest, most sensual kiss she'd ever experienced.

The *only* kiss she'd ever experienced, for that matter.

Her eyes fluttered closed as she gave in to the unbridled passion, her hands reaching up and running over the muscled planes of his back as she responded with all the pent-up emotion that'd been simmering inside her belly ever since...

Her hands stilled.

Ever since...

...meeting Bade.

Cashel pulled back, his eyes growing wide as he took in her tear-stained cheeks. "Shit, Fia, I'm sorry. I... I don't know what came over me." He winced. "I mean, I do, but I shouldn't have –"

"Don't," Fia interrupted. "Don't apologize. You didn't do anything wrong."

"And yet, you're crying," he replied. "So, clearly I didn't do something *right*."

Her heart squeezed painfully as she stared up at his anguished expression. "Actually, I think it was a little too right." She felt her cheeks heat as she added, "It... it felt wonderful." His face lit up, and she swallowed hard, hating that she needed to finish what needed saying. "It felt wonderful," she repeated. "I'm just not sure I'm ready to feel that with someone other than..." She drifted off, feeling awkward.

"With someone other than Bade," Cashel finished for her, his face falling. He pushed himself up to a sitting position, and she followed suit, stealing glimpses at him out of the corner of her eye as she twisted her hands together in her lap.

"I love him," she whispered, shrugging helplessly.

"We can't save him," Cashel replied, his voice hard. "Not without the sash."

"I know."

"You'll never be able to have a life with him. Not like you could with me."

"I know that, too."

He let out a shaky laugh. "You're stubborn as hell, you know *that*?"

She smiled, reaching over and taking his hand in hers. "I'm aware."

His hand squeezed hers gently. Standing up with an awkward shuffle-hop, he pulled her off the bed so that they stood face-to-face. Holding her hand captive in his own, he used the other to brush back an errant strand of red hair, his fingers grazing her cheek ever so slightly. Her lips parted instinctively, her breath coming just a tad too quickly. His eyes twinkled mischievously as he looked down at her.

"You said you weren't ready, and I understand. I do. But," he grinned, "you should also understand that doesn't mean I'm giving up. I'm just as stubborn as you are." He bent down, dropping a quick kiss on her forehead before releasing her hand and heading toward the door. "I'll wake up the kids while you get dressed," he called over his shoulder before disappearing into the hallway and leaving her standing, flustered and confused, by the bed. Her fingertips traced her swollen lips, lingering there as she recalled the pleasure they'd felt just moments before.

Why had she stopped him again?

Chapter Twenty-Six

"I asked Maddie about getting a wagon, something we can use to get back to Lochless and see the kids off before moving on to the capital. She thought I might try down at the livery. Figured I head over there after breakfast. With any luck, we could be on our way by noon."

Cashel looked around the table with a satisfied grin, and Fia tried to swallow the sudden burst of panic that kicked in at the thought of leaving. Rosie and Cole certainly seemed excited at the prospect of a quick departure, and who could blame them? They had something to look forward to, something good to hope for. While she, on the other hand...

I'm not ready to give up, she realized. *There must have been something we missed, some kind of a sign.* Her feet bounced nervously under the table as she scrambled to think. *I need more time.*

"Clothes!"

Cashel stopped mid-sip of his coffee, looking perplexed. "I'm sorry?"

"The kids need new clothes," she stated, gesturing toward the two of them for good measure. "We can't just send them off in these rags, can we? Without even a change of clothes for wash days?"

Cashel looked over at the young Haverdashes, taking in their worn outfits, patches of which were almost threadbare from overuse. "I see what you mean." He thought for a moment. "Perhaps we can get them some new things once we reach Lochless. I seem to recall there being a number of shops. I'm sure they'll have something that'll suit."

Fia shook her head. "No, I really think we should get some things made here, before we leave. Not only is Rosie's dress about to fall apart at the seams, it's too recognizable. What if someone realizes she's from the asylum? There'll be questions." She pursed her lips. "Do you really want to deal with questions?"

"I guess not," Cashel replied with a groan. "But where are they going to get anything around here?"

"I'm sure Maddie can refer me to someone who'd be willing to whip up an outfit or two for the right price," Fia insisted. "With enough incentive, they may even get them done in a day or two." She looked over at the siblings, who were following the conversation with silent interest. "How would you like something made to your actual measurements for once?"

Cole shrugged, stuffing another biscuit in his mouth as he did. Crumbs dusted the front of his shirt, but he didn't pay them any mind as he answered, mouth half full, "Whatever's fine with me. It's just clothes." Rosie, however, was looking back at Fia with stars in her eyes.

"If it's not too much trouble..." She looked as if she wanted to say more but held herself in check. Fia grinned triumphantly.

"It's settled! A fresh set of clothes will be arranged for each of you before we go. I'll see to it myself."

"Oh, thank you," Rosie breathed.

Cole mumbled something that could have been a thank you, as well, but it was difficult to tell around all the food.

"I guess that's that, then." Cashel pushed his chair back and rose, using the table to steady himself. "I'll see to the wagon, and you all see about getting fitted for clothes. Something simple that be can done quick."

"It's a plan," Fia replied, giving him a reassuring smile. Mentally, she calculated just how long her errand would take. Hopefully, there would be time for her to slip off that afternoon and return to the cave without anyone knowing. For all his support, she was certain Cashel would label her a lovesick fool for not giving up. They'd dug until they'd hit rock, overturned every stone, anything they could think of to find that mysterious little box. And yet, she just couldn't shake the feeling that there was something they were missing. *One more look, that's all I need. One more look, and then I can leave without any regrets.*

∞∞∞

The clothing took longer to arrange than she thought, and it was well into mid-day by the time she made it back to the beach. Alone and with a lantern in tow, she made her way down the coast toward the cave, her excitement increasing with each step.

There has to have been something we missed. There just has to be.

"Or perhaps this is just wishful thinking?" Artemis's voice in her head was gentle, but there was no hiding the underlying note of pity.

Perhaps, she thought. *But given the fate of Lehi lies in the balance, you'll forgive me double checking.*

Artemis was silent for a moment before responding. "The fate of Lehi? Or the fate of your first love?"

Excuse me?

"I'm just saying. It's true the sash could be of use to stopping Bade's invasion, provided Luxeos can actually create a potion powerful enough to destroy the hagrüs *and* you're successful in getting Bade to drink it. But, let's be honest, the odds of that happening are minimal, at best. What's really driving you back to that cave? Besides your desire to save Lehi?"

Fia slowed her pace, the truth of Artemis's words sitting heavy on her shoulders. *I guess I'm just not ready to give up. Not on Lehi,* she admitted hastily, before Artemis could jump back in. *But on Bade. He was my savior, my refuge in the dark.* She took a calming breath, turning her agitated gaze to the sea. *He was my first love, and knowing what I know now... I wouldn't be able to live with myself if I simply turned my back on him and went on with my life. I just couldn't.*

"Isn't that what he did to you?"

...

"And anyway, what about Cashel?"

What about *Cashel?*

"You're attracted to him."

I am not!

"Really? You're attempting to lie to me? You do know I'm privy to your every thought, should I care to listen."

Ugh, fine. Yes, I'm attracted to Cashel. Who wouldn't be? He's kind, compassionate, brave, not to mention maddeningly hand-some.

"And he saved your life, at the risk of his own."

Trust me, I know. So, yeah. I admire Cashel.

"And kissed him..."

He kissed me first, if I recall.

"What I recall is you kissing him back, quite emphatically, I might add."

So I got caught up in the moment. What's your point?

"My point is, you have feelings for him. And I don't just mean admiration. I mean, deep, emotional feelings that rival the ones you're so desperately holding onto for Bade."

...I don't... I don't want to discuss this right now...

"That's not a denial."

Artemis. Please. Can we just go and check out the cave one last time? Without reading anything deeper into it?

"Fine. All I ask is that you think about what I've said. Cashel would be good for you."

Maybe so, but would I be good for him? I doubt it.

"You're too hard on yourself. It's one of the things holding you back from greatness."

And you're too forgiving, Artemis. I'm not the hero in this story.

"You could be."

Right. She shook her head. *Can we drop this now? Please?*

"As you wish, Shendri. Go do what you need to do."

Thank you. She closed her eyes, feeling Artemis's warmth inside her chest. *Really. Thank you.*

He didn't answer, but the warmth swelled, spreading down to her toes and putting a smile on her lips. With renewed energy, she pushed on, until at last the opening of the cave stood before her. Stopping only to light her lantern, she crept into the cave and looked around, holding the light up as she inspected the main chamber.

"I can't imagine having a baby in place like this," she muttered to herself, scanning the rough walls and damp floor. "And all alone, as well. Lunares must have been terrified." She crept further in, studiously checking every nook and cranny.

Nothing.

There could still be something in the back chamber. That's where she said she buried it, after all.

Slipping through the narrow tunnel, she made her way into the small room. The floor was a mess after their furious digging, with dirt and rocks piled all around the edges. Dropping to her knees, she scraped her hands over the uncovered rock, feeling for anything they might have missed. The rough stone grated against her fingertips, tearing at the skin, but she ignored the pain as she continued to scrape and sift through every inch of loose dirt.

Still nothing.

Frustrated tears slid down her face as she folded in on herself. "Why isn't it here?" She smacked the floor with her fist, scraping her knuckles in the process. "Damn it." She pressed the injured hand against her mouth as she mentally cursed the night she'd fallen into the sea. If only she hadn't made the jump, hadn't spoken to Lunares and set off on this ridiculous quest. If only she hadn't been given hope, just to have it stripped away.

"I've done everything you told me to do," she cried, squeezing her eyes shut as she pictured the moon goddess's ethereal face shimmering in the moonlit water. "Why isn't it here? What did we miss?"

Silence. Of course.

"I wish you could tell me what we did wrong," she whispered, wiping her filthy hand across her eyes as she slowly rose to her feet. "I wish..."

She froze, struck by a sudden idea. Sure, it was a little crazy, but what did she have to lose? Maddie's warning floated through her mind as she snatched up her lantern and scurried through the narrow passageway. She grinned at the memory, one last kernel of hope blossoming in her heart as she ran through the cave and out into the late afternoon sun. The sea lay before her, both beautiful and treacherous in all of its untamed glory.

No one swims in the sea because an evil spirit lives there. That's what Maddie had told them. But what if it wasn't evil? What if it *was* actually Lunares? "No more wishing for something I can't have," she whispered, streaking across the sand to the shore. Vaguely she registered a distant shout coming from down the beach, but she ignored it, focused on her new goal. "I'll get those answers if I have to swim the entire sea to do it."

I'm coming, Lunares.

Chapter Twenty-Seven

Cashel cursed as his wooden leg struggled to find purchase in the sand. Stupid thing wasn't made for beach walking, that's for sure. Maybe when he got back to Mihala, he'd have Trekklin make him a new one. Something with a little caeruleum worked into it would be nice. It'd certainly make hunting down stubborn Shendri a bit easier. Training on the beach the kids had said. Right. Like he was buying that.

She just can't give him up, can she? Even with a perfectly good Mihalan prince staring her in the face, practically begging *for her affection, she still has to chase down any chance of reuniting with that damnable demigod. As if he even deserves her! Ha! Not bloody likely.*

He kicked at the sand with his good leg, instantly regretting the childish move as his balance was thrown off, and he started to topple over. Righting himself, he swore as he noticed Fia running out of the cave.

Please tell me she didn't see me looking like an ass just now.

Apparently she didn't, as she never even glanced his way during her full-speed run down to the water's edge. *What the hell is she doing?*

"Fia!"

Either she couldn't hear him or she was choosing to ignore him, her feet only slowing for a brief moment as she pulled her shoes off and tossed them aside without actually stopping. She ran into the water, jumping over the smaller waves as they rolled in toward the shore. Her movements slowed as she got further out and the water rose to her waist, but still she didn't stop.

It wasn't until she dove into an oncoming wave, her body

disappearing from sight for a few tense moments, that Cashel managed to snap himself out of his confused stupor.

"Fia!" He ran clumsily through the sand toward the water. "Fia! What are you doing in there? It's dangerous!"

She disappeared under another wave, and he thought his heart might explode altogether before he finally spotted a flash of red hair bobbing in the distance. He quickly shucked off his boots and shirt before stepping into the sea himself. "Fia!"

She turned this time, meeting his gaze and shouting, "I need to find Lunares! She'll know –"

Her words were cut off as a wave came crashing down over her head, pulling her under. Cashel swore, stumbling through the water as he desperately tried to reach her. The waves pushed back at him, attempting to trip him in his haste, but he dug his good foot into the sandy floor as he pressed on, miraculously maintaining his balance for once. Fia popped back up, arms flailing wildly, before being sucked back down once again.

He dove forward, cutting through the oncoming wave and plunging headfirst into the cold water. Swimming furiously, he continued, diving into each wave, until he reached the place he'd last seen her come up. Adrenaline pumped through his veins as he dove under and began searching, even as his own body was tossed about by the increasingly strong waves. A flash of lightning lit the sky as he surfaced, and for the first time he noticed just how dark it'd gotten. In his distraction, he hadn't seen the gathering storm clouds. Now, they were just one more weight on his already frazzled nerves.

The booming *crack* of thunder made his blood run cold.

Where are you, Fia?!

He dove down again, twisting and turning in the dark water until his lungs screamed at him for air. This time when he resurfaced, he caught a glimpse of red disappearing into the water off to his right.

There!

He veered right, arms cutting through the water with every bit of strength he had. Diving into the water, he saw Fia's body being tossed about like a limp ragdoll. His stomach dropped as he realized she wasn't even attempting to reach the surface anymore. He reached out and hooked one arm around her waist as he pulled her to the surface. Her head rolled to the side as they emerged, her body limp in his arms.

"Hang in there, Fia." He started the slow, laborious swim back to shore, his wooden leg dragging behind like a dead weight. Rain began to fall, but he barely noticed as he pressed on. By the time he crawled onto the beach, dragging a disturbingly limp Fia along with him, it was coming down in sheets.

He rolled Fia onto her back in the sand as he tried to remember what Trekklin had taught him about reviving someone after they'd drowned.

Air. She needs air.

He tipped her chin back and pinched her nose closed, his hands shaking as he did. Taking a deep breath and throwing up a prayer to any goddesses who might be listening, he bent down and pressed his lips against her blue ones as he let it out, filling her lungs. He waited a moment, then did it again.

"Come on, Fia. Breathe for me."

As if on cue, she jerked, then coughed up water as her eyes blinked open, staring up at him in confusion. "Cashel?" she rasped. "What happened? Where's Lunares?"

Exhilaration at seeing her alive was quickly replaced by rage as he looked down at her. "What happened? *What happened*?" he growled. "You almost died, that's what happened! You –" He cut himself off, pushing the anger down long enough to acknowledge they were both soaked to the bone and not getting any drier. He may never get truly cold, but Fia's face was a ghastly mix of blue and white and her entire body was trembling. "You need to get out of the rain." He pushed himself up, struggling to his feet. "Can you move, or do you need me to carry you?"

"I th-think I can walk." She started to sit up, and he reached down to help pull her to her feet. "Th-thank you," she stuttered over chattering teeth.

He wrapped an arm around her, guiding her toward the cave

while attempting to shield her from the storm that continued to rage around them. They trudged slowly across the sand to the opening of the cave and ducked inside, breathing a collective sigh of relief as they collapsed onto the ground.

"We should get a fire going, warm you up," Cashel said, looking over at the abandoned fire ring the Haverdashes had used during their stay there. A partially-burnt log was all that remained, but if they could get it lit, it'd be better than nothing. "I don't suppose Artemis could light that for us?" he asked.

Fia blinked tired eyes as she wearily turned her gaze toward the sad little ring. "I don't think I can bring him out yet," she admitted. "I'm so tired." Her head drooped, falling forward and hiding her face behind a curtain of red hair. "I just... I can't do it anymore."

Her voice was so forlorn, Cashel felt the last of his anger give way to concern. "No worries. We'll just have to warm you up the old-fashioned way, is all." Scooting behind her, he pulled her back against his bare chest, his arms wrapping around her in a firm hug. "A little Mihalan heat will bring the color back to those cheeks in no time."

Her body relaxed into his arms as she curled into him, turning just enough so that she could rest her cheek against his chest. She sighed. "That is nice." A pause. "You're nice." Her hand drifted to his abdomen, gently tracing one of the many blue markings curving their way up toward his chest. "Why are you so nice to me, Cashel? All I seem to do is cause you more trouble."

"You've certainly managed to scare me shitless on more than one occasion," he replied. "But all of that worry and stress is nothing compared to the joy of being with you," he added. "And I wouldn't trade that for anything."

"Truly?" she whispered.

"Truly," he confirmed. He took a deep breath, stealing his nerves as he confessed, "It's not just that I enjoy being with you, Fia. I mean, I do. Obviously. But it's more than that. I...," he swallowed. "I love you."

She was quiet for a long moment, and he felt his stomach

drop at the prolonged silence. *What did you expect? She literally threw herself into the sea out of love for Bade. What makes you think she'd want to hear your pathetic confessions? Idiot. You –*

He broke off his mental admonishment at the feel of warm tears sliding down his chest. He brushed Fia's hair back as he searched her face, his heart aching at the sight of her tears as they fell unchecked down her cheeks.

"Fia? What's wrong? Was it something I said?"

She nodded against his chest. "You... you said you loved me," she whispered.

"I did. I mean, I do. Love you, that is." He cringed. "Sorry. I'm an idiot."

"No, you're not. It's just..." She lifted her head off his chest, looking up and meeting his worried gaze. "No one's ever said that to me before." She dropped her gaze to the side. "I've never been good enough," she admitted.

"What are you talking about?" he scoffed. "Of course, you're good enough."

"That's not what my parents thought."

"To hell with your parents! They were bloody idiots not to recognize the gift they'd been given having you."

"And the mesdames at the asylum," she continued. "They were always punishing me for something or other I'd managed to screw up. I never seemed to do anything right in their eyes."

"Bitches, the lot of them."

"The earl and his wife didn't blink an eye before sending me off with the baron. Clearly, I wasn't that great of a servant for them, either."

"The baron was a powerful man. I doubt they would have parted with you as easily to anyone else."

"Maybe." She hesitated, her body tensing. "And then there was the baron himself." She swallowed. "If there had been any doubt left in my mind of how little I mattered in this world, he would have certainly beaten it out of me."

"If he weren't already dead, I'd beat a hell of a lot more out of him," Cashel growled. "But Fia, you have to remember that man was insane. He couldn't have seen the worth in anyone if he tried. And you, Fia, you are worthy of love. I promise you that."

"Bade didn't think so," she whispered.

He bit back a curse. "You don't know that for certain," he admitted grudgingly.

"He sent me away."

"For your own good," he countered. "You just refuse to see it. You've been living in the shadow of evil men for so long, it's blinded you to all of the good. To all of the love," he added, cupping her face in his hands and wiping away the last of her tears. "You are loved, Fia, more than you realize. And it's not just me. It's Lily and Maya and Luxeos and, hell, I'd wager even Josselyn loves you like a sister by now. They all love you, Fia."

She shook her head in denial, though the tension in her body eased. "But I failed them," she reminded him. "When they needed me most, I let them down."

"Everyone makes mistakes, that's part of life. Besides, look how much stronger they've become since you arrived. Look at Lily! She was able to shield an entire army from that crazy woman's lightning attacks. Some of that was due to her own hard work, but a lot of it was you. You make them stronger, Fia, and that's pretty damn amazing in its own right. *You're* amazing."

"You think I'm amazing?"

"Hell yes, I do!" He threw his hands up in the air. "Why, the first time I met you, you literally threw yourself in front of an arrow in order to save someone you loved. That in itself is pretty damn amazing. And the way you train with the other Shendri? You give everything you have and more in those sessions, never cutting corners or giving up halfway. You're a natural leader, even if you can't seem to see it yourself." He stopped to catch his breath, and her eyes began to kindle with a low-burning light as she stared up at him. His heart swelled at the sight, and he hurried to continue, not wanting to see them dim. "And then there's the kids, Rosie and Cole. You don't even know them, yet you never even hesitated to offer your help, because that's the kind of person you are. You lift everyone else up without a thought to yourself. Which is admirable, but Fia – " He paused, holding her gaze as he prayed his next words would reach her, despite the protective walls she'd built around her heart. "Even with everything you do and all of the people who love you, none of it will ever be enough until you can truly love yourself."

He leaned down, pressing his forehead against hers. "Forget the words of evil men, and see yourself for who you truly are. Accept yourself, Fia, and love yourself like I love you."

She remained silent, and he pulled back so that he could see her face, worried how his words might have affected her. Her eyes were closed, her lips moving silently. Was she talking to Artemis? Their silent conversations always left him frustratingly confused, but if the dragon could help her, it would be well worth it.

He watched her intently as she continued her strange mediation. Recalling how cold she'd been, he scooped up her hands, thinking to warm them in his own while he waited, but to his surprise, he found they'd grown warm.

Make that quite warm.

He frowned as he stared down at them, then let out a curse as he dropped them from his hands altogether, palms stinging from the unexpected heat. *She's burning up!* He scooted back in alarm as smoke began to pour out around her. Her eyes flew open, and he was once again taken aback when he saw they were flickering with orange and red flames. He scrambled to his feet as she rose, turning toward the opening of the cave and walking out into the rain.

"Fia?! What are you doing? What's happening?"

He limped out of the cave, then stopped as she held up a hand, gesturing for him to stay back.

"I saw it," she said, her voice carrying clearly over the storm, despite the pounding rain and howling wind. "I saw Artemis's home." She looked over her shoulder at him, and her face was radiant with wonder. "The sky above his mountains were filled with the most beautiful lights, green and pink and blue, and they rippled when he flew through them, like waves on the sea. It was the most beautiful place I've ever seen, and it's all right here, inside of me." She touched her chest in wonderment, the smoke continuing to build up around her until he lost sight of her altogether. He started to take a step forward, then froze as smoke shot forcefully in every direction, pushing him back onto the sand. He blinked as it slowly cleared, revealing Fia once more.

Fia, who was currently climbing onto the back of a massive dragon.

She looked down from her perch, and even from a distance he could tell she was beaming. "Well?" she called. "Are you just gonna lie there all evening or are you gonna come for a ride?"

He only hesitated a moment before letting out a whoop and scrambling to his feet. "Hell yeah, I'm gonna ride a dragon!"

Chapter Twenty-Eight

They started the trip back to the port in Lochless the very next morning. With the recovery of Artemis's true form, Fia and Cashel had agreed that a return to Eldour and the rest of the Shendri would be in everyone's best interests. Cashel had been uncertain at first, but Fia had convinced him of her new confidence. She wasn't the weak shadow of a girl she'd been upon their departure. Having finally accepted herself for who she was and connecting with Artemis on a deeper level, she felt confident that she could stay strong in the face of their adversaries. Even if one of them was the man she loved.

Or, had loved, anyway.

Honestly, she was no longer certain where her true feelings lay. The love she'd felt for Bade had seemed so strong, so unbreakable, but now... she cast a furtive glance at Cashel, who sat beside her in the donkey cart he'd procured for their trip, reins held loosely in his hands.

Now, she wasn't so sure.

She held tight to the cart's seat as it bumped along. The road was narrow and full of dips and crags that threatened to throw her into the air at any moment. Cashel, however, didn't seem to have any trouble keeping his seat, but perhaps it was his sheer girth that kept him glued to it. After all, the man was built like a fortress.

A sexy, muscular fortress that could kiss like the devil himself.

And was in love with her.

She swallowed, turning her attention to the siblings stretched out in the back. "You two alright back there?"

"My backside's going to be bruised for a week," Rosie replied. "But I've seen worse."

"Yeah, but does he have to hit *every* hole along the way?" Cole grouched. "I'd swear he was doing it on purpose."

"I'm doing no such thing," Cashel denied. "You Lowlanders are all just soft, is all."

"Lowlanders?" Rosie asked, twisting in her seat to look up at them. "What do you mean by that?"

Cashel shrugged, keeping his eyes on the road. Fia leaned back, lowering her voice to a conspiratorial whisper. "Cashel here is from Mihala, a secret village hidden deep in the Endless Mountains."

"Really?" Cole's eyes grew as large as dinner plates.

Cashel sighed. "You do know what the word *secret* means, don't you Fia?"

"Sure, I do," Fia replied, winking at the young ones. "But I also know these guys can keep one. Can't you?"

"You bet I can!" Cole sat up straight, nodding profusely. Rosie simply looked bemused.

"I thought the mountains were cursed. Why would you want to live there?"

"It's a long story," Cashel muttered. He shot Fia a hard look. "One we don't have time for at the moment, am I right?"

"Whatever," Fia huffed, then grinned. "But you can at least admit to being royalty, can't you? Hmm, Prince Cashel?"

Cashel grunted, looking annoyed.

"Prince Cashel? That's it?" Rosie asked. "Don't you have a surname?"

"Mihalans don't use surnames," Cashel stated. "They're un-necessary and superfluous."

Rosie seemed to consider that. "But how do you keep track of your relations, then?"

"Everyone in Mihala is my relation," Cashel replied. "We're all one family."

"So, you're saying you're all inbred?" Cole snorted. "Planning on marrying your sister anytime soon, or are you holding out for a cousin?"

"It's not like that." Cashel threw Fia an exasperated look. "Help me out here, would ya?"

She laughed. "Don't look at me. I haven't the faintest idea how marriage works in Mihala. Although, given your royal status and all, I assume you need to marry a Mihalan lady. Hopefully *not* your sister, though, 'cause, well, gross." She shuddered. "Not to mention Edmund would skin you alive if you did."

"Once and for all, we do not marry our siblings. I'll admit the cousin thing isn't completely uncommon – we are a limited number, after all – but we do have some standards." He shifted in his seat, casting a sideways glance at Fia. "And when it comes to my own betrothal, I'll be given complete freedom in my choice, be the lady Mihalan or not." He cleared his throat as he returned his attention to the road ahead. "Assuming the lady in question doesn't object, of course."

"And who would object to such a fine specimen as yourself?" Fia teased. "A girl would have to be crazy to turn down a prince."

"Or in love with someone else," he countered with a rueful smile, meeting her gaze briefly. Her breath caught and she dropped her gaze, the implications of his words doing funny things to her stomach. *Surely he isn't implying he'd like to marry me.* She chanced a peek at his profile. *Is he?* It wasn't all that preposterous of a thought – he had declared his love for her the other night, after all. She tried to picture herself married to Cashel. Assuming peace was someday restored, would they live in Mihala? She knew little about the hidden mountain village aside from its access to caeruleum. She had, in fact, assisted Bade in mining the precious resource from the outer edges of the mountain. Or rather, Artemis had, his celestial fire helping to break through the Mihalans' barriers protecting it.

She cringed as guilt over her past-actions trickled in. She'd been so naive then, willing to do anything Bade asked without question. What a fool she'd been.

But no more.

She sat up straighter, pushing the past back where it belonged – in the past. She was a new woman now, a warrior of light. She would not allow herself to fall back into the darkness again.

"Are we almost there yet?" Cole whined. "It feels like we've been in this cart for a million years, already."

"Don't exaggerate," his sister Rosie scolded. "It's only been a few hours. I'm sure you'll survive a bit longer."

"Doubt it," Cole grumbled.

Cashel chuckled. "Don't worry, buddy, we're almost there. You'll be stretching your legs before you know it."

"Yes!" Cole pumped his fist in the air, his previous lethargy all but forgotten as he climbed to his feet and peered over Cashel and Fia's shoulders at the road ahead. "I haven't been to Lochless in years!" he said excitely. "Does it still smell like dead fish and sailor butt?"

"Cole!" Rosie rebuked, smacking him in the hip.

"What?" He looked down at his sister in confusion.

"You're being crass," she hissed.

"Why? I was just telling the truth. Last time we came down to see Uncle Jake off, the whole place reeked. You said so yourself!"

"It did smell pretty bad when we arrived," Fia admitted, interrupting the siblings' impending argument. "Though I'm not entirely sure I know what a sailor's butt smells like. I'll let you be the judge of that, Cole."

"That's easy, they smell like sh –" Cole broke off with a gasp as Rosie elbowed him in the side, having stood up herself.

"What was that?" she asked, ignoring her younger brother as she pointed ahead of them, past the treeline.

"What was what?" Cashel replied, looking in the direction she indicated. Fia did as well, squinting her eyes in an attempt to see through the thinning trees.

"I thought I heard something," Rosie explained. "There!" she shouted as a low boom sounded from the other side of the trees. "There it is again!"

Fia tensed, glancing over at Cashel. His expression was tight as he met her eyes. The sound could have come from any number of things, really, but this close to the shore...

"I'll fly up with Artemis and check it out," she stated as Cashel slowed the cart to a halt. He nodded.

"Good idea."

"Who's Artemis?" Cole asked, leaning forward and sticking his face next to Fia's.

Right. The kids didn't know about the whole Shendri thing. Ugh. This was so not the time to get into a lengthy explanation.

"Let's just say I'm a magical warrior with a dragon living inside me and leave it at that for now." She gave the siblings a hopeful look. "Yeah?"

The two kids exchanged glances. "A dragon?" Rosie repeated, eyeing Fia skeptically. "Like, a real, live dragon?"

"Yup."

"Mmm, 'kay. If you say so."

Fia stood up and hopped down to the ground before looking over her shoulder with a mischievous grin. "I can do more than say so," she countered. "I can show you."

Smoke poured out as Artemis emerged, forming his massive body beneath her so that she rose up with him, straddling his back as he solidified. She peered down at the siblings' faces staring up at her with open mouths.

"Rosalind and Cole Haverdash, meet my counterpart, Artemis."

Cole rubbed his eyes. "Did that really just happen?"

Fia grinned. "Yup."

"That thing has been inside you this entire time?"

"He has."

Cole let out a low whistle. "Amazing."

Rosie nodded her agreement, still too stunned to manage actual words.

Fia patted the side of Artemis's neck. "Alright, Artemis. Let's see what's happening on the other side of these trees, yeah?" Artemis flew up, carrying her over the treetops until she had a clear view of Lochless's harbor and the Valiant Sea stretching out beside it.

A sea full of ships.

The smile fell from her lips as she urged Artemis closer, squinting to make out the flags waving from the assorted fleet as they attacked the harbor, their cannons tearing the coastline to bits. Several flew a dark green flag decorated with a coiled snake. The Sea Snakes – a bloodthirsty group of pirates that'd been happily doing Bade's dirty work over the past few years. Other ships bore a black flag with a simple "D" painted across the center. The Dredgers – an Antos-based mercenary group known for tearing up the mainland. Apparently, they'd been granted their sea legs, as well. Spectacular.

She watched as several of the ships lowered boats into the water, each one filled to the brim with armed men. Without waiting to see more, she directed Artemis to head back down to the others.

Cashel stepped forward as they landed. "How bad is it?"

Fia grimaced. "There's gotta be at least twelve ships out there. A mix of Sea Snakes and Dredgers, all bent on destroying the town. We've got to do something."

"Agreed." He nodded toward the kids. "But what're we going to do about them? We can't take them in there with us. It's too dangerous."

"Hey!" Cole interjected. "I can fight! Rosie, too. Give us some knives and we'd tear those pirates to shreds! Our Uncle Ja –"

"Absolutely not," Cashel barked, cutting him off. "You're too young."

"Am not!"

"Cole," Rosie whispered, grabbing her brother's arm. "Just listen to someone for once in your life. Those are real pirates out there. Pirates who would kill us on sight. This isn't just some stupid game."

"Your sister's right," Fia added gently. "We need you two to stay here, with the cart. Move it off the road and into the trees. Or, better yet, take it back to Nimrey and warn them about the attack." She gave him a solemn look. "Can you do that for me,

Cole? Do you think you can drive this cart all the way back there? It's pretty far…"

He straightened his shoulders. "Course, I can. I've driven wagons plenty before."

She nodded. "Good. Then I'll count on you to spread the word." She glanced over at Rosie. "And to stay safe until we return for you." Seeing the worry in the girl's eyes, she added, "We *will* come for you. I promise."

"You shouldn't make promises like that," Rosie whispered, though her eyes brightened with hope all the same.

"Why not?" She winked. "I'm the dragon Shendri. I can do anything I put my mind to. Now, you guys get going. Cashel and I have business to take care of."

"Stay safe," Rosie called out as Cole shouted, "Kick their asses!", spurring the donkey into motion and steering it back around the way they'd come.

Cashel climbed up behind Fia on Artemis's back. "You have any weapons?"

She nodded. "I've got my daggers, one on each leg. And you?"

"Got my sword, a knife in my belt and another in my boot. Not the best for going against firearms, but what can you do."

"We are sitting on top of a dragon," Fia reminded him. "A fire-breathing dragon? I'd consider that a pretty formidable weapon right there."

"Fair enough," Cashel admitted. "So, what are we waiting for, then? Let's burn those assholes down."

Chapter Twenty-Nine

The pirates didn't see them coming until just before Artemis began raining fire down on their ships. Those who remained on board alternated between running around in a panic and attempting to shoot Artemis down. Cashel and Fia stayed low as a mix of bullets and arrows flew past.

It didn't last long, however, as the first ship was engulfed in flames, followed quickly by a second and third. Sea Snakes and Dredgers alike dove into the water, abandoning their ships as they sought refuge from the inferno. The ships furthest out turned in retreat, leaving the others to fend for themselves. Cashel let out an exhilarated whoop. It felt pretty damn good to be the ones doing the chasing for once.

As the last remaining ship crumbled, they turned toward shore, where the villagers and sailors were doing their best to fend off the horde of attackers who'd made their way onto land.

"Better not use fire here," Fia warned as they flew over the fighting. "We don't want to hurt any of the islanders." Artemis bobbed his head before diving down and snatching up one of the Sea Snakes in his massive jaw and throwing him to the side.

"I'm going in," Fia yelled, shifting her body around and preparing to jump into the fray. Cashel caught her arm.

"Are you sure that's a good idea? These guys are ruthless fighters, and your combat skills aren't the greatest." He cringed at the last part, not wanting to hurt her feelings, but more so not wanting her to die doing something foolish.

She turned her head, looking back at him. "Things have changed. I've changed. Trust me, I've got this."

His fingers tightened their grip on her arm briefly, not

wanting to let her go, but ultimately, he knew it wasn't his call. Releasing her, he nodded and reached down to draw his sword. "Alright, but I'm going in, too."

He waited for her to protest, to say something about his leg, but she simply nodded as she returned her attention to the chaos below. And then she leaped, flying into the air with such grace that Cashel couldn't help but stare after her in awe. Her twin blades glinted in the sun as she landed atop a Dredger's shoulders, like some kind of crazed monkey, before deftly slicing him to shreds.

Amazing.

He didn't have long to gape, however, as a mix of pirates and mercenaries streamed in. It was a testament to their nerves that they could charge headfirst toward a dragon such as they were, but Cashel had doubts about their overall intelligence as Artemis nipped and pecked at the various offerings.

Sliding down the dragon's side, he stumbled a bit on the landing and might have been impaled right then and there had Artemis not swung his neck around and snatched the approaching Dredger up just before the tip of his blade made contact with Cashel's gut. *Come on, man. You're better than this.* With an ear-splitting Mihalan yell, he charged into the fray, taking out a pirate before they could land a fatal blow on the villager they had cornered. Energy coursed through his veins, spurring him on, and he soon found himself in a familiar rhythm. If his footwork was a bit slower than before, it didn't seem to matter, as they were soon chasing down the last few mercenaries, who'd finally seen the light and started to run for it. Fia tore after them like a rabid fox, and he couldn't help but chuckle as he watched her frenzied form in action.

Better not get on her bad side again.

The laughter died on his lips, however, at the sharp sound of a girl's scream. Twisting around, Cashel spied Rosie being pulled toward the water by one of the remaining Sea Snakes. A big beast of a man, his meaty hand was locked around the poor girl's wrist as he forced her along with him. In his other hand he held a double-barreled firearm, and he swung it around wildly as he ran for one of the rowboats lining the shore.

What the hell is she doing here?!

Cashel half-ran, half-hobbled after the pair, his heart pounding furiously with each broken step. Fia soon caught up with his staggered gait, and they ground to a halt beside each other as the pirate whipped around to face them, the barrel of his gun shifting so that it was pressed against the back of Rosie's head.

"Not another step, or I'll blow her head off!"

"Hurt her, and my dragon here will eat you for lunch," Fia countered with a growl.

The man visibly trembled, his eyes shooting up toward Artemis as he swept around in a wide circle above, puffs of smoke coming from his nostrils. "You tell that beast to get the hell away from me or the girl dies!"

"She dies, and you'll be following right behind," Cashel warned, keeping his voice even. "Let her go, and we'll let you live."

"Like hell you will," the man snapped as he tracked Artemis's hulking form. Jerking his gaze away from the dragon, he turned it toward Fia, eyes flaring. "You! I know who you are! You're one of those Shendri warriors the boss warned us about." His eyes narrowed, and his grip on Rosie's arm loosened as he swung his firearm around, training on Fia, instead.

"That creature up there is bound to you, isn't it? Which means, all I've gotta do is kill you, then no more dragon."

His words were followed by a flurry of actions, most of them blurring together as Cashel focused on the only thing that mattered in that moment – Fia. There was a loud *crack* as the firearm discharged, but Cashel was already moving as he threw himself in front of Fia. His hands gripped her arms as the bullet tore into his side, burning his flesh. Her eyes met his, and he could see the stunned terror of the moment reflecting back at him.

Pained screams sounded from behind him, and he turned his head just in time to see Artemis lifting the pirate high into the air with his talons before dropping him onto an outcropping of jagged rocks. Vaguely, he noticed Rosie being held by her brother as they stared at the bloody show, but his attention soon returned to the searing pain in his side and the woman attempting to examine it with shaking hands.

"I'm fine," he murmured, gently pushing her hands away. She looked up at him, and her tear-stained face wrenched at his heart. "It's fine," he reassured her. "Just a scratch."

"That's a hell of a lot more than a scratch, you idiot," she shot back.

"Says you," he replied, keeping his voice light despite the pain radiating through his side. He pulled off his shirt and proceeded to tear it into strips. Using a few to pad the wound, he handed the longest one to Fia. "Tie this around my waist for me?"

She glared at him through her tears, although it didn't stop her from complying as she deftly tied the makeshift bandage in place.

"See? No big deal. The bullet just scratched me, no harm done."

"No harm done?" she repeated angrily. "*No harm done*? You're bleeding all over the place, Cashel!"

He shrugged. "I'm Mihalan. We heal quickly."

"You shouldn't have to heal at all," Fia argued, her hands balling into fists at her side. "You've already sacrificed your leg for my sake. When are you going to stop risking your life for me?"

He brushed his thumb over her cheek, wiping away a tear. "Never," he said simply. "So long as there's life in my body, I will continue to throw myself in front of anything meant to harm you." She blinked up at him through her tears, and he lifted the corner of his mouth in a slight smile. "I love you, Fia. More than life itself."

She stared up at him for a long moment before lifting her still shaking hands and placing them on either side of his face. "I'm starting to believe you mean that," she whispered. Pushing herself up onto her tiptoes, she pressed a tentative kiss against his lips, freezing him in place as all rational thought flew from his mind.

He was still trying to put two thoughts together as she slowly pulled away, a shy smile hovering on the very lips that had just stolen his wits away.

"I... you..." He swallowed. "You kissed me."

Her smile deepened. "So it would seem."

"Wh..why? I mean, thank you." *Thank you? Did I just say thank you?!* "I mean, it... it was nice," he finished lamely.

The corners of her eyes crinkled in amusement, but before she could say anything they were interrupted when Cole appeared at their side. He wrung his hands nervously as he stared down at his worn shoes.

"I'm sorry. It was my fault we came back." He dragged his fearful gaze up to meet Cashel's eyes. "It's my fault you got shot."

"Don't listen to him," Rosie said, stepping up behind her brother and placing a hand on his shoulder. "It was my idea to come back, not his."

"But I was the driver," Cole argued. "That makes it my fault."

"You were only doing what I told you to do," Rosie shot back. "And I'm the eldest, which makes it my responsibility." She looked back and forth between Cashel and Fia with a solemn expression. "I didn't want to leave you two. You're the first people to show us any kindness since our parents died, and I... I didn't want to chance losing that. I'm sorry. If I hadn't made Cole turn around, you never would have gotten injured."

Fia smiled, reaching out to brush a stray wisp of hair away from the girl's face. "It's okay. It was only a scratch, right, Cashel?" She winked at him, and the tiny gesture effectively turned his brain to mush.

"Hmm?"

She gave him a pointed look. "Your injury, it was no big deal, right?"

"Oh! That. Right, no big deal at all. I barely feel a thing."

Rosie looked at him doubtfully. "Well, I'm sorry either way. I shouldn't have put Cole at risk like that, either. It was pretty thoughtless of me."

"Me? At risk? Ha!" Cole puffed up his chest. "Didn't you see me take that pirate out after he fired off that shot? Knocked him right off his feet!"

"Did you really?" Cashel gave him an approving look. "Well done!"

Cole flushed. "Aw, it was nothing, really. You shoulda seen Rosie here! Nailed the guy right in his you-know-where! And then Artemis comes down and snatches him off the ground like a bloody eagle going after a rabbit! It was amazing!"

"Speaking of Artemis, I should probably call him back in before he scares the poor villagers to death," Fia said, looking around at the people watching them with wary eyes.

"Not a bad idea, seeing as we still need to book passage on one of their ships," Cashel agreed.

"Two ships," Fia reminded him. "We promised to see these guys off to Orphan Island."

"Or maybe..." Rosie bit her lip. "Maybe we could come with you?"

Cashel shook his head. "Absolutely not. We're heading back into a war zone. It wouldn't be safe."

"Oh. Okay." Rosie's face fell, and Cole slipped his little hand into hers. Cashel's heart squeezed at her obvious disappointment, but what was he supposed to do? It would be far too dangerous for them in Eldour, what with Bade and the lightning witch hovering outside the border, waiting to strike the moment Luxeos's shields fell apart.

"I'm sorry," he said. "If things were different..."

"*When* things are different," Fia interjected. "I'll come back for you, myself. If you'll have me, that is."

Rosie and Cole exchanged excited glances. "You mean it?" Cole asked. "You'll really come back?"

"It's a promise."

Fia stuck her hand out, and he took it, shaking it with solemn seriousness. When he released it, Rosie lunged past him, throwing her arms around Fia and hugging her tightly. Turning her head to the side, she caught Cashel's eye as she continued to cling to Fia. "What about you? Will you come back, too, or will you be too busy doing princely things?"

He smiled. "Seeing as I'm not planning on letting this one," he nodded toward Fia, "out of my sight for the foreseeable future, I guess I'll have to."

"Don't listen to him," Fia said, giving him a look. "He wants to come back for you just as much as I do."

Cashel flushed. "Lies, all of it. I'm a cold-hearted warrior, through and through."

"Ha!" Fia laughed. "Is that why you were willing to dig around in a dark cave for hours on end? 'Cause you're just sooo cold-hearted?"

"Do you mind? I'm trying to build a new rep here." They grinned at each other, and Cashel felt the last bit of pain fade away as he lost himself in her smile. He would have continued to stand there grinning like an idiot if Cole hadn't cleared his throat, bringing his attention back to the young boy who was looking suddenly nervous.

"Um, about the cave," the boy started, shuffling his feet. "You know how you said you were looking for a treasure in a little box? Something really valuable?"

"Yeah. What about it?"

"Well, um..." Cole peeked at his sister, whose face was growing increasingly ashen.

"Oh, Cole, you didn't," she cried.

He flushed as he pulled a small wooden box out of his pocket and held it out toward Cashel. "Please don't change your mind about coming back. Rosie really likes you two, and I swear she didn't know I took it. No one was looking when I uncovered it during my turn at digging, and I just couldn't help myself. We needed money to get to Orphan Island, and I wasn't sure you'd keep your promise about helping us." He hung his head. "I'm sorry."

Cashel stared at the box for a moment before taking it. Fia stepped closer, her eyes wide as she stared down at it. "I hate to break it to you," Cole said. "But there isn't any treasure inside.

Just a strip of cloth."

Fia's hand trembled as she reached out and lifted the box's lid. Sure enough, a dark blue strip of silk was folded up inside. "This is it," she whispered. "Lunares's sash." She looked up at Cashel. "Do you know what this means?"

His stomach sank. Finding Lunares's sash meant they might actually be able to make a counter-potion strong enough to kill the hagrüs without hurting Bade.

Who was most likely in love with Fia.

Who was probably still in love with him.

Awesome.

Fia's smile faltered at his blank expression, and he forced himself to smile back at her. "Looks like we might be able to save Lehi, after all."

Chapter Thirty

The Banris' home in Tallis

"We need to make a move and soon." Josselyn looked around the table. "I say we strike tomorrow."

"Yes!" Maya shouted, slamming her fist on the table. "Finally!"

"Do you really think we're strong enough?" Lily asked. "The last time we took them on, Bade froze the entire battlefield with just a few words."

"A spell you and Suzaku broke," Maya reminded her.

"Only just," Lily replied. "And as soon as we brought it down, that woman began conjuring balls of lightning from her fingertips. Add in an entire army of trained Antoski soldiers, and I think you can see why I'd be a bit hesitant to jump back in."

Luxeos leaned back in her chair, watching the three Shendri argue over the logistics of riding out into battle. Their protective bubble had been surrounded by Antoski for over a week now, with an army laying in wait on land and a fleet of ships lingering in the sea outside the harbor. The moment the shields dropped, they'd converge upon Tallis from every angle. They were sitting ducks.

A tremor ran down her spine, sending pinpricks of pain through her overworked body. As cool and calm as she may appear on the outside, inwardly she was spread as thin as the butter on a poor man's toast. It was unlikely she'd be able to hold the barrier much longer.

Not with Lumeria attacking it with relentless precision.

"Josselyn is right," she stated, interrupting the heated discussion. "If we don't go on the offensive soon, we'll be overrun.

Better to begin on our own terms."

"Thank you," Josselyn exclaimed. "That's exactly what I'm saying."

"But what about the woman?" Lily asked. "We still haven't learned anything about her. If we just knew a little more, we might be able to target her weaknesses. Let me do some more scouting with Suzu before we go rushing into anything."

"There's no need for scouting," Luxeos said with a defeated sigh. "I already know who she is."

"What?!"

The Shendri's voices overlapped each other as they all stared at Luxeos in shock.

"You know who she is?" Josselyn gave her a bewildered look. "Why didn't you say something sooner?"

"Yeah, what the hell, Luxeos?" Maya added, crossing her arms over her chest. Lily reached out and covered Luxeos's hand with her own.

"I'm sure Luxeos had a good reason for keeping it to herself." She gave the goddess a reassuring look. "Didn't you?"

"I'm afraid my reason for staying silent has been a rather selfish one," Luxeos admitted. She hesitated, her mouth twisting from the bitter taste of her confession. Forcing herself to continue, she whispered, "She's my daughter, you see."

A hush fell over the table as the Shendri were stunned into silence. Luxeos wrung her hands together. "Her name is Lumeria," she offered when no one spoke up. "Her father, Jet, was the king of Mihala."

More silence.

"You had a baby," Josselyn stated, breaking the silence at last.

"That's right."

"With the king of Mihala," she added.

"Yes."

"When?" she asked incredulously. "Where? *How*?"

Maya snorted. "Well, you see, Joss, when a man and a woman love each other – "

"I'm well aware of where babies come from, Maya," Josselyn

snapped. "What I want to know is how the goddess of the sun ends up impregnated by a Mihalan king!"

"Lunares was impregnated by an island villager," Lily pointed out.

Luxeos shrugged. "Goddesses are actually incredibly fertile, as it turns out. Had I known as much, I wouldn't have been quite so frequent with my mortal dalliances."

"I'm so not hearing this," Josselyn groaned.

"I think it's great," Maya argued. "The goddess of the sun knew what she wanted and went for it. Hell yeah."

"You guys." Lily nodded toward Luxeos. "Do you think you could keep your comments to yourselves for the time being? I'd like to hear the rest of the story."

"The rest of the story." Luxeos winced. "I'm afraid it doesn't paint me in the best of lights."

Lily squeezed the goddess's hand. "It's okay, Luxeos. You can tell us."

"I suppose I must," she sighed. "Seeing as my frivolous past is at the root of our current problems." She let her gaze drift off to the far side of the terrace, where a gentle breeze rustled the ivy leaves that covered the red brick wall separating them from the rest of the city. "It all began five hundred and thirty-two years ago..."

Chapter Thirty-One

"It was the night of the summer solstice, and Lunares had just blessed the four mountains of Mihala with the gift of caeruleum cores. The Mihalans were hosting a celebration, and both Lunares and I were the guests of honor."

Luxeos paused, glancing at the three young women listening with rapt attention. "It wasn't uncommon in those days for us to mingle with the people of Mihala from time to time, as they were the closest to immortal beings that the human race had managed, thus far."

"Did you hear that, Joss?" Maya whispered. "I'm practically a goddess. That's way higher than a mere queen."

"Shut it, merc, I'm trying to listen to the story," Josselyn whispered back, kicking Maya's shin underneath the table.

Lily sighed. "Please, continue."

The sun goddess graced them with a fond smile before allowing her gaze to drift off once more, memories from a past era playing out before her eyes as vividly as if they'd just occurred.

"The king at that time had been courting my favor for years, and I'll admit I'd long been tempted by his smooth words and rugged physique. He really was an exceptional specimen. Add in a little too much caeruleum-infused wine, and, well... one thing led to another..."

"What do you mean?" Maya asked innocently. "What kind of things?"

It was Lily's turn to kick Maya under the table this time. With a glare in the wolf Shendri's direction, she prompted, "So, you ended up pregnant with the king's baby?"

Luxeos nodded. "Jet was thrilled. To have his first-born conceived by a goddess? It was more than he'd ever hoped for."

"And how did you feel about it?" Lily asked, sensing the goddess's hesitancy.

"I'm ashamed to admit I was rather upset when I realized what had happened. I mean, I was the goddess of the sun, for goodness sake. I could hardly raise a half-human in the sacred realm of the gods. The child would never have been able to survive there, it would've been much too frail. So, I distanced myself from the idea of a child, building an emotional wall so thick that by the time I gave birth to a baby girl, I handed her off to her father and returned to the heavens without looking back."

"You never considered staying and raising her in Mihala?" Josselyn asked.

"That's exactly what Lunares asked me," Luxeos replied sadly. "She never understood how I could turn my back on my own daughter so easily. As you know, she went on to give her very life for her own child." She sighed. "She always was the most human of us all. But, never mind that. What's important here is the child, Lumeria."

Pushing back from the table, she stood up and began pacing across the terrace floor. The three Shendri followed her movements with their eyes as they remained motionless, waiting for her to continue.

"As a demigoddess and Mihalan princess, she was raised with full access to both the mountain's caeruleum and the complete library of ancient magical texts. She began training with the royal enchanters when she was eight years old and became a full-fledged enchantress by the time she was sixteen. With the addition of her inherited powers, she soon became the most powerful being in all Lehi. A fact which she took more than a little pride in."

"As you know, the Mihalans have always considered themselves to be superior to the rest of Lehi. Usually this superiority led to an attitude of pity in regards to the Lowlanders, but in Lumeria's case it became more of a disgust. She despised everything about the Lowlanders, and as she grew more and more powerful, she began to lash out."

She paused, a shudder running down her back as the memory of those bloody scenes flashed through her mind. "She grew violent," she whispered. "Viciously so. I confronted Jet about it, but he didn't want to listen. She was his pride and joy. He refused to recognize the evil that twisted her heart. But then came the incident with the river..."

"The witch in the mountain!" Maya exclaimed. She looked around at the others. "She poisoned the Border River and would have destroyed an entire harvest if she hadn't been caught and sealed in the mountain. Or so the story is told in Myr," she added. "Was that her? Was that Lumeria?"

Luxeos nodded. "Fortunately, the Mihalans uncovered her actions before too much harm had been done, but it ended up being the event that opened Jet's eyes to his daughter's true nature. He finally agreed that something needed to be done. Neither of us had the heart to kill our own daughter, so we agreed to imprison her, instead. In retrospect, a quick death would have been far more humane than the centuries of solitude we forced upon her, trapped in that cave under the river all by herself. Had I known she was immortal..."

She shook her head. "But no one really knew anything about the children of gods at that time. Lumeria was the first to ever be conceived. I never imagined she'd inherit my immortality."

"Wait. Does that mean she can't be killed?" Josselyn asked. "Because that's going to be a serious problem if it does."

"Honestly? I don't know," Luxeos admitted. "Although it's possible she's simply immune to the human weaknesses of sickness and aging. That doesn't necessarily mean she can't be killed."

"I'll have Trekklin make me a few more of those caeruleum-tipped arrows," Maya stated. "We'll see who can't be killed then."

"Just make sure you don't shoot one of us by mistake," Josselyn muttered.

"My aim is perfect," Maya retorted. "I only shot Fia because she jumped in the line of fire."

"So you say," Josselyn teased. "It's not like any of us were there to witness it."

"She has a point," Lily chimed in innocently, causing Maya to jump to her feet.

"What? You guys need a demonstration? Someone get me my bow! I'll show you how perfect my aim is!"

"Okay, *Edmund*," Josselyn laughed.

Luxeos smiled to herself, leaving the three young warriors to their ridiculousness as she accepted the welcome distraction from the past. Strolling around the outer edge of the terrace, she took a moment to breathe and relax her aching shoulders. The constant strain from holding the barrier in place against Lumeria's attacks had taken quite the toll on her body. *I doubt I could hold it in place much longer if I tried. Thank goodness they're planning to –*

Her train of thought was abruptly cut off as a burst of flames shot across her line of sight, followed by an enormous green and black dragon. The vision disappeared as quickly as it had come, and she blinked, stumbling backward and dropping to the ground as her body gave way to the shock.

"Luxeos?!"

"Oh my goodness, are you okay?"

She waved a hand as all three women rushed to her side. "I'm fine," she murmured distractedly. Closing her eyes, she focused on the distinct light of the dragon Shendri until her face became clear in her mind. A laugh escaped her lips at the sight, and she opened her eyes to look up at the others in excitement.

"Fia's returned!"

Chapter Thirty-Two

Do you think they're dead?

"More or less."

More or less? How is that even possible? Either they're dead or they're alive.

"Their ships were just reduced to cinders in the middle of the sea. Unless they're well enough to swim ashore, then they're more or less dead."

Fair enough.

"You're doing it again, aren't you?" Cashel groaned, dropping his forehead onto the back of Fia's head as they coasted over the harbor and landed inside Tallis's shipyard amid the roaring cheers of those gathered nearby. "You know it drives me crazy when you have conversations with Artemis inside your head."

"It's not my fault you weren't blessed with a celestial beast," Fia retorted, waving at the crowd of people rushing in to greet them.

"That doesn't make it any less irritating."

"Eh, you'll live." She slid down off Artemis's back. "Now, I'd suggest you hop down before he disappears completely." Cashel hurried to follow suit, and soon the great dragon was nothing more than a wisp of smoke. A broad-shouldered man wearing the Eldorian colors stepped forward to greet them, a wide grin on his weathered face.

"You two are a sight for sore eyes." He nodded toward the water. "Thanks for clearing out the rubbish in the harbor. I was getting rather sick of seeing those flags lurking in our waters."

"Happy to do it," Fia replied. "Captain Melbrooke, was it?"

The older man grinned, holding out his hand and shaking

hers with unbridled enthusiasm. "Impressive memory. I don't think we've met more than in passing. Not that I'd forget the dragon Shendri herself." He turned to offer his hand to Cashel. "And King Malachite's son, Cashel. Another honor."

Cashel shook the captain's hand. "Thank you, sir. Likewise."

The captain let out a low whistle as he turned toward the harbor. "That dragon of yours sure did a number on the Antoski's naval fleet. I can't wait to see him open fire on those bastards crowding us in on the western side. No pun intended," he added, then chuckled. "Well, okay, maybe it was intended. I'm just happy to see you've recovered. Things were looking pretty bleak up until now, if I'm honest, but with a dragon leading the charge, I'd say we have a damn good chance of turning things around."

Fia and Cashel exchanged looks. "Right, well, that's probably something we should discuss with Her Majesty," Fia said in an attempt to side-step the issue. She didn't want to lie to the captain, but there was no way she was going to tell him she was working on an alternative plan. One that didn't involve Artemis burning down the legions of soldiers hovering outside their barrier walls. "Do you know where we might find her?"

"Aye. She and His Majesty have been staying with the magistrate, Mr. Jonathan Banri. I believe the rest of the Shendri are there, as well. Would you like me to take you there?"

"A ride would be appreciated, thank you." She gave him a rueful grin. "I suspect flying there on Artemis might be a bit over the top."

"Maybe just a bit." The captain's eyes twinkled as he waved to a nearby wagon, calling them over. "But it would be an amazing sight to see, nonetheless." The wagon pulled to a stop beside them, and he gestured for them to climb in. "Now, let's get you two to Their Majesties so we can see an end to this war once and for all."

The tension in the Banri's parlor was palpable as Fia stood in front of the others, anxiously waiting for someone to say something. Anything, really. Having just relayed her story about Lunares and the hagrüs, the silence that now hung in their air was downright suffocating. A warm hand wrapped around hers, and she relaxed as the comforting gesture washed over her.

Thank goodness for Cashel.

"I truly believe saving Bade is our best chance at saving Lehi," she stated. "If we turn him to our side, he could help us take out Lumeria. Or, at the very least, stay out of our way."

"You know what else would get Bade out of our way?" Maya asked. "Killing him. That would definitely keep him out of our way for good."

"He doesn't deserve to die," Fia insisted.

"Tell that to the hundreds he's killed," Maya retorted. "I suspect they'd feel differently."

"I told you – that wasn't his doing. It was the hagrüs!"

"So says his mother," Maya snapped. "Who I'm sure is completely unbiased."

Fia ground her teeth in frustration. "If you want my help taking down Lumeria, you'll have to at least let me try to free him."

"Are you serious right now?" Maya shouted, throwing her hands into the air. "You came all the way back here just to take his side *again*?! Gods, I thought you were supposed to be our leader!"

"Easy, Maya," Edmund murmured, placing a calming hand on her shoulder. A hand that Maya promptly tossed to the side with a growl.

"Stay out of it, Edmund."

"Yes, ma'am."

He took a hasty step back, joining the other men behind the settee. Alex smirked as Edmund slid into place beside him. "Wimp."

"I don't see you jumping in."

"That's 'cause I'm not an idiot like a certain knight I know."

"He has a point," Draven muttered, adding his two cents. "Knights aren't exactly known for their brain power."

"And here I thought we were getting to be friends," Edmund huffed.

"Delusional, too," Alex muttered. "Classic knight."

"If you three are quite finished," Josselyn interrupted. "I'd say we have somewhat more important matters to discuss?" She rose off the settee and turned to face the other Shendri. "Fia's plan has merit, and if it can finally bring us together with a common goal, then I say we go for it. Assuming, that is, that you can actually make this counter potion?" she added, turning to address Luxeos, who'd been quietly taking everything in from the corner.

"I believe I am familiar with the potion Lunares was referring to," Luxeos said. She ran a finger over the celestial sash Fia had given her at the beginning of her story. "And she was correct about the sash. Given that it's made from the same heavenly material as the tainted robes that created Bade's hagrüs, it'll be an integral part in undoing the curse. There is, however, one thing she failed to mention, and I'm afraid it will make the creation of this potion almost impossible. Especially if you wish to administer it on the next full moon."

"What do you mean?" Fia asked. "What's missing?"

"Caeruleum."

"Well, that's not so hard to get, is it? Didn't Trekklin bring a supply of caeruleum with him?"

"He did," Luxeos said. "But I'm afraid it's all been used to help maintain the barrier. The only caeruleum left is in Mihala."

Cashel wrapped his arms around Fia from behind as she silently processed Luxeos's words. "I'm so sorry, Fia," he whispered. "I know how much you wanted this."

"You're right. I do want this. And what's more, I will make it happen." She twisted around to face him. "Artemis can fly me to Mihala and back before the full moon, I'm certain of it." She lifted her chin as she met his gaze square on. "That is, if you're willing to show us the way?"

Chapter Thirty-Three

The royal castle in Eldon

Darius... James... Anthony...

Bade gripped the back of the chair he stood behind as his head began to pound. *Ignore it. You can do this. You can remember.* He took a deep breath in, fighting past the pain. *There was Darius, the young duke of Westford. He would have sat there, just beside me.* His eyes slid to the right, falling on the empty chair to his right. *He was always by my side.* A fresh wave of pain flooded his head, stripping away the sandy-haired image he'd almost been able to conjure.

"Damn it!" He grabbed an empty goblet and threw it across the long table with all his might, wincing as the resulting clatter added to the almost unbearable pain in his temples. "Just let me have this," he shouted, his voice bouncing off the walls in the dark room. "Please," he added, whispering this time. Let me remember them."

He closed his eyes and focused on clearing his mind. A thin beam of moonlight broke through the window, lighting his face and easing the pain. *Next to Darius would have been James. He was a commoner, like me, but brilliant. His head for numbers was extraordinary.* The pain threatened to return as he pictured a young man with dark brown curls and a rounded face, his eyes bright and eager as he listened to the others chatter on around him. He pushed it back, focusing on the soothing feel of moonlight on his skin.

Anthony would have sat to my left, leading the conversation with grand speeches of revolution and fighting for the common man. His gut clenched as he recalled the last time he'd seen his old friend, his vacant eyes staring back at him from a mutilated corpse. Killed by the king's knights for nothing more than speaking his mind. It'd been his death that had driven Bade to seek more drastic means of obtaining power. *And I got it. All the power in the world rests on the tip of my tongue, and what have I done with it?* He stared down at his hands. *I've destroyed the very people I sought to help.*

"Change can only occur once the lands have been cleansed."

Bade cringed as the creature's voiced wormed its way into his mind, making his thoughts grow muddled.

"Stop it," he whispered. "Stop trying to confuse me."

"Confuse you?" the creature hissed. "If anything, I'm trying to give you some much needed clarity. How can you expect to see the bigger picture, when you keep drowning yourself in the past? This maudlin attitude of yours makes me sick."

The fog grew thicker with each insidious word, and Bade felt himself being pulled under the creature's spell. The big picture, yes. Yes, that made sense. He needed to stop romanticizing the past and start looking to the future. He needed to –

"No!" He slapped himself across the face before stumbling toward the window, desperately seeking the moon's comforting beams. "You're wrong," he rasped, falling to his knees in the circle of moonlight. "This is wrong."

"It's what your mother wanted..."

"I don't believe you," he whispered. "She wouldn't have wanted this."

"Of course she would. After what that man did to her? To *you*?!"

The fog crept back in, insistent. Was the creature right? Was this the way? Someone cleared their throat, and Bade lifted his heavy head to look over his shoulder at the door. A footman stood there, nervously fidgeting with a sealed scroll that he held in front of himself like a shield.

"You needed something?" Bade asked, not bothering to rise. Everything felt far too heavy, and he found he really didn't care what this man thought, anyway.

"I, uh, yes, Your Majesty," the footman stuttered.

"I hate that title," Bade muttered. "Don't call me it."

The footman shuffled his feet nervously. "Y-yes, Your... uh, sir." He held up the scroll. "We've had a message from the barrier."

"I see." Bade sighed. He really didn't want to be bothered with Lumeria's ramblings at the moment, but it wouldn't do to put it off. "Go on, then. Read it."

"Yes, sir." The footman broke the seal with shaky hands and quickly unfurled the parchment. Clearing his throat again, he read, "I'm pleased to report that Lumeria's continued attacks on the barrier wall are beginning to take effect. We expect a complete breakdown in the next few days, at which time our army will be poised to take the city. We don't anticipate any problems, however, it would be wise if you came in person to ensure everything goes smoothly, especially given that the dragon Shendri appeared in the harbor with a fully restored dragon and obliterated our entire fleet. While Lumeria is confident she can handle the Shendri on her own, should they decide to attack, I believe it would be prudent to have you both present. Signed General Brackett."

"So she's rediscovered her dragon," Bade murmured, turning back to bathe his face in the moonlight. "Damn." *I'd been hoping she'd stay tucked away out of sight until the worst of it was over. Now, she'll be front and center along with the other Shendri warriors.* His chest tightened at the thought. If Lumeria didn't kill her, the creature surely would. It despised Fia for being his so-called weakness. *Am I just to sit back and watch the creature kill the only woman I've ever* – He checked himself mid-thought. It wouldn't do to acknowledge any deeper feelings, whatever they may be. He couldn't allow the creature any more power than it already had.

"Sir?" the footman prompted, reminding Bade of his lingering presence.

"You may go," he replied, waving a hand over his shoulder.

"Yes, sir. It's just, um, there's a postscript. Shall I read that, too?"

"Obviously," Bade drawled, reining in his rising temper. *What kind of simpleton doesn't read the damned postscript?*

"I-it mentions the, uh, dragon Shendri again. Says that witnesses stated she wasn't alone during the attack on the fleet. There was a-another rider with her."

An eerie calm settled over Bade's person as he processed the man's words. "Oh?"

"Y-yes, sir. It says they believed him to be one of the Mihalan princes. They weren't sure which one."

An image of the Mihalan man from the battle in Merin danced into his mind, taunting him. The man had been clearly protective of Fia at the time, a fact which Bade had used to ensure her safety. He'd stolen Bade's role as her savior when Lumeria had attempted to kill her. Had he stolen his place on the dragon, as well?

His hands shook, and he clenched them in his lap.

"Leave me," he growled, sending the footman scurrying away. As soon as he heard the door close behind him, he stood and began pacing the length of the room, his entire body trembling with bitter jealousy.

It should be me riding behind her.

My arms wrapped around her, holding her.

He stopped beside the table, grasping its side before flipping it over with a resounding crash. His chest heaved as he stared at the wreckage, and he could feel his mind coming unhinged as the creature crept back in, drawn by the increasingly violent thoughts fighting their way to the surface. Its return reminded Bade of the reason he'd sent Fia away to begin with.

To protect her from the creature.

Stepping around the table, he cast his gaze over the mess of scattered silverware and broken glass. A particularly jagged piece caught his eye, and he bent down, allowing the tips of his fingers to brush over the sharp edge before slipping it into his hand.

"Perhaps I can still protect her..." he murmured, eyeing the shard of glass as a spark of desperate hope lit his chest on fire. "Perhaps I can..." His hand jerked, thrusting the glass toward his abdomen. The tip scratched at the hard plane of his stomach before his body locked into place, preventing him from finishing the one task that might have actually been worth something in his lifetime. He stared down at his frozen hand in despair. Once a failure, always a failure.

"Surely you didn't think I'd let you end it like that?" the creature hissed. "Fool." It forced Bade's hand open, allowing the shard of glass to fall onto the floor. Bade watched in a daze as the glass shattered, the pieces blurring together as his mind began to fall under the creature's thrall once more. *My friends are dead and buried, my ideals stripped from my control. My only love has found someone who might actually deserve her. There is nothing left for me now but to watch helplessly as the creature attempts to destroy all that is good in this world.*

I really am a fool.

"You're wrong about one thing," the creature whispered.

"And just what is that?" Bade muttered despondently.

"That you must watch," the creature purred. "I assure you, that is entirely unnecessary."

"What do you mean?"

"Give yourself over to me completely, and I can spare you the pain of watching your beloved Fia die."

"You already control my every move," Bade spat out disgustedly. "What's left to give?"

"Your mind." The creature paused. "And your moonlight."

"My moonlight?"

"Surely you've noticed the way you're drawn to those pitiful beams? Grasping at them like a drowning man. They won't be enough, you know. All they'll do is keep you awake when you want nothing more than to sleep. Give yourself over to me, and I will give you that peace you want so badly."

Bade's eyes flickered over to the window, tracing the thin trails of light streaming through it. It was a tempting offer. Cowardly, perhaps, but tempting.

"Tell me what to do."

Chapter Thirty-Four

Somewhere in the Endless Mountains

"Let's stop here for the night," Fia yawned, gesturing down at a small meadow nestled between the mountains' rocky cliffs. "Artemis and I could both use some rest before I pass out and he disappears from beneath us."

"Rest sounds good," Cashel agreed. "As does not falling into thin air."

Artemis glided down between the mountains and landed in the tall grass of the meadow, where he vanished in a cloud of smoke the moment Fia's and Cashel's feet touched the ground. Fia dropped onto the soft grass with an exhausted sigh, sprawling out on her back as she stared up into the starry sky. "Who knew sustaining a dragon in flight for almost twenty hours would be so hard?"

"Right? Sounds easy enough to me," Cashel teased, setting their supplies down. "Should I try to make a fire, or do you think you'll be warm enough without one?"

"I think I'll be fine so long as I have a warm, Mihalan blanket to wrap up in," Fia murmured, her eyes already beginning to close.

"I don't think we brought any blankets from Mihala," Cashel replied, digging into his pack. "Just this old wool one from the Banri's," he added, pulling out a blanket roll and tossing it beside her in the grass.

Fia didn't even look as she grabbed the blanket and chucked it back at Cashel's head. "Your brain must be full of wool if you think that's the blanket I was referring to."

"Okay, I'm lost," Cashel stated. "What other blankets do you think we have in here?"

Fia rolled her eyes as she pushed herself upright. "I'm talking about you, ya big dolt."

Cashel froze mid-search, and a hint of red crept up the back of his neck as he studiously avoided her gaze. "Oh."

"Yeaaah," Fia replied, drawing the word out as she studied Cashel's profile in confusion. Why was he acting so weird all of a sudden? *Come to think of it, he was quiet pretty much the entire flight here.* "So, are you going to keep me warm tonight or what?" She forced a teasing note into her voice. "I mean, you're always bragging about how hot you are. Might as well put it to good use."

"Oh, uh, right." He let out a nervous chuckle. "That makes sense."

"I usually do." Fia cocked her head to the side as he continued to stare blankly into the supply pack. "Is something wrong? 'Cause I can make do with the blanket if you're uncomfortable. I just thought, seeing as we've already slept together once..." She shrugged, feeling suddenly self-conscious. "I thought it'd be nice," she mumbled, dropping her gaze and picking at the grass by her feet.

There was a soft shuffling of feet as Cashel stood and walked over. He lowered himself onto the ground beside her with a sigh, his leg brushing against hers as he reached over to drop the blanket back into her lap.

"How about we do two blankets?"

Fia swallowed against the sudden lump in her throat. "Two sounds good."

"Yeah," Cashel whispered, his voice coming out a touch raw. "It sounds pretty good to me, too." He laid back on the grass, his arm stretching out to wrap around Fia's shoulders as she followed suit. His bare skin was warm to the touch, and she snuggled against his chest with a contented sigh.

"This is nice," she murmured, her eyelids growing heavy as the exhaustion of the day's flight settled in. Cashel pulled the wool blanket over them both, tucking the edges in around her.

His hand stilled briefly as it brushed her own, and she caught hold of it, weaving their fingers together. He pulled her closer in response, his arms tightening around her.

"I'm going to miss this," he whispered.

"Miss what?" Fia asked sleepily, her eyes already closed. "Sleeping on the ground in the middle of the mountains?"

He let out a soft laugh, and Fia smiled as his chest vibrated against her back. "Not the location so much as the company. Who knows when I'll get the chance to hold you like this again?"

"Why's that?" she asked. "You planning to run off on me, Cash?"

"Of course not. It's just... you know... things will be different." He paused, then added, "If you succeed in destroying the hagrüs, Bade will be free. The two of you could have a life together, if you wanted." He swallowed. "Do you? Want that, I mean."

Do I want a life with Bade?

Images of the handsome demigod flooded her mind, preventing her from responding. A pair of silvery-blue eyes pinned her to the ground, and she would have been lying if she said they didn't still stir the butterflies in her stomach. Bade had been so much to her. From the moment he'd stepped into that fiery room and ended the baron's miserable existence, she'd been in awe. True, he'd been a bit aloof and unreadable most days, but those nights... those nights had been her most cherished memories. They'd been her first taste of what love could be like, and she would never forget that. Bade had been her first true love, and that love would never fully fade.

But Cashel...

She twisted in his arms so that she could meet his eyes, and the worry she found there pricked painfully at her heart. This man, this beautiful, giving man, had no idea just how much she'd come to care for him. He couldn't, or else he wouldn't be lying there with such a heartbreaking expression, discussing her future with another man.

"What I want," she whispered, sliding her hand up and

around the back of his neck. "Is right here in front of me."

Cashel's eyes glistened as he stared back at her in wonder. "Truly? You'll stay?"

Fia gave his head a gentle tug downward as she pushed herself up to meet his lips. "You're my home now, Cashel," she whispered, her mouth inches away from his own. "You couldn't shake me if you tried."

He closed the distance between them, swallowing her last word in a kiss so full of passion and longing it made her toes curl on instinct. She met his passion with her own, desperate kisses, hands grasping at his back as she tried to close a distance that wasn't there. Cashel groaned as he pulled away, his head dropping onto her shoulder.

"If we do that much longer, I'm going to end up breaking some very strict Mihalan laws," he whispered regretfully.

"Boooo," Fia teased, dropping a soft kiss on the side of his neck. "Berg wouldn't care. Maybe I should fly back to Eldour and see what he's up to right now. You two are twins, after all."

"Not. Funny," Cashel growled, tickling her sides.

She laughed as she swatted his hands away. "I thought it was."

"Yeah, well, you're lucky I love you," he retorted, giving up his attack in order to wrap her back in his arms. "Or I'd never let you off so easy." Her laughter turned into a contented sigh as she let his warmth surround her.

"I am pretty lucky, aren't I?"

Chapter Thirty-Five

How was it possible to be on the cusp of an inevitable battle, and still be more blissfully happy than you'd ever been in your life? It seemed like an impossibility, and yet, Cashel couldn't help but feel buoyant as Artemis touched down outside the natural mountain wall that guarded Mihala from the outside world. He hurried to dismount, and reached up to catch Fia as she slid down behind him.

"This is it," he said, taking her hand and pulling her toward the rock wall. "The hidden kingdom of Mihala."

"It's a bit more... mountainous than I pictured," Fia replied, looking over the wall in confusion.

"Just wait until you're inside," Cashel assured her. "No matter where you've been, I guarantee you've never been anywhere as beautiful as Mihala."

"And how exactly *do* we get inside? Climb? If it's on the other side of this wall, wouldn't it be easier if Artemis simply flew us over?"

"Wouldn't work," he replied. "There's a barrier covering the top that even Artemis couldn't break through. And unlike the one surrounding Tallis, it hasn't been adapted to allow entrance to friends and allies." He pressed the palm of his hand flat against the wall, drawing upon the essence of the mountain as he did, and grinned in anticipation as the outline of a door began to light up. "The only ones who can open a door to Mihala are the Mihalans."

Fia gaped at the newly formed door. "Now *that* is a security system," she murmured, reaching out to trace the door's handle. "No wonder King Malachite didn't have any qualms about bringing his entire army to Eldour. Honestly, I'm surprised you even have one at all."

Cashel reached around her to open the door, waiting patiently as she slowly made her way in, her gaze sweeping from side to side as she took in the wide tunnel that would lead them to the hidden city. Blue light flickered out of wall-mounted lanterns, creating a soft glow that illuminated the thick, wooden door on the other end of the tunnel.

"We've always believed it's better to be prepared," he explained. "Besides, the Mihalan fighting techniques are a part of our heritage. It's considered an honor to be trained for the guard." They stopped outside the final door, and Cashel looked down at Fia, one hand firmly gripping the handle, the other lifting hers for a brief kiss.

"Welcome to Mihala, Fia." He pulled the door open with a dramatic flourish, and they both squinted into the bright light that met them. "Sorry." He winced as he guided them forward. "I forgot about the light. It's meant to throw off any intruders upon entrance, should they manage to make it this far."

"It's certainly effective," she replied, rubbing a hand over her eyes as the light began to dim.

"Yeah, sorry about th –"

The words died on his tongue as his vision cleared, revealing the Great Tree that held his kingdom's city. Or, what was left of it anyway.

"Bloody hell."

Cashel hardly registered Fia's muttered curse as he gazed, dumbfounded, at the charred stump rising out from the center of the Caeruleum Lake.

Gone.

The Great Tree, the castle, the homes, all of it gone. The muscles in his leg convulsed, forcing him to his knees as his body began to tremble.

The people.

His stomach roiled, the bile bubbling its way up his throat.

Where were all the people?

Chapter Thirty-Six

What in Lehi happened here?

Fia alternated between staring at the ruined stump in horror and staring at Cashel in worried silence. More than once she opened her mouth to say something, then immediately closed it. What did you say to someone whose home had been wiped away? What could she possibly say that would be of any use in that moment?

Nothing.

She placed a hesitant hand on his shoulder, hoping the contact would do her speaking for her and remind him she was there. Cashel's hands clenched into tight fists, his knuckles whitening under the strain. He muttered something illegible, and she leaned closer. "What's that?"

"He did this," Cashel growled, louder this time.

Fia didn't need to ask who he was talking about to know it was Bade's face Cashel wanted to pummel those fists into.

"It wasn't him, it was the hagrüs –"

"I don't give a damn about the hagrüs, Fia!" Cashel burst out, cutting off her weak attempts of reasoning and shrugging her hand away. "My entire home has been reduced to a damn stump! Bade, the hagrüs, they're one and the same as far as I'm concerned. A dead man."

"I know you're hurting right now," Fia said, an edge of desperation creeping into her voice. "But if we follow through with the plan, we can end this destruction. The potion will kill the hagrüs once and for all. I promise."

"You know what else would kill the hagrüs? My sword in Bade's gut."

"He'd never let you get close enough," Fia argued. "You'd die trying, and then where will we be? You have to trust me on this, Cashel. There's a good man hidden in there. You have to let me reach him."

He let out a humorless laugh as he pushed himself back up. Walking over to the edge of the lake, he stared out over the ruined trunk of his once great kingdom. "Is that what you told Maya when the Haven was attacked? That deep down he was a good man, if only you looked? Did you try to talk her out of her revenge, as well?"

Fia's stomach felt as if it were lined in lead as she whispered, "Yes."

He nodded. "And when she tried to kill him back in Antos? You stopped her. Threw yourself in front of the arrow that would have killed him. I thought it was noble, oddly enough. Touching, even. The way you gave everything you had to protect the one you loved." He paused. "Do you know how I feel about that now, Fia?"

She swallowed. "No."

He slowly turned until he was looking her square in the eye, and her heart constricted at the coldness reflecting back at her. "I'm disgusted. Disgusted that you allowed that bastard to live for even one more moment. That you allowed him to do this," he spat. "This," he jabbed a finger at the ruined tree, "this is on you."

Fia's face paled. "You don't mean that," she whispered, hot tears pricking at the corners of her eyes. She blinked them away as she forced herself to stay calm. *He's upset. He doesn't mean it.*

"Don't I?" He shook his head, looking away. "I don't think I know what anything means anymore."

"Cashel, please." She reached for his arm, but stopped short at the sound of voices calling out from the other side of the lake. The two of them turned in unison to seek out the source, and Fia let out a joyous cry as she spotted a group of people coming out from what must have been one of the caeruleum caves. "Cashel, look! They're alive!"

"They're alive," Cashel murmured numbly. Tears streamed

from his eyes as he stared across the water. "They're alive," he repeated, louder this time as reality began to set in. He let out a sharp laugh before scooping Fia up into his arms and squeezing her in a tight hug. "They're alive!"

She hesitated for a moment, uncertain, before lifting her arms to return the embrace. "Thank the goddesses," she whispered. "Come on," she added as he finally set her back down. "I'll give you lift over."

He nodded, his gaze returning to the mass of Mihalans waving frantically from the other side of the lake. "Thank you."

∞∞∞

There was a flurry of greetings and people talking over each other as the pair dismounted from Artemis's back outside the cave's opening. The Mihalans took the large dragon in stride, moving closer to the beast than most would ever dare as they rushed forward to greet their prince. An older woman in a flowing, sleeveless gown the color of sunset was the first to reach him, and she enveloped him in a firm hug the moment his feet touched the ground.

"Prince Cashel, thank goodness you're alive. We've feared the worst since that witch came and so effortlessly destroyed our homes. Please tell me Lehi hasn't been overtaken."

"All but Tallis and the islands, I'm afraid," Cashel replied. "But Anaria, what happened here? I had thought this place impenetrable, and yet the Great Tree has been reduced to rubble. Did Bade do this?"

"Bade, yes, he was here," the woman stated, her expression darkening. "But it was the witch who destroyed the tree with her conjured lightning. It was difficult to make out from where we hid, but we could hear her vicious laughter grow louder with each explosion and we saw the flash of each blow through the slits in the rock." She shuddered. "I'm only grateful we were able to evacuate to the hidden storage caves before she arrived, for I'm certain she would have killed each and every one of us given the chance."

"When I saw the destruction, I assumed the worst," Cashel admitted. "I've never been more glad to be mistaken." He paused as confusion colored his face. "How did you manage to evacuate everyone into the caves before they arrived? Did a scout see them coming?"

The woman, Anaria, shook her head. "It was the strangest thing, actually. A voice warned us of their approach." She touched her temple. "In here. It was a man's voice," she added. "Deep and soothing. He said someone was coming to destroy Mihala, and if we valued our lives, we would hide. That fighting back would only result in the death of our people." Fia's breath caught at the woman's words, her heart pounding at their meaning. *It was Bade's voice, it had to have been.* Anaria continued, oblivious to Fia's building excitement. "His words were so compelling, we couldn't help but do as instructed." She glanced around the crowd gathered around them. "It's thanks to his warning that we're standing here today. Without the Guard, we could never have fought back against such immense power."

"You would have had trouble regardless," Cashel said, tapping his hand against his wooden leg. "I've tasted the witch's power firsthand. She's not one to be messed with."

The woman dropped her gaze to Cashel's leg and tutted. Fia could tell she was about to ask how it had happened, so she hurried to jump in before they went completely off topic.

"It was Bade," she interjected. "He was the one that warned you."

"The demigod responsible for the destruction of the Lowlands?" Anaria replied skeptically. "Why would he warn us? He stood by the witch's side while she tore our kingdom apart."

There was a murmur of agreement from the crowd, and Fia gave Cashel a beseeching look. "He must have wanted to spare the Mihalans, but the hagrüs wouldn't allow him to interfere directly. So he warned them of Lumeria's approach, instead."

Cashel nodded slowly. "As much as I hate to admit it, you may be right. He used a similar technique when we were in Roshka, compelling me to keep you safe from Lumeria's attacks. Not that I wouldn't have done it, anyway," he added hastily.

"You see? He does have good inside him," Fia stated. "We have to at least try to save him."

Cashel's face darkened. "I still think we'd all be better off if someone simply ended his existence. Hagrüs or not, he's been at the root of too much destruction to ignore."

Fia crossed her arms over her chest as she glared at him in annoyance. "You're just being stubborn."

"Better stubborn than stupidly naive."

"Are you saying I'm stupid now?"

"No, I'm saying you're stupidly naive. There's a difference."

"Why are you suddenly being such an asshole about this? I thought you came here to support me."

"Oh, I don't know, maybe since Bade unleashed a half-crazed witch on us, then stood by and watched as she decimated my entire village? Not to mention countless other villages across Lehi?" Cashel let out a frustrated growl. "Gods, Fia, why do you have to be so damn blind when it comes to Bade? The only way this nightmare is going to end is when he's dead and buried."

There was a long silence as Fia stood there staring at the ground, speechless and trembling. *Just when I thought someone was truly on my side, I'm slapped in the face with how wrong I was.*

Anaria cleared her throat. "You, uh, must be hungry after such a long flight. We don't have much left to offer in the way of variation, but there's plenty of fish to go around. Should I fix you something?"

"Food would be great, thank you, Anaria," Cashel said, his previously hard expression softening to one of contrition as he cast surreptitious glances in Fia's direction. She pressed her lips into a firm line, ignoring him.

"I'm good, thanks." She turned toward Artemis and he lowered his head in response to her silent plea. *Get me out of here.* Hoisting herself up onto the dragon's back, she called down, "I think I'll just get some air. I won't go far."

"You should eat something," Cashel argued. "You can't sustain Artemis on air alone."

"I have rations in my pack if I need them."

"Ah, right." Cashel hesitated, looking uncertain. "Would you like me to come with you?"

Fia swallowed, turning her face so he wouldn't see how much she was hurting. "We'll be fine on our own," she assured him. "I just need some space to think." Artemis pushed off the rock floor and swept into the sky, leaving Cashel and the Mihalans behind them. Fia leaned against his scaly back as she wrapped her arms around his neck.

Thank goodness for you, Artemis.

Chapter Thirty-Seven

Cashel stood in the mouth of the cave, watching as Artemis flew laps around the Caeruleum Lake. At least he didn't have to worry about Fia ditching him and heading back to Eldour alone. With the barrier in place, they wouldn't be able to leave Mihala on their own. Still, it pained him to see her so upset. And it straight out gutted him knowing it was his own careless words that'd caused it.

The dragon eventually dipped down and landed out of sight on the other side of the ruined tree. Cashel eyed the water as he contemplated swimming out and joining them. Sure, she'd said she would be fine on her own, but would she really? Flashes of her jumping off the rail of the ship invaded his mind, and he had just about made up his mind to dive in and follow her when Anaria's voice piped up from behind, startling him.

"Give her time. She'll come around when she's ready."

"You don't know that," he replied, shoulders drooping. "I said some pretty horrible things today."

"What? That bit about being stupidly naive?" Anaria waved her hand dismissively. "Not your most princely moment, to be sure, but nothing she won't forgive in due time. I wouldn't worry about it too much."

"I wish that were all, but..." He sighed. "Earlier, before we saw you all here, I... I told her it was her fault."

Anaria shot him a hard look. "That *what* was her fault?"

"All of it," he whispered, his face burning with shame. "I was so angry, the words just slipped out. I didn't really mean it."

"Hmm." She studied him before turning and gesturing for him to follow her into the cave. "Let's get you some fish. You must be famished."

"That's it? No wise words, no dressing down for being a cruel jerk?" he exclaimed, following along behind her. The other villagers had already returned to their various chores, but they all looked up and nodded as he walked past them down the winding cavern tunnel.

"Just because I'm old doesn't mean I have all the answers, you know, " she retorted. "Besides," she paused as she stopped to face him. "I've known you since you were in swaddling clothes, Your Highness, and I've never once heard you say something you didn't mean. Not even to that ridiculous brother of yours," she added. "The goddesses help us all when he ascends to the throne one day. Not that there are any thrones left to ascend to."

Cashel brushed aside the thought of his brother's future reign as he took in the meaning of Anaria's words. "You think I meant it? That Fia's responsible for what's happening in Lehi right now?"

"I think there's at least a small part of you that believes that, yes."

"But that's crazy! She would never hurt innocent people the way Bade has."

Anaria shrugged. "I won't claim to know the girl's character, but I am aware of her connection to Bade. Trekklin and Berg told us everything they saw that day in Antos, when Princess Maya attempted to kill Bade but the young dragon Shendri took the caeruleum arrow in his place. She may not be doing it intentionally, but that doesn't mean people haven't suffered due to her interference."

Cashel opened his mouth to protest and Anaria raised a pointed brow when nothing came out, resuming her quick pace through the tunnel. He trailed silently behind her, mentally scolding himself for not being able to come up with a better defense. He'd been wrong to accuse Fia of having anything to do with the destruction of his kingdom... hadn't he?

Or was it just the hurt you inflicted on her that's making you eat your words?

An uncomfortable feeling crept over him at the thought. He'd been drawn to Fia from the moment he'd met her, and his attachment had only grown stronger over time, to the point where he was making declarations of love in the pouring rain. Had his feelings blinded him to the truth? *I can forgive her past, but can I ignore the fact that her need to save Bade may only prolong the war? We should be back in Tallis right now, fighting back, not flying off on some quest to save someone who probably doesn't even want to be saved.*

Anaria stopped in front of a stack of crates piled neatly against the wall of the tunnel, and he had to catch himself to keep from bumping into her, he was so distracted. "Sorry," he mumbled.

"No need to apologize, Your Highness," she replied, opening one of the crates on top and pulling out a handful of small, dried fish. She handed them over before digging into a barrel and pulling out a wrinkled, old apple. "You have every reason to be distracted," she continued, tossing him the fruit. "You're obviously smitten with the girl, despite her poor decision making skills."

"What? No." Cashel flushed. "I mean, what makes you think that?"

She chuckled. "I've known you your entire life, Your Highness. Did you really think I wouldn't notice the way you look at her? Good goddess, even when you're arguing, I can hear the heat behind your words. The question is, does she feel the same?"

"She says she does..."

"But?"

"But," he drawled, "There's Bade."

"And you think she still loves him," Anaria supplied.

"I don't think she can help it," he admitted. "He's too close, too important for her to write off. It's like he imprinted himself on her very core when he took her from Roshka, and as much as she says she wants to save Lehi, I'm afraid she's too blind to see that ending him completely is the only real way to do that. All she can think about is saving him from the hagrüs that may or may not be controlling him. It's just so... so frustrating!"

"A hagrüs?" Anaria gave him a sharp look. "If there's a hagrüs controlling that demigod, then all the more reason to destroy them both. No one will be spared if it gains control. They're cruel, bloodthirsty creatures." She poked him in the chest. "You have to kill him. Mercy may usually be a virtue, but in this case, it will be our doom. Do you understand?"

"You want me to kill Bade." A heavy weight settled on Cashel's shoulders as he thought of Fia's face should he succeed in doing so. "How? I'm no match for a demigod, with or without a wooden leg. And Fia – she'd never let me try." He shook his head. "With Artemis returned to full strength, there's no way I could get past the two of them."

"So you don't get past them," Anaria countered. "You stay with them until an opportunity presents itself. Then, you strike."

"Fia isn't going to want me around when she goes after Bade," Cashel argued. "Not after the things I've said."

"So apologize," Anaria huffed. "Make nice with the girl, win her trust. Whatever you have to do, do it. So long as Bade ends up dead in the end, that's all that matters."

She made an excellent point, and yet...

"If I betray her trust like that, that's it. She'll never forgive me."

Anaria gave him a hard look. "And if you don't, we all may die. Have you considered the fact that Bade might actually kill the dragon Shendri himself, should she continue to throw herself at his feet? Then where would we be? Bade's not the only monster we have to worry about, you know. The witch that destroyed our village isn't going to go down easy. We'll need every one of the Shendri warriors working together to defeat her. Kill Bade, and allow Fia to live long enough to stand by her sister Shendri." Her voice softened, and she placed a gnarled hand on his arm. "It's the right thing to do, Your Highness. You see that, yes?"

He sighed. "I do."

"Good." She nodded toward the way they came. "Now, go

make nice."

"Right." He stared down the tunnel, reluctance holding him in place. "I'll need something first," he said. "A peace offering to help bring her around."

"And what's that?" Anaria asked.

"Caeruleum."

"The witch destroyed most of it when she attacked the mines with her lightning," Anaria lamented. "But," she pulled a necklace with a blue pendant out from the neckline of her dress, "I still have a small piece here, if you think that will be enough."

"It doesn't really matter if it is," Cashel replied, accepting the pendant. "It doesn't need to work. It just needs to get us on our way back to Tallis."

"Then, good luck. The fate of Lehi lies in your capable hands." She smiled. "I know we can count on you, Prince Cashel."

He bowed. "I won't let you down, Anaria."

The only person I'll be letting down is Fia. His hand clenched around the caeruleum pendant. *So, why does it feel like she's the only person who matters?*

Chapter Thirty-Eight

"I can't believe she destroyed the entire tree." Fia picked her way through the wreckage, heart heavy. "Do you think this is my fault, Artemis? Should I have just let Maya kill him when she had the chance?"

The great dragon hummed, his deep tone rumbling through her mind with comforting familiarity. "You weren't aware of everything he was doing at the time," he argued. "He hid the evil well."

Fia made a noncommittal noise. "What about in Merin? Josselyn had him, and I froze her in place. The only time I managed to effectively tap into my abilities as the lead Shendri, mind you," she added.

"It was the first time you'd seen him since leaving Antos," Artemis countered. "And you loved him. It's natural you'd want to protect him."

She kicked the base of the blackened stump in frustration. "Is that what you're doing to me, Artemis? Protecting me? Because I don't need protection right now, I need honesty."

"I am always honest, Shendri," Artemis replied. "I've never disapproved of your actions. They were done out of love." He paused. "The question is – does Bade truly deserve it?"

Fia wiped at a stray tear as she leaned her back against the stump and closed her eyes, blocking out the wreckage that surrounded her. "Probably not," she admitted. "But I can't seem to give up on him. Ever since Lunares's spirit reached out to me, it's all I can think about. Saving Bade." She groaned. "I'm the leader of the Shendri. I should be trying to save Lehi, not the possessed demigod bent on destroying it."

"When you put it like that," Artemis murmured, "perhaps your priorities are a bit misplaced..."

"Ha!" Fia slumped onto the ground, dropping her head into her hands. "More like a lot out of place. Gods, I'm the worst."

"You know that isn't true," Artemis chided.

"Fine, I'm not the worst," Fia conceded. "Just the worst possible leader of the Shendri."

"That's fair."

She snorted. "I knew I'd break you eventually."

"See? You can do anything you put your mind to."

"Riiight." She sighed, lifting her head to look out over the water. "I want to save him, Artemis. But I want to save Lehi, too."

"So, do it," Artemis rumbled. "Save them both. Show Cashel and all the other Shendri what you're capable of."

Fia smiled as the weight slowly lifted from her shoulders. "You truly believe I can do it? That I can save Bade without abandoning everyone else?"

"I believe you will do everything in your power to make it happen," Artemis replied. "And should you fail, you will do whatever is necessary to save this world."

"Meaning if I can't save him, you expect me to kill him?" Fia cringed. "Let's hope it doesn't come to that."

"Indeed," Artemis agreed. "And what of the witch? Didn't I hear Maya telling you she was Luxeos's daughter? And a former Mihalan princess, as well?"

"That's right. I forgot." Fia ran a hand over the charred root at her side. "I can't believe a Mihalan could do something like this to her own home." She paused. "Although, now that I think about it, it does explain how she and Bade were able to get through the barrier. With her Mihalan skin shifting abilities, she would've been able to walk right through the front door. I should probably mention that to Anaria before we head back to Tallis. Not that I think Lumeria will be coming back here anytime soon. She's going to be too busy dying to make any extended trips."

"That would make traveling rather difficult for anyone," Artemis mused. "She won't be defeated easily, though."

Fia flexed her hands as she imagined the feel of her twin daggers there. The change she'd felt upon reconnecting with Artemis had been staggering. Her body felt stronger, more agile, her reflexes sharper than ever. Powerful.

"I may not be the leader the others would wish for, but I'm not the weak link anymore, either," she stated emphatically. "Between the four of us, we can definitely take her down."

"Whose demise are you plotting over here by yourself?"

Fia yelped as Cashel appeared at her side as if from nowhere. "Geez, Cashel. What have I said about making a little noise when you walk?" She gave an awkward laugh as she tried not to look as uncomfortable as she felt upon seeing him. "You startled me half to death."

"Well, that's no good. You're never going to take anyone down if you're already half dead." He lowered himself onto the broken remains of the dock, casting her a furtive glance. "Mind if I join you?"

"Suit yourself," she replied. "And I'm not by myself. I'm with Artemis."

"Ah, right. I keep forgetting he's still here, even when he isn't really *here*." Cashel rubbed a hand over the back of his head. "Or he's in some kind of magical realm inside of you? The whole thing kind of boggles my mind."

"It's definitely a bit hard to grasp," Fia admitted. "The idea that I have an entire mountain range somewhere inside me is pretty crazy, and I've actually seen it."

"The things a goddess can create with nothing more than the power of her robes," Cashel mused. Clearing his throat, he added, "So, uh, who're we killing? Not me, I hope."

"You *were* kind of an ass earlier," Fia pointed out. "But no, I'm not planning to murder you in your sleep over it. Especially seeing as you were somewhat justified in your assery."

"My *assery*?" Cashel's lips twitched.

"You heard me."

"Well, please consider this my formal apology." He grew serious as he added, "I never should have said those things to you.

Nothing that happened here is your fault. I was a jerk to even suggest it."

Fia peeked up at him, hesitant. "Really?"

"Really." He caught her gaze, and she felt the tension in her chest ease with each moment he held it. "Forgive me?"

"Yes," she breathed, blinking up at him. "Can you forgive me for wanting to save Bade after everything he's done? I'll understand if you don't," she hurried to add. "But it would mean a lot to me if you could at least see where I'm coming from. He's... important to me."

Cashel tensed, his expression freezing in place as he stared back at her. After a long, stilted moment he nodded, eyes darting off to the side. "I can do that. In fact, I..." he paused, fingers tapping restlessly against the wooden surface of his artificial leg. "I'd like to help," he finally muttered, his voice only just audible.

"You want to help?" Fia repeated, too surprised to process this sudden change in attitude. His slight nod of confirmation prompted her to add, "With Bade?"

"That's right."

"You want to assist me in saving the demigod who played a role in destroying your home?" Fia couldn't help but clarify. "The same demigod you were all revved up to kill not even an hour ago?"

He cleared his throat. "Yes."

"Why? I thought you hated him."

"Well, why not? If you're right, and you can end this war with a simple elixir as opposed to people dying on a battlefield, then who cares if I hate the guy? I can't let my personal feelings get in the way of an opportunity for peace."

"I guess that makes sense." Fia eyed him skeptically. "Although, getting through to Bade won't necessarily end the war. Lumeria isn't going to just pack up and go back to her mountain prison, even if Bade does change sides. If anything, I'd expect her to become even more vicious than before."

"Are you trying to talk me out of supporting you?" Cashel asked, laughing softly. "I thought this was what you wanted."

"Well, yeah…"

"And didn't you say that once you killed the hagrüs, Bade would help us defeat the witch himself?"

"Yes, but I wasn't sure you really believed me."

"I'm here, aren't I? I brought you to Mihala so you could get the caeruleum you needed."

"Only because I threatened not to fight with the other Shendri unless we tried this first. The sooner you got me here, the sooner you could get me back. That doesn't mean you agreed with my plan."

He sighed. "Does it really matter what I thought back then? Or whether I believe that deep down Bade has a soul worth saving? I believe in you, Fia." He lifted his hand, and she caught sight of a silver chain dangling from his fingers.

"Is that what I think it is?" she asked, reaching out to trace the curved, blue stone embedded into the necklace's round pendant. It warmed to her touch, and she gasped as it began to emit a soft, blue glow.

"Caeruleum," Cashel confirmed. "The only piece that survived the attack."

"It's beautiful," Fia murmured.

"Almost as beautiful as its new owner," Cashel said, draping the chain over her neck. "Let's hope its power matches yours, as well. We're going to need it."

Chapter Thirty-Nine

As eager as they were to be on their way back to Tallis, the need to rest and refuel forced them to spend the night in Mihala. With a long, two-day flight ahead of them, Fia would need to be as fresh as possible to maintain Artemis's solidified form. So, they stayed, and that evening found themselves seated around one of the many fires burning around the Great Tree's ruined stump. Anaria joined them at their fire, along with several of the other elders, all of whom took turns grilling Cashel and her about the situation in Eldour. While Fia understood their desire for news, she couldn't help but send wistful glances toward their neighboring fire, where a far more youthful crowd laughed and teased and even occasionally broke into song. There was a girl there who looked to be about Rosie's age, and Fia found herself tuning out the elders' war talk as she thought about the Haverdashs' faces as they'd parted. Cole's had been hopeful, but Rosie's...

She's seen too much darkness to believe there will ever truly be a happy ending. As much as I want to save Bade and put an end to Lumeria and the hagrüs's reign of terror, deep down I know how hard that's going to be. Cashel and I will be lucky if we come out of this alive. Her stomach clenched. *I'm going to be the death of us all, aren't I?*

"You okay?" Cashel nudged her side, his voice low as he leaned toward her.

She blinked, pushing her increasingly morbid thoughts to the side. She wasn't that weak, self-loathing girl anymore. She could do this. "I was just missing Rosie, is all." She forced out a laugh. "Cole, too, the scamp. I can't believe how attached I feel to them after just a few days. It's crazy."

"You haven't had a lot of family in your life," Cashel pointed out. "It makes sense that you'd want to keep your new one close."

"My new family," Fia mused, turning the words over in her mouth. She smiled, enjoying the way they felt on her tongue. "Are you part of my new family, too?"

"If you'll have me."

"Of course, I'll have you," she laughed. "After everything we've been through together, how could I not?" He grew quiet, and she looked up at him in confusion. "Cash?"

He gave her a half-hearted smile. "We should get some rest. Got a couple of long days ahead of us, especially if we want to get back before the full moon. It's going to be close."

"Artemis will get us there in time."

"Still. Best to get some sleep while we can, right?" He stood up and offered her a hand, which she took in mild bewilderment.

Is it just me, or is he acting weird?

She didn't say anything, however, as he led her over to one of the boats, and she let it go entirely as he looked up with a wink, and asked, "I don't suppose you're in need of a fine Mihalan blanket tonight, are you?"

She grinned. "It *is* a bit chilly. You think you can find one that'll be warm enough?"

He pulled her down into the boat, wrapping one arm around her waist as the other reached up to smooth back a stray lock of hair. "I think I can manage," he murmured, lowering his head until his lips captured hers.

She allowed herself to be drawn in, giving in to the comforting warmth of his embrace, and when he reluctantly pulled away, she smiled up at him with all of the love she'd found for this remarkable, young man and whispered, "I'm so glad we're in this together."

The light that had burned so brightly in his eyes just moments prior dimmed, and he pulled her against his chest, burying his face in her hair.

"Yeah," he whispered roughly. "So am I."

∞ ∞ ∞

They left Mihala early the next day, with promises to send help back as soon as things were settled. The likelihood of failure was left unspoken, as everyone sent the trio off with words of hope. But despite their refusal to voice it, the possibility sat in Fia's stomach like a stone, a constant reminder of everything she had to lose should she fail to destroy the hagrüs. Her pensiveness combined with Cashel's increasingly laconic attitude made for a long and silent flight, and it seemed that even Artemis drew a breath of relief when the first glimpses of the Valiant Sea sparkled in the distance.

A relief that was soon shattered as the sounds of battle reached their ears, and Fia's hopes crumbled into irreparable bits. There would be no seeking Bade out in the light of the full moon, no magical elixirs to free him from the creature who'd taken root inside his mind. Lumeria had succeeded in tearing down the barrier, and all of their endeavors were now nothing more than wasted energy.

"We're too late."

Chapter Forty

Earlier that evening, Tallis

"We can't wait any longer. The barrier is starting to crack, and the Antoski army won't waste any time in attacking once it's down." Josselyn drew her sword as a swirl of black shadows poured out of her chest, and Kella growled in agreement as she solidified at Joss's side. They stood facing the barrier along with Lily, Maya, and Luxeos, no more than a quarter mile past the last of the wattle and daub houses that lay scattered about the outskirts of the city. The Antoski army was camped on the other side, filling the open fields in an arc from one rocky bluff to another. "We should strike first," Josselyn continued. "Take the fight to the fields and keep them away from the city. It's the only way to keep the people safe."

"Are you sure you don't want to wait for Fia to return?" Lily asked, craning her neck for a better view of the sky on the other side of the weakening barrier. "We'd be a lot stronger with her fighting alongside us."

"We undoubtedly would, but there's no way I'm going to risk the lives of my people by sitting around and waiting on some lovesick fool who can't get her priorities straight," Josselyn snapped. Cursing, she growled, "I never should have let her run off to Mihala."

"Leave Fia be," Luxeos interjected as she stepped forward and placed a calming hand on Josselyn's arm. "At least she has the conviction to fight for the people she loves. If I had shown even a fraction of her devotion to my own child, we wouldn't be in the mess we're in now. A mistake I plan to rectify myself." She lifted her chin. "I'm going with you."

"Are you serious?" Maya exclaimed from her perch atop Kitsune's back. "You look like the slightest breeze could topple you over. No offense or anything, but I'm not sure you'd be much use on the battlefield."

"You do look awfully tired," Lily added gently. "Are you sure you wouldn't be better off staying at the Banri's? My sisters will be there, and I'd feel a lot better knowing you were with them."

"I may be a bit tired, as Maya so *tactfully* pointed out," Luxeos argued, "But I still have enough strength to amplify your power in Fia's place, at least for a short while."

"Really?" Maya's eyebrows shot up in surprise. "You can do that?"

"I am the original creator of the Shendri warriors," Luxeos retorted. "Is it really that surprising that I would be able to influence your powers?"

"That's right," Josselyn inserted. "You did something like that for Lily and me back in Eldon, when Prince Stefan was attempting to force my hand in marriage." She looked over at Lily. "That's when Suzu recovered her true form as a phoenix, isn't that right?"

"That's true," Lily confirmed. "If Luxeos believes she's strong enough, then I say we take her up on her offer. We're certainly going to need every advantage we can get going head-to-head against both Bade and Lumeria."

"You've got that right," Josselyn muttered, then raised her voice as she turned and shouted toward their own small army, where Alex was currently doing a weapons and armor inspection alongside General Townsend. "Hey, Your Majesty! Get your butt over here for a moment, would ya?"

"How regal," Maya muttered, and Lily covered her mouth with her hand, eyes dancing.

"It was effective, wasn't it?" Josseyln retorted, watching Alex break away from the general and head their way with an amused expression on his handsome, if scarred, face.

"Yes, Your Majesty?" he asked, crossing his arms over his chest as he grinned at his wife. "And how may I be of service to you?"

Josselyn met his grin with a fleeting one of her own, but she soon grew serious as she spoke of the impending battle. "Lumeria and Bade are the most formidable targets, so we'll need to take them out as soon as possible. Bade, in particular, will have to be dealt with quickly, or else he may well turn our own army against us. Lily," she turned to face the phoenix Shendri, "you'll need to get a shield around him as soon as you can."

"You want me to protect him?" Lily asked, looking confused.

"No, I want you to restrain him," Josselyn explained. "See if you can contain his magic inside the shield's bubble."

"Okay," Lily said, rubbing her hands together nervously. "I think we can manage that, right Suzu?" There was a flash of light as the phoenix materialized, flames flickering briefly on her wings before settling into her usual deep red plumage. She circled Lily, brushing the tips of her feathers against her shoulders in passing, before landing atop Kella's sleek back. The enormous hellcat looked less than pleased to be used as a perch, although she kept her annoyance to a growled huff.

"Excellent." Josselyn turned back to Alex. "I want you to assign both Edmund and Draven to guard Lily while she's maintaining the shield. She'll be too preoccupied to fend off any attackers herself."

"'Cause she'd *totally* be able to, otherwise," Maya teased.

"Hey now," Lily protested weakly. "My knife training has improved a lot over the last few months."

"Define improved," Maya laughed.

"Well," Lily hemmed, "I don't cut myself handling them anymore, so that's gotta count for something, right?"

Maya snorted, but Josselyn cut her off with a look. "Maya, I want you and Kitsu running circles around Lumeria. Fire as many arrows as you can to keep her distracted, but maintain your speed. If she hits you with one of those light orbs of hers, you're toast."

"Move fast and kill the witch, gotcha." Maya's face lit with a vicious grin, and her eyes darkened until they were almost completely black. "I am so ready for this."

"Have I mentioned how perfect you and Edmund are for each other? Cocky bastards," Josselyn muttered, before adding, "If you get a hit on her, great, but I suspect it's going to take more than a few arrows to bring her down. Which is where Kella and I come in. Once she's distracted, we'll attack her head-on. Between Kella's jaws and my sword, we'll hopefully be able to take her out for good."

"I think what you meant to say was *our* swords," Alex interjected, jaw clenched as he stared stonily at his wife. "Like hell you're facing a lightning-throwing, wind-commanding demigoddess without me. Not again."

"You know I'd have you with me if I could," Josselyn started, "but –"

"But nothing," Alex growled. "I'll fight alongside you, and I'll die alongside you, should it come to that. Your aunt and the duke can fight over the throne all they want, so long as I'm with you."

"Alex, please," Josselyn whispered softly.

"I'm fighting, Joss. Deal with it."

Josselyn screwed her face up in frustration before letting out a deep breath. "Alright," she conceded. "You can fight with us. But," she added, "I want you guarding Luxeos. If she's going to be channeling her energy into our powers, she'll need someone to look out for her, same as Lily."

Alex looked like he wanted to argue, but after a brief moment he nodded. "Assuming you'll be close to her, then fine. I'll be Luxeos's guard." His lips tipped into a crooked smile. "I certainly have plenty of training."

Josselyn returned his smile. "That you do."

"So, uh, is that it?" Maya interrupted. "Or do we have to keep watching you two make doe eyes at each other?"

"That's just about it," Josselyn replied, narrowing her eyes at Maya. "General Townsend can order his men to attack as he sees fit. Hopefully, they'll be able to hold back the soldiers until we've had a chance to deal with their leaders."

"It won't be easy," Lily murmured, looking out past the barrier wall at the encampment beyond. "They'll be out numbered almost ten-to-one."

"Not the best odds," Maya agreed, glancing up at the sky. "We could really use a little backup, preferably of the fire-breathing variety."

Josselyn's expression darkened as she, too, looked to the empty sky. "I wouldn't hold my breath."

Chapter Forty-One

Less than an hour later the army was assembled, and everyone waited anxiously in front of the barrier as Luxeos spoke the words that would bring what remained of it down, thus signaling the start of the battle. Lily allowed herself to sink back into Draven's arms as they sat astride his horse, memorizing the feel of his chest against her back and trying not to think about the fact that it may very well be the last time she felt his warmth surround her.

"It's going to be alright," Draven whispered in her ear. "Edmund and I will keep you safe, I promise."

Her throat tightened. "But who will keep you safe?"

"As if I'd allow myself to be killed when I've been charged with your safety?" he scoffed. "Not happening, love."

"I'm going to hold you to that," she whispered.

"Aye, and I'm going to hold *you* when this is over, and make you my wife once and for all. I'm done waiting."

"I do love a good wedding."

"I thought you might," he said, his chest rumbling behind her back.

She smiled, savoring the feel of his laughter and tucking it deep inside, so it might stay with her throughout the upcoming madness. "I love you, Draven," she whispered.

"And I you," he rumbled in return. "With all my heart."

∞ ∞ ∞

The barrier came down in a burst of light, one that flared out in the eyes of the waiting army, blinding them. Maya and Kitsune didn't waste a moment as they streaked forward, firing shot after shot into the front lines as they raced to the outer edge. Luxeos's strength surged through them, pumping Kitsu's legs and Maya's arms as they worked in perfect tandem. Thoughts of Edmund swirled through her mind, heightened by the warmth that even now remained on her lips from their parting kiss, but she pushed them down with the force of a hardened mercenary. Edmund was a warrior in his own right. He didn't need her compromising her performance with thoughts of his safety.

The Antoski roared to life as Townsend's men descended upon them, and soon the sound of clashing metal rang across the field. Kella's hulking form caught Maya's eye as both she and Josselyn fought their way through the throng of soldiers, Kella's razor sharp claws and Josselyn's blade cutting a wide swath through the center.

Heading for Lumeria, Maya thought, straining her eyes for a glimpse of the golden-haired terror. A piercing cackle rose over the din, and Maya grinned as she steered Maya toward its source. *Gotcha.* She continued to fire off shots as they moved, picking off as many soldiers as she could before she finally caught sight of her real target – Lumeria, demigoddess of the sun and soon-to-be dead woman. She stood at the back, a languid smile on her face as she swirled a ball of light above her open palm. Bade stood beside her, casually surveying the scene before him. *Arrogant bastard, watching everything unfold as if it were some sort of play. These are real people out here dying, damn it.* She aimed her bow at his impassive face. *Eat shit and die, asshole.*

His silvery-blue eyes glanced her way, almost as if he could hear her very thoughts, and her fingers froze around the arrow's shaft, unable to move. Kitsune jerked to a stop beneath her, and Maya went flying over the wolf's head at the sudden change in momentum. Landing with a thud on the grass, she tried to sit up, but it was as if the weight of the world was bearing down on her from above. Darkness crept in from the sides, attempting to snuff out her vision, but she fought it off, gritting her teeth in determination. *No. I'm not going to let him control me like this. Not again. Fight it, Maya. You've got this.*

A phoenix's call rent the air, and Maya grinned as the weight dispersed. *Thatta girl, Lily! Cage that bastard in.* Springing back to her feet, Maya reached up and grabbed Kitusune's fur as the wolf moved beside her. She swung back on as the wolf picked up speed and grinned at the enraged look on Bade's face as he pushed at the shield's walls.

Now, where was I?

A crackling sphere of light whizzed over her shoulder, singeing the loose wisps of hair and sending Maya's heart into overdrive. *Right.* She nocked another arrow. *Time to kill the witch.*

That's it, Maya, keep her distracted. Josselyn ducked beneath a swinging blade before plunging her sword into another soldier's belly. Kella roared beside her as an Antoski blade clipped her flank, and she swatted her massive paw through the oncoming soldiers in retribution, her sharp claws tearing through their metal armor as if it were made of nothing but cheap tin. They pushed forward, eyes on the prize, as the crazed demigoddess threw ball after ball of crackling light at Maya and Kitsu's blurred figures. Josselyn grimaced when she saw just how close the deadly spheres were coming to their target, and she pushed forward with renewed vigor.

You hit left, and I'll take her from the right, Josselyn projected, parrying another blow without bothering to look. Her eyes were fixed on Lumeria – everyone else was nothing more than an annoyance.

"On it," Kella's voice growled in response, the vibrations

from her low tone filling Josselyn's body with an added layer of anticipatory energy. As if on cue, Luxeos channeled a surge of power her way, propelling Josselyn into action with inhuman strength.

One, two, three, strike.

Kella pounced as Josselyn charged, and the demigoddess screamed in fury as they descended on her. Wind shot from her core in every direction, pushing Josselyn and Kella back, but only just. Josselyn dug her heels into the soft soil, resisting the force of the wind as it battered against her. She inched forward, her determined gaze unwavering as she closed the distance between them.

The wind cut off as quickly as it began, and Josselyn darted forward, poised to strike. A flash of light was all the warning she had before Lumeria attacked, lobbing the lethal orb straight at Josselyn's face. Josselyn slid to the ground as it flew over her head, and she sliced at Lumeria's legs with all the force she could muster. Her blade struck bone before it was brought to a stop. Lumeria's sun-filled eyes gleamed as she bent over, grasping the blade of Josselyn's sword despite the way the sharp metal cut into the palm of her hand as she whispered a single word.

"Grendalah."

A jolt of lightning shot up Josselyn's arm and into her chest, slamming her down against the ground where she continued to spasm in the most unbearable pain she'd ever felt. Kella's enraged form bore down on top of the smirking witch from above, tearing at Lumeria's neck with her massive jaw.

The resulting scream of pain was almost enough to numb Josselyn's own. Almost.

That's it, Kella. Tear her bloody throat out.

But it was the hellcat who fell to the ground, whimpering in pain, leaving a bloodied and unhinged Lumeria laughing over her massive form. Huge gouges were missing from her shoulder and neck, and blood poured out at a disturbing rate. The delirious witch placed her hand over the wounds and they began to sizzle and smoke beneath her touch. When she finally dropped her hand, the holes remained but the blood had been hardened into a black sludge.

"Is that the best you can do, Shendri?" she cackled. "Scrape my shins and sic your cat on me?" She tsked. "I'm far too fabulous to be beaten by such rudimentary tricks."

Josselyn snarled, forcing herself to her feet as the spasms died down to a dull ache. She lifted her sword, then cursed. All that remained clutched in the hand was the hilt – the entire blade had shattered under Lumeria's touch. *Bloody hell.*

"Not so tough without your precious sword are you?" Lumeria taunted. She leaned toward Josselyn, only to jump back as an arrow pierced her shoulder blade. "Damn it, that hurt!" she yelled, breaking off the arrow's shaft and turning to glare at the white blur racing in and out of sight. "Stupid wolf," she muttered, sending a gust of wind their way that swirled around them, lifting them off the ground and holding them captive. "I should have killed the pesky mongrel the moment she stepped into my prison." Light burned to life in her palms, and she narrowed her eyes at Josselyn. "No matter. I'll just kill the both of you now. And then, I'll kill your little blonde friend over there, too. That is, if Bade doesn't break down her pathetic little shield and kill her himself first."

"You'll do no such thing." Luxeos appeared at Josselyn's side, frowning sternly at her estranged daughter. Alex slid into place on Josseyln's other side, his profile grimly determined.

Lumeria's eyes lit with recognition, and her mouth spread into a wide grin. "Mother! What a delightful surprise! I'd be happy to add your death to my agenda, as well."

"You don't have to do this, Lumeria," Luxeos's pleaded. "Kill me, and let them go. I'm the one who wronged you. Take your vengeance and be done."

"Oh, I'm definitely going to kill you," Lumeria stated. "Although, I don't see why that has to interfere with the rest of my fun. But hey, I'll be sure to make a beautiful memorial with your bones once it's all over. It'll look wonderful in my garden."

"Lumeria, please –"

"Nope, done talking now," Lumeria interrupted. Flicking her wrist with all the care one would give to shooing away a fly, she sent a ball of light sailing into Luxeos's stomach. The goddess's eyes widened briefly as the orb made contact, and Josselyn felt her own stomach heave as she watched the vicious light shoot straight through the goddess's torso and out the other side. A scream tore from her lips as she watched Luxeos fall to the ground.

"Well, that was a bit anticlimactic, wasn't it?" Lumeria mused, staring down at her mother's corpse. "In hindsight, I really should have savored the moment more." She slid her gaze back to Josselyn, who could feel Alex tensing beside her.

Please don't make me watch him die, too, Josselyn prayed, frantically trying to come up with a plan to stop the monster leering at her with blatant blood lust.

"Uh oh, looks like your little friend over there is starting to struggle with that little shield of hers," Lumeria commented, her voice dripping with false concern. "I'd better hurry up if I want a chance at her, too." She pulled her hand back, aiming the other sphere of light at Josseyln's face. "Bye bye, then."

The light flew.

Josselyn lunged.

Alex swung.

Kella swiped.

And as Josselyn's dagger, previously tucked away in her boot, slid into the witch's stomach, Alex's sword struck the witch's side, and Kella's claws sank into the back of her leg. Pinned as she was, Lumeria could barely turn her head in time to see the dragon swooping down behind her before he bit off her head.

Chapter Forty-Two

"Ugh. She tastes as vile as she acts." Artemis paused. "Or, acted rather."

I can only imagine, Fia projected as she hastily took in the lay of the battlefield. Josselyn had fallen forward onto her hands and knees beside Lumeria's decapitated body, and Fia winced when she saw the bloody mess formerly known as Josselyn's shoulder. Apparently, she hadn't been able to avoid Lumeria's attack completely. Alex hovered over her, one eye on the fighting, the other on Josselyn. The Antoski swarming the field gave them a wide berth, none of them attacking the king and queen, despite their vulnerable position. It would seem none of them were too keen on coming within range of Artemis's massive jaw. At least, not while their remaining leader was still being restrained. From the waves of fatigue radiating off of Lily's form, however, Fia suspected their respite would soon be ending.

Time to act.

"I'm going in after Bade," she shouted, sliding down off of Artemis's back. "Artemis, start clearing the field. You'll want to take out as many Antoski as possible should Lily's shield break while I'm in there."

Cashel dropped down beside her and drew his sword. "I'm coming with you."

"Lily won't be able to block his power on the inside," Fia warned. "He'll control you the moment you step in there."

"I could say the same for you," he argued. "What makes you think you'll be any different?"

She took a deep breath, eyeing the man inside the shield – the first man she'd ever loved, now the man she would need to kill.

E.P. STAVS

"Because I'm the dragon Shendri, that's why," she stated, never taking her eyes off of Bade as she strode forward, daggers in hand. "Tell Maya to work the field – I'll deal with Bade."

"If you're sure…"

Her hands tightened around the daggers' hilts, and she hesitated for a brief moment outside the shield's wall. "I can do this," she whispered, as much to herself as to Cashel. She thought he might have said something in return, but the words were lost as she stepped through the wall.

And froze, limbs locking into place.

"If it isn't little Fia, the dragon Shendri herself. Come to greet your lover?" Bade smirked as he walked toward her. "Or perhaps you had something else in mind," he murmured, running a finger over the blade of one of her daggers before pulling them both out of her hands completely. She ground her teeth as she tried to resist, but her arms only seemed to grow heavier the more she tried to move them.

He tossed one of the daggers on the ground, but kept the other, tracing the tip down the side of her face with just enough pressure to draw blood.

A pained cry caught in her throat, but she swallowed it down, focusing all of her energy on regaining control. *I can fight this. Come on.* The muscles in her jaw loosened in response, and she found her voice as she stared back into Bade's emotionless gaze.

"Are you really going to let this creature hurt me like this?" She glanced up at the sky and drew strength from the sight of the moon, big and bright and so close to being full. *Please, let it be enough.* "I know you don't want to hurt me," she continued, returning her attention to Bade. "It's the hagrüs that's doing it. But you don't have to let it, Bade. You can stop it. I know you can."

Bade – no, the hagrüs – smiled, his face full of fake sympathy. "So, you've uncovered the demigod's secret, have you?" He tsked, drawing the tip of the dagger down across the other side of her face and eliciting a hiss of pain from between her teeth. "Unfortunately, your precious Bade is no longer with us. It's just me now." His smile stretched even wider as his blade moved down to her neck, where it rested precariously on her rapidly pounding pulse. "And, as you can see, I have no problem with hurting anyone. Or killing them, for that matter," he added, pressing the blade a touch harder. "And the moment your little Shendri sister loses control of this makeshift prison, I'll kill every last person who dares to stand in my way."

"I won't let you do that," Fia hissed, blocking out everything but the tingling in her legs and arms. *Move, damn it. MOVE!*

"I'm afraid you won't have much choice," the hagrüs replied. "Seeing as I'm about to slit your throat open."

Beads of sweat broke out across Fia's forehead as she attempted to remain calm and focused, but it was kind of hard to think about moving your legs with a dagger pressed against your throat. Even if she could move, how would she manage to escape without getting herself killed? The pressure on her neck increased, and she squeezed her eyes shut, bracing herself for the inevitable.

It never came.

The dagger remained motionless against her skin, and she cracked her eyes open to see the hagrüs's smile had fallen, replaced instead with enraged frustration.

"Get back down in your hole," he hissed. "You wanted oblivion, and I gave it to you. It's too late to change your mind."

What in the world? Fia's brow knitted as she watched the creature struggle with itself. A thrill of hope pricked at her heart as she realized the hagrüs wasn't talking to her. *That's it, Bade. Fight!*

"Get your hands off her!"

The hagrüs jerked his head around as Cashel came charging toward it, sword raised, and Fia took the opportunity to drop back, having finally regained control over her body. The hagrüs snarled as he froze Cashel in place, the statue of a warrior in motion, then turned its disdainful gaze toward Fia. She sank into a fighting position as she met his gaze, and he smirked in response.

"You'd attack a god with your fists? Cocky little thing, aren't you?" He tossed her dagger onto the ground and spread his arms out wide. "Well, come on then. Show me the strength of the dragon Shendri."

She darted forward, striking at his smug face, but he dodged her fist effortlessly, catching her wrist as it brushed past and muttering, "Adendiah." Her entire body grew heavy at the utterance, and he sneered in disgust as she faltered forward, her free hand clutching onto his shoulder in support. "It's no wonder he sent you away when he did. You're absolutely pathetic."

"He sent me away to save me from *you*," Fia growled, pushing back against the weight of his words with every fiber in her being. *I've been controlled too much for one lifetime. Never again.* With a burst of strength, she drove her knee forward into his leg, causing him to stumble backward. Shifting slightly, she swept the same leg back, catching his own and forcing him to the ground as she followed, driving her knee into his chest.

The look on his face was priceless.

Pinning him to the ground, she leaned forward so that their faces were mere inches apart and whispered, "I know you're in there."

"I'm going to destroy –"

His words broke off with a strangled gasp, and uncertainty flooded his face.

"Fight him, Bade," Fia whispered. "Even without a counter-potion, I know you're strong enough to defeat him." She leaned down, pressing a kiss against his lips as her hand reached out the side, grappling for the discarded dagger. Her fingers brushed steel, and she slid them down to the hilt. She clutched the weapon in her hand and raised it, poising it above his heart as she reluctantly dragged her lips away from his with a soft whisper. "I'm sorry."

The dagger plunged into the demigod's heart, and she followed it down, laying atop Bade's body as it convulsed beneath her. Choked sobs wracked her body as she held him, one hand wrapped around the dagger's hilt, the other grasping at the fabric of his shirt.

"I'm sorry," she sobbed, repeating the words over and over as his body grew still beneath her. "I'm so sorry."

Someone touched her shoulder, and she vaguely registered Cashel's voice as he wrapped his hand around her forearm, urging her upward. "It's over, Fia," he soothed. "You did it."

She blinked against the tears as she sat up, her legs still straddling Bade's body, and she fought against the urge to vomit as she watched the blood ooze out around the dagger's handle. Her eyes narrowed, and she looked closer. Blood and... was that smoke?

Acrid, black smoke poured out of the wound in Bade's chest, and she flinched away from it as it rose up toward the sky. A low moan followed, and she gasped as she looked down and found a pair of sorrow-filled eyes gazing up at her.

"You're alive," she breathed. "How?"

His eyes darted around, taking in the battle that still waged in the fields beside them. "Oh gods," he whispered. "What have I done?" He murmured something indiscernible under his breath, and the fighting stopped abruptly as soldiers looked around in confusion.

"Bade, you're alive," Fia repeated, drawing his attention back. "How is this possible?"

He lifted his hand, touching the dagger that remained embedded in his chest. "You missed my heart," he murmured distractedly, his eyes darting around once again before coming back to meet hers. "There's so much blood," he whispered. "Too much."

"What do you mean?" she asked, but he shook his head wordlessly as regret etched across his features.

Cashel pulled at her arm again, more forcibly this time, and she allowed herself to be lifted to her feet. She glanced at Cashel's profile and froze when she saw his sword was pointed at Bade's neck. "What are you doing?"

"We can't let him live, Fia," Cashel stated. "You know what happened two-hundred years ago. The Shendri thought they'd won then, too. We can't take a chance of history repeating itself."

"It's different this time," she argued. "The hagrüs is dead."

"It doesn't matter," Cashel said, refusing to meet her eyes as he stepped forward, sword in hand. "I refuse to take chances with my people's lives. This ends now."

"But – "

"He's right." Bade's voice interrupted her protests, and she looked down to find him smiling weakly up at her. "He should kill me." He paused. "I *want* him to kill me."

"But, it's different now," Fia insisted, tears spilling down her cheeks as she looked desperately from one man to the other. "You can start a new life, make amends. You have so much goodness inside you, I just know you can make things better. You – "

But he was already shaking his head. "It's too late, Fia. I'm sorry." Looking past her, he nodded at Cashel. "Do it."

Cashel's face tightened, and Fia thought for a moment he might reconsider, but then he was moving, thrusting his sword downward...

...and into the ground.

Her heart swelled as he cursed and spun away, leaving his sword sticking out of the ground beside Bade's neck.

"Go," he demanded, keeping his back turned to them both. "Get on a ship and leave this place for good."

Fia thought her face might split she was grinning so hard, but Bade merely looked tired as he slowly rose to his feet. "You should have Lily heal that chest wound, first," she said, eagerly looking around for the phoenix Shendri and spotting her kneeling beside a wounded soldier with a battered Draven hovering over her shoulder. Soldiers huddled in groups around the battlefield, confused and uncertain, and Fia noticed them casting curious glances their way.

"I imagine she has more important matters to attend to than this," Bade said quietly. "Besides, it's already healing on its own. If I pulled the blade out, it'd probably close up completely."

"What?" She looked at the dagger in surprise. "How?"

He shrugged. "A mix of my own powers, and this," he added,

pulling his shirt down and revealing a crescent-shaped, black mark on his chest. He lifted the caeruleum necklace she'd forgotten she was even wearing. "I believe this was what gave me the added strength to force the creature in front of your blade. I thank you for that." He dropped the pendant, and turned away, facing the sea. "He's a good man. He'll give you the family you deserve."

"He is," Fia whispered. "And so are you."

Bade's mouth curved in a slight smile. "You always did see the best in me, Fia." He glanced over at her before turning back to the water. "You always claimed I was your savior, but really, it was the other way around. You saved me, Fia, and I'll never forget that. Thank you." He walked over to the bluff, stopping only when he reached the very edge. Fia followed, confusion turning to sorrow as she realized his intentions.

"You don't have to do this," she whispered.

"Yes, I do." He turned to face her, his eyes shining with a new light as he bent down and placed a gentle kiss on her forehead. "Live as hard as you can," he whispered. "And if you ever need me, just look to the sea and I'll be there. I promise."

"I love you," she sobbed, and he smiled back at her.

"I love you, too."

And then he was gone, falling through the air toward the crashing waves below. Fia watched through blurry eyes as his body broke the surface of the water, and he disappeared into its dark depths. A beautiful, blue light swirled through the waves, circling the place where he'd sank, and Fia couldn't help the smile that made its way through the tears as she realized Lunares would finally be able to hold her baby boy at last.

"Goodbye, Bade," she whispered, wiping her eyes. "May you both find the peace you crave." Strong arms wrapped around her from behind, and she melted into them. "Thank you for giving him the choice, Cashel. You didn't have to."

He rested his chin on her head, tucking her even closer against him.

"Yeah, I did." He sighed. "You were right. He did have goodness inside him."

She smiled as she watched the light split in two as it swirled its way back out to sea. "He does."

Chapter Forty-Three

"We're gathered here today to say goodbye to the goddess Luxeos, whose sacrifice gave us the ability to defend ourselves against those who would destroy our world." Her royal Highness Josselyn deLure, hellcat Shendri and ruling queen of Eldour, stood beneath a tree in the castle gardens as she faced the solemn faces of her sister Shendri, all of whom had gathered around the marble dais upon which their former mentor had been laid. Luxeos looked as peaceful as though asleep, with her arms crossed and eyes closed. The only sign of her demise lay in the slight dip of her flowing, white dress as it gaped down into the hole of her abdomen.

"She left her home in the heavens for the sake of the humans she loved so dearly," Josselyn continued. "And now, more than two centuries later, it's about time she returned." She looked around at the others, and they nodded. As one, they released their beasts, and the smoke and shadows, the white and silver lights, all entwined as one above Luxeos's body. The celestial swirls dove down and wove around the goddess's body, and she began to float above the dias as they sunk into her skin, until all at once she erupted into a burst of light so bright that the four young women had to shield their eyes against it. As it slowly dimmed, they lifted their heads to watch as the light drifted upward, wending its way back up to the heavens. Bearing the goddess home.

"I'm going to miss you, Kella," Josselyn whispered, watching the light sink into the night sky. She could hear the others murmuring similar goodbyes as they watched their beasts return home, and her breath hitched when she saw the lights arrange themselves into four distinct constellations – a dragon, a wolf, a phoenix, and, lastly, a hellcat.

The lights winked, and she smiled as warmth spread through her chest. *Gone, but not out of sight.*

"So, now what do we do?" Maya asked.

Josselyn shrugged. "Whatever we want, I suppose."

"Well, maybe not anything we want," Lily teased through watery eyes. "You are still the queen of Eldour, are you not?"

"Oh right." Josselyn gave her a crooked smile. "That."

"I suspect Alex is going to try to fill her belly with heirs now that they don't have to worry about Kella being passed on to the next generation," Maya stated.

Josselyn paled. "Don't even suggest it. I'm not ready to be a mom, yet."

"I think you'd be a great mother," Lily reassured her.

"Can we not talk about this?" Josselyn complained, and the others chuckled.

"How about we just live our lives and let the rest fall into place," Fia suggested, taking Josselyn's hand and giving it a squeeze. "I know that's what I'm planning to do."

Josselyn grinned. "Sounds good to me."

Epilogue

A salty breeze brushed Fia's hair away from her face as she stood at *Serendipity*'s bow and gazed into the moonlit water below. It'd been over a year since Bade disappeared into those same, silky depths, but she could still feel his presence, following her as she journeyed westward to Tentalla and the new life that awaited there. She'd been looking forward to the change ever since they'd laid Luxeos to rest, but rebuilding Mihala had taken priority. It would be many years before the Great Tree rose to its former heights, but as the mountains' cores continued to produce new caeruleum, the enriched water of the lake would help it grow.

And then there'd been Lily and Maya's double wedding, and all the festivities that went along with it. Fia had found the whole thing a little overwhelming, but fortunately most people had been focused on the bridal couples, not to mention the newly pregnant queen. And she'd finally been able to spend some quality time with Lily's sisters, which was nice. Rosemary was a bit much at times, but she'd found Violet's dry humor and intelligent conversation to be quite refreshing. Honestly, Fia had to admit she was going to miss all of her newfound friends back in Lehi. Especially considering this would be a one-way trip – you could only count on a demigod's spirit to provide safe passage so often. And getting Josselyn to arrange a ship for them? No simple task. Although, being a war hero certainly helped.

The familiar sound of a wooden leg tapping its way across the deck brought a smile to her face, and she turned to greet her husband as he approached. There was a knowing light in his eyes as he looked over her shoulder at the glimmer of moonlight that seemed to propel them forward. Pulling her close, he took a moment to worship her lips before wrapping her in an embrace and gazing out over the sea.

"And how is our watery friend this evening?" he asked, dropping a kiss on the tip of her ear. She leaned into him, soaking up his warmth.

"Well, I believe," she replied. "And the kids? Did they manage to settle down?"

"They're doing well enough, although I think Cole's going to have a rough time of it."

Fia grimaced. "Is he still puking?"

"Not so much anymore, but he's pretty green around the gills." He chuckled softly. "I think the hardest part for him is realizing his dream of finding his uncle and becoming a pirate might not be quite as appealing as he once thought."

"Yeah, not exactly the best career choice for someone prone to seasickness," Fia agreed. "I'm sure he'll find plenty of ways to keep us on our toes once we reach land, though."

"No doubt," Cashel laughed. "Thank goodness for Rosie is all I can say."

Fia hummed in agreement as she snuggled back against Cashel's chest. "We'll deal with whatever trouble he manages to get himself into together." She smiled to herself. "As a family."

My family.

Live Hard

The thoughts and actions of this book's characters are based entirely in fantasy. Suicide is never the answer - if you're having harmful thoughts, please seek help!

National Suicide Prevention Lifeline (US)
(800) 273 - 8255

National Suicide Helpline UK
0800 - 689 - 5652

Lifeline (Australia)
13 - 11 - 14

Join the Live Hard Movement: Live Hard is dedicated to providing love and light within the darkness of those affected by the depth of depression and suicide.

https://livehardmovement.com/

In loving memory of Ian James Chavez
February 7, 2003 - May 8, 2017

Like What You Read?

If you enjoyed "The Moonlit Warrior" (or even if you didn't), please consider leaving a review on Amazon or Goodreads. Even a few words can make a difference in helping an author's work get noticed!

Thanks so much for reading!

∞ ∞ ∞

To stay informed of any new releases check out epstavs.com and follow E.P. Stavs on Amazon.

Twitter: @e_stavs

Instagram: @e.p.stavs

Acknowledgement

First off, I'd like to thank all the readers who've taken this journey with me from start to finish - I hope you enjoyed the ride! To my editors and proofreaders, Blake and Christy, thank you so much for helping me find all the bumps along the way. To my beta readers, Allison, Ewan, Becky, Aliya, and Michele - thank you for all your input on what did and didn't work. I appreciate you all! To my parents, Robert and Lynne - thank you for continuing to be my biggest fans. I love you both so much!

To my family, Michael, Kaitlin, and Melanie - thank you for constantly inspiring me and filling my life with sunshine and love. I never could have made it all the way through without you guys. And lastly, to my Lord and Savior, thank you for blessing me with this wonderful life. I'm sure I don't deserve it, but I'll enjoy it all the same.

About The Author

E.p. Stavs

Erin grew up in various parts of Upstate New York, where she became a regular at the public libraries, checking out book upon book upon book. Not even bedtime could stop her from reading, thanks to a handy flashlight kept close by.

Erin married her husband, Michael, in the Fall of 2007, and the couple moved across country to Seattle, Washington soon after, where Erin worked as a math teacher. When baby girl number one came along, however, she decided she'd had more than enough teaching to last a lifetime and decided to be a stay-at-home mom, instead. Five years and two daughters later, she finally found the time and motivation to follow through on her ultimate dream – writing books of her very own.

When she's not reading, writing, or mom-ing, Erin enjoys taking long walks with her headphones on, playing video games with her husband, and taking that first sip of coffee in the morning. So good.

Made in the USA
Middletown, DE
14 August 2021